OUT OF Bounds

ANN JACOBS

ELLORA'S CAVE
ROMANTICA PUBLISHING

What the critics are saying...

5 Cupids "OUT OF BOUNDS is a fantastic read. MS. JACOBS has done a great job in creating characters and a storyline that just touches your heart. […] I just loved the gut wrenching emotion in this book. […] OUT OF BOUNDS is a great and unique read. […] It has twists and turns—and passages brimming with emotion that will just enthrall you. This is a great dramatic erotic novel that encompasses an unexpected and torrid attraction between two seemingly different people, yet with an underlying tender and bittersweet love story." ~ *Cupids Library Reviews*

5 Hearts "Ms. Jacobs penned with *Out of Bounds* another great and very emotional story. It's a tale of betrayal, misunderstanding, trust and real love. The whole story is very well written and you won't be able to stop reading until you reach the last page. The story is an absolute emotional roller-coaster ride for the heroine as well as the hero. […] *Out of Bounds* is loosely connected with *Wrong place, wrong time*, but it can be read as a stand-alone, although this reviewer recommends reading both books, because it's a great story."
~ *Love Romances Reviews*

An Ellora's Cave Romantica Publication

www.ellorascave.com

Out of Bounds

ISBN 9781419958731
ALL RIGHTS RESERVED.
Out of Bounds Copyright © 2006 Ann Jacobs
Edited by Sue-Ellen Gower.
Cover art by Syneca.

This book printed in the U.S.A. by Jasmine-Jade Enterprises, LLC.

Electronic book Publication August 2006
Trade paperback Publication February 2009

With the exception of quotes used in reviews, this book may not be reproduced or used in whole or in part by any means existing without written permission from the publisher, Ellora's Cave Publishing, Inc.® 1056 Home Avenue, Akron OH 44310-3502.

Warning: The unauthorized reproduction or distribution of this copyrighted work is illegal. Criminal copyright infringement, including infringement without monetary gain, is investigated by the FBI and is punishable by up to 5 years in federal prison and a fine of $250,000.
(http://www.fbi.gov/ipr/)

This book is a work of fiction and any resemblance to persons, living or dead, or places, events or locales is purely coincidental. The characters are productions of the author's imagination and used fictitiously.

OUT OF BOUNDS
☙

Trademarks Acknowledgement

☙

The author acknowledges the trademarked status and trademark owners of the following wordmarks mentioned in this work of fiction:

AstroTurf: AstroTurf, LLC
Camaro: General Motors Corporation
Ferrari: Ferrari S.p.A
Greyhound: Greyhound Corporation, The
iPod: Apple Computer, Inc.
Jacuzzi: Jacuzzi Inc.
Limoges: Bernardaud Porcelaines de Limoges, S.A.
Little League Baseball: Little League Baseball, Inc.
Mercedes: Daimler Chrysler AG
Nautilus: Nautilus, Inc.
Nike: Nike, Inc.
Rolex: Rolex Watch U.S.A., Inc.
Salvation Army: Salvation Army, The
Southern Living: Southern Living, Inc.
Sports Illustrated: Time Inc.
UPS: United Parcel Service, Inc.
Xbox 360: Microsoft Corporation

Chapter One

Do I know your father? Hell, unless I'm sadly mistaken, I am your father.

Brand Carendon felt as if he'd just been ground into AstroTurf by a three-hundred-pound tackle. Every muscle in his body tensed as he stared first at the kid then at the dog-eared piece of paper in his hand.

"Mr. Carendon?"

"Sorry." Brand looked again at the copy of a birth certificate that had been issued eleven years ago in Fulton County, Georgia. Suddenly conscious of his near nudity, he set the paper down and knotted a damp towel more firmly about his waist. "Where's your mother?"

"At work." The boy shrugged.

Brand's day had started out with a light preseason workout under the hot Florida sun. He'd felt good throwing passes on the field, relaxed afterward in this damp locker room with its familiar smell of sweat and leather. As a matter of fact, he'd gotten so comfortable he'd damn near gone to sleep while a trainer worked the kinks out of his shoulders, until an old teammate had come in, two boys close on his heels.

He'd have pegged the smaller boy as former teammate Speed Johnson's son anywhere. He was a dead ringer for Speed, right down to his toothy grin, short-cropped kinky hair and oversize hands on a compact body. What had bugged Brand was the feeling he'd gotten—a feeling he should have recognized the gangly, dark-haired boy as well. Turned out he'd been right.

But what the fuck? Hadn't Dani told the boy anything? When Brand spoke again, he tried to sound casual. "Can't your mother get in touch with your dad for you?"

Dave stood there, shifting from one foot to the other as if uncertain what he should say. "I've asked her to. She won't. She says he didn't want me or her."

Brand clenched his fists so hard his nails damn near drew blood. It burned his ass that all his son knew about him was his name—his first name that nobody ever used at that. Trying to maintain his cool, he looked again at the dog-eared copy of a birth certificate that said Dani Murdock had delivered a son and named David Carendon as the father.

"She must have liked him, though. She named me after him."

Bullshit. While he'd been nursing a broken heart at college on March 18, eleven years ago, Dani had been in Atlanta's charity hospital giving birth to the baby she'd told his mother she was going to abort. It was all Brand could do to avoid letting out a string of curses that would burn the kid's ears. His own kid, apparently.

"Do you know my father?"

He hated the plaintive sound of Dave's voice, the hopeful look that was fading from his face. Brand had to find Dani, find out what the fuck was going on. But he had to say something now. "I'm not sure. Give me your address and phone number. I'll do some checking and get back to you."

The boy's smile came back, full force. "You'll help me find him?"

"I'll do all I can." Years had passed. He'd changed and so, he was sure, had Dani. "I'm sure finding your dad means a lot to you." Watching Dave blink back tears brought moisture to Brand's eyes.

"Wouldn't you hate not knowing anything about your father? If you didn't know what he looked like, if you couldn't understand why he wasn't around like other kids' dads? I never even knew his name until I saw it there." Tears ran down David's cheeks now, but he brushed them away, obviously embarrassed to have been caught crying.

"Yeah, son, I'd hate that, too." Brand's own throat felt tight, and he wasn't at all sure it was sweat and not a tear making its way down his cheek. He reached out, patted the boy's thin shoulder. "I'll see what I can find out, and I'll get back with you soon. Go find Roger. I need to talk to his dad."

* * * * *

Fortunately Speed had been able to tell him where Dani worked. Ironic, Brand thought, that he and Dani both had crossed paths with Speed at different times during the years since they'd seen each other. Brand sped across the bridge between Tampa and St. Petersburg and got off I-275 at a downtown exit. He found the distinctive-looking high-rise, parked and went inside. Bursting with nervous energy, he stalked the downstairs lobby of the building where Dani worked as a secretary for an investment house. It was all he could do to keep from storming her office, wait until she got off work.

He'd loved her once, hated her after she'd walked away from him without a backward glance. Her parting note had hit him harder than any monster linebacker ever had, and that was saying a lot. It still hurt when he thought about how Dani had denied their love, their marriage and their unborn child in one terse note she'd left with his mother.

Twelve years had gone by, and he thought he'd put that all behind him, but he still remembered every word of that damn note. He'd never been able to banish the memory of her looking up at him, adoration in her dark eyes, as though he'd been the most important thing in her world.

Her desertion had changed him, hardened his attitude toward women and steeled his determination to control his own destiny—not to give in to anybody's demands.

Particularly his mother's. He had a sneaking suspicion she'd done or said something that had encouraged Dani to go.

He'd always had the feeling it wouldn't have taken a lot to trigger the insecurities that had made him feel so protective of her. Insecurities fed by the disdain of nearly everyone in their hometown for her because of her mother who'd kept herself in booze by a little informal prostitution...and the tumbledown shack where they'd lived with her alcoholic grandfather. Part of him still wanted to protect her, even from his own righteous anger.

He wondered if he'd recognize her now. But he had no doubt she'd know who he was, considering his mug was pasted all over ads and newspapers so often even perfect strangers recognized him. Used to having people treat him like some kind of celebrity because he could throw a football, Brand ignored stares from passersby. Mindlessly, he scrawled his name on various scraps of paper thrust his way, his gaze focused all the while on the sea of faces that swarmed out of the elevators.

Then he saw her.

She still took his breath away. He swore under his breath, told himself to drag his gaze away from the girl who once made him feel ten feet tall when she'd looked up at him with those soft, dark eyes. The tiny, dark-haired waif who'd taught him the hard way that when it came to women, he needed to be in control.

He wanted to throttle her. He wanted her to suffer at least as much as she'd made him hurt when she walked out. Most of all, he wanted to punish her for letting him believe for all these years that she'd destroyed his child.

Fuck. He wanted to strip off the drab brown dress that didn't quite manage to disguise her dynamite body, tie her to the nearest bed and make her admit what his hard-on told him loud and clear. That the chemistry was still there between them, as strong as ever. He'd bury himself balls deep in her hot, wet pussy. Just once more he'd sample the heat and softness he'd never been able to forget no matter how hard or with how many women he'd tried.

He stood beside a marble support beam until Dani passed by. Then, matching his pace with hers, he stayed behind her until they were outside on a brick patio. Certain she would have bolted given half a chance, he reached out and grasped her arm.

"Remember me?"

He sounded calm enough, but his big hand clasped her arm like a vise.

Even before he spun her around to face him, Dani knew who he was. The one man on earth she'd never forget. The man she'd never expected to see again.

"Brand." Her cheeks turned icy cold in spite of the summer's oppressive heat.

"We need to talk. Shall it be here or somewhere in private?" Brand motioned toward one of the outdoor tables.

"We have nothing to say to each other."

"Yes, we do." Brand sounded deadly calm, as if... No! He couldn't have found out about David, could he? "What about that lounge across the street?"

"I have to get home." She tugged with all her strength, but she couldn't get free from his iron-like hold. Not until he decided to let her go.

"I'll follow you. Where's your car parked?"

"I take the bus. The stop's over there." She pointed toward the covered benches at the corner.

"Come on. I'll drive you." Not giving her time to protest, he herded her to the curb and unlocked the passenger door of a low, sleek-looking sports car.

"I've never seen a car like this before."

He opened the door. "It's a Ferrari." None too gently, he settled her inside. Before getting into the driver's seat, he retrieved a parking ticket from under a windshield wiper and tossed it carelessly onto the dash. "Like it?"

She glanced at the dark wood dash, touched the butter-soft leather seat, fastened her seat belt. "It's nice. It had to have cost a fortune."

"I can afford it." He turned the key, started the motor.

Dani started to comment but held her tongue. No need to point out they came from different worlds. That had been clear from the day they'd met at the ice cream stand where she'd been working. She'd made her choice, walked out of his life when his mother had made it clear she'd never fit in his world and he'd never want to live in hers.

"Why are you here?" Dani couldn't quite control the tremor in her voice, but she had to know.

"Your son came to me today and asked me to help him find his father." Brand's fierce expression and cold, emotionless voice sent chills down her spine. "Speed Johnson brought Dave over to the Marlins' training camp this morning."

"I've never told him. How did he know?" Perhaps if she could keep her wits about her, she could —

"He didn't. Not until he saw his birth certificate. It has my name on it."

"How? Oh, God, his Little League baseball coach must have given it to him to bring back home. But that was months ago."

"Do you hate me so damn much you don't even want our son even knowing who I am?" He swore under his breath as he maneuvered through downtown traffic.

"I don't hate you. I never hated you." Dani could hardly speak. She could barely make out the sound of her own voice above the engine's roar. This time she raised her voice, practically shouted. "I didn't even hate you when you had your mother send me away."

Brand swerved, barely avoiding hitting a motorcycle on the on ramp to the Interstate. "Damn it, I can't listen to this while I'm driving. Tell me where we can go, then shut up until we get there."

Dani didn't even consider arguing. Brand might have the same dark brown hair, the same compelling eyes, but this wasn't the boy she'd loved. He was a fierce, scowling stranger, and he intimidated her.

"Take the next exit. There's a little restaurant a couple of blocks west. It should be quiet enough. I can't stay long, though. Dave's over at Roger's house, and they'll be ready for supper soon."

Brand turned off I-275 and followed her directions. She didn't say another word until a hostess had seated them at a corner table in the small Mexican restaurant and lounge. It was all she could do to hold onto her shaky self-control.

* * * * *

Brand needed a drink. He imagined Dani did, too, so he ordered a glass of white wine for her, a beer for himself.

The soft light from a fat candle in the center of the table cast shadows on the face that had haunted his dreams. He told himself the tension in his gut was signaling hunger, not desire. His cock wasn't listening.

"Do you come here often?" he asked.

"I've never been here before. Some of the women at the office talk about it. I thought it sounded like your kind of place."

"And what's my kind of place, Dani?"

"Upscale? Popular? I don't know." She wove her fingers together, staring down at them as though she couldn't bear to look at him.

The waiter interrupted them to deliver their drinks. He waited for Brand to produce a credit card then scurried away.

"Why don't you repeat what you were saying just before I damn near killed that poor motorcyclist?" Brand sipped his beer, watched Dani toy with the stem of her wineglass.

"I just told you I never hated you, not even when you had your mother send me away."

What the fuck? He'd always suspected his mother had done or said something to make Dani go, but had the woman actually persuaded Dani he wanted her to leave him? For a minute he wanted to comfort her, wipe that terrified expression from her face. But damn it, she should have trusted him. It was all he could do not to shout out his frustration, his anger. "Damn it, I didn't have my mother send you away. All I did was leave you at my parents' house for a couple of hours. While I was getting my high-school coach to help me make arrangements for married housing at the university, you disappeared."

"Didn't you get my note?"

Brand barely suppressed a particularly foul four-letter word. "That note? It hardly explained anything. Mother told me you'd decided you wanted an abortion, that you didn't want to be bothered with me or the baby."

Her hand shook so hard, wine sloshed over the rim of her glass before she managed to set it down. "Your mother said you'd offered to marry me out of a misguided sense of honor, and you were miserable at the thought of having to spend your life with someone like me. She said if I had an ounce of decency I'd walk away." Her words, hardly more than a whisper, trailed off entirely.

"Bull. If I hadn't wanted to marry you, I wouldn't have. I didn't have to marry you to take care of my responsibility to our child. I thought you knew me better than that." Brand massaged his throbbing temple. "Obviously, you didn't have an abortion. You had our baby and made damn sure I didn't find out about him. You denied my son the chance to have a father. You denied me my child."

"I did what I thought you wanted. But I couldn't bring myself to kill my baby."

"What about Dave? Did you think you could bring him up without him ever wondering about me?"

"I didn't know it would bother him not to know his father."

"I don't believe you believe that."

"You know me better than I know myself, do you?" she spat out, as if she hated him now as much as she'd once professed to love him. "I've devoted my life to my son. I've loved him since the nurse put him in my arms at the hospital. Everything I've done, I've done for him."

Brand pictured the boy's tousled dark hair. He'd looked more than ready for a trip to the barber. Clean but faded jeans and shirt, and scuffed, ratty tennis shoes—his clothes had yelled "cheap" as surely as if they'd been able to talk.

Jesus. He'd stormed across Tampa Bay to find her, full of righteous anger. Now he just felt drained. And guilty. Dani didn't look as if she spent much on her own wardrobe, either. He assessed her drab, brown dress, the plastic digital watch that was her only piece of jewelry. When he met her gaze, he noticed tiny lines at the corners of dark eyes that reminded him of a trapped doe staring down a hunter.

Maybe he ought to share some of the blame. Brand sighed and handed her his cell phone. "This isn't going to be quick and easy. You'd better arrange for the Johnsons to keep Dave a while longer. I'm sure they won't mind. I'll order us something to eat."

Brand signaled the waiter and ordered the house special, not even bothering to find out what it was.

Chapter Two

Dani tried to focus on a picture hanging above their table while she waited for Callie Johnson to answer the phone. Despite everything, the sight of Brand still made her feel tingly and hot, deep inside. She'd been telling herself for years that she was over him. Apparently she'd been lying. At the sound of her friend's cheery voice, she asked if Dave could stay a couple of hours longer.

"Will Dave be okay?" Brand asked when Dani handed back the phone.

"He'll be fine. Callie said she'd feed him." Brand looked good enough to eat in loose-fitting cotton pants and an open-collared polo shirt that gave her a tantalizing view of the light brown curls on his chest. He was huge, so much bigger now than she remembered. He'd filled out in maturity where he had been gangly as a youth. Powerful muscles rippled every time he moved, strained against the short sleeves of his shirt.

"Good. I ordered something here for us. Look, I might as well go right to the bottom line. I want to be part of my son's life. I *am* going to be part of his life. It would be best if we set aside our personal feelings and agree on this."

Dani forced herself to look at him. For a moment she drowned in blue eyes so dark they matched the night sky. Then fear took over. Her cheeks grew hot, and she looked away. She shuddered, certain that given a choice, their son would rather be with his football hero dad than with her. Then she remembered. Brand wasn't single. "How will your wife feel about having a stepchild?" she asked bluntly.

"I'm not married."

"You married Marilee Sheridan right after you finished college. I saw your wedding pictures in the Atlanta paper."

"We got a divorce less than two years after that. Did you stop reading the papers?" He sounded put out. Did he hate that she'd kept up with his activities, or was it that she'd quit doing it after a while that had him scowling. "In case you don't already know, we had a daughter. She's six."

That little girl might have been theirs if she'd waited instead of running away. If she hadn't let Brand's snooty mother intimidate her. Tears threatened to spill from Dani's eyes. "I didn't know."

"Well, now you do. Marilee and I made better friends than lovers. We should never have married. We didn't even manage to stay together long enough for me to see LeeAnn take her first step. Our mothers wanted us to marry, a hell of a lot more than Marilee or I ever did." He shrugged, but said nothing more while the waiter was tossing their salad.

Brand wolfed down his food, but Dani pushed it around on her plate. She was far too nervous to be hungry. "Doesn't stress affect your appetite?"

"After I saw Dave, I wasn't thinking very clearly. Instead of eating lunch, I drove straight to Tampa and paced the lobby of the building where you work. I wanted to be sure to catch you when you came downstairs."

"Oh."

When he'd refilled his plate, he shot her a grin that reminded her of the Brand she'd once loved. "I was out in the hot sun all morning doing passing drills. It may not sound like work, but it burns a lot of calories."

"That's what Dave watched you do this morning?"

"Yeah." Brand smiled. If Dani hadn't deceived him and kept his son away from him for more than eleven years, he might actually enjoy her company.

He'd thought if he ever saw her again, he'd feel nothing at all. But he did. He told himself his only emotion was resentment, but he'd be damned if he didn't want to reach out and touch her satiny, olive skin. He'd make her submit to the pleasures they'd discovered together so long ago. The fiery passion that had made their youthful affair inevitable still smoldered beneath all the questions that remained to be answered.

"I guess Dave knows now that you're his father," Dani said, a frown emphasizing the faint lines around her soft, velvety lips.

"Not yet. Hell, Dani, I had to see you first. I had to be sure. I'm not such a bastard I wouldn't give you the chance to tell him."

"I can't believe he doesn't know. After all, he came to you. He saw your name on his birth certificate."

"That birth certificate only has my first name on it. Since I go by Brand, not David, he didn't make the connection." He wondered then if Dave did know, and if his son was hurt because he hadn't immediately acknowledged their relationship. Suddenly it hit him that Dave's last name was Murdock.

Brand reached across the table, took Dani's hand. At that moment all he wanted was to wipe away the pain he saw in her dark eyes. "I want my son to have my name. All it will take are affidavits from both of us stating that I'm his father, and that we want him to have my name."

Dani pulled her hand back. "You'll take him away from me." It wasn't a question. It was a flat declaration. Brand watched her fight to retain control, felt his own eyes moisten when she lost it. Tears ran down her cheeks. As Dave had this morning, she fought back those tears, only she lost and tried to look away, battling them ineffectively with her napkin.

"I want to be my boy's father. I don't want to take him away from his mother. From what little I've seen, you've done a good job raising him. I want to be there for him, too."

"He's going to hate me when he finds out you're his father. Dave practically idolizes Speed Johnson just because he used to play pro football a long time ago. You're every boy's hero, a big name quarterback."

She twisted her hands together. Brand wondered if she felt, as he did, that her world was suddenly being wrenched apart. "Instead of telling him he has a father any boy would kill to be related to, I've deliberately kept your identity secret."

"He'll still love you." He took her hand again. Retaining it more firmly this time, he rubbed her damp palm with his thumb. He wished he could do something more to allay her fear.

"It's not just that. You're everything I'm not. Famous, rich, well educated. You've got a family tree you can trace back forever." Her shoulders sagged, as if she thought she had nothing that would recommend her over Brand to a young boy.

Self-doubt had plagued her years ago, even though she'd had more determination to succeed than anyone he'd ever met. Remembering that helped him shed the remnants of his anger. "Listen to me. Dave won't hate you. I don't want him to be angry with you. Hell, if he hates anybody, it will probably be me."

"I don't think so. I know I should have told him about you as soon as he was old enough to start asking questions. I tried several times, but I just couldn't talk about it. About us."

He met her gaze, guessed how she must be hurting. Her expression reminded him of the agony he'd gone through after he'd lost her and their unborn baby. He'd fucking like to strangle his mother for having driven Dani away.

While the waiter served them, Brand reached under the little table and stroked her knee. He knew he shouldn't, but he gave her thigh a reassuring squeeze before moving his hand back to his own lap.

As they ate, he tried to convince himself all he should feel was resentment, but he couldn't help wanting her now, any more than he'd been able to when he was seventeen and in love.

Dani hardly ate a bite. She sat quietly, pushing food around on her plate. Her dark eyes, still sparkling with tears, seemed to see into his soul. He wanted to reach out and smooth the fall of dark brown hair that shadowed her cheek.

"Could we tell Dave together?" she asked, breaking the silence.

"I'd like that."

She looked up from her plate, met his gaze. "When?"

"Tonight. No need to put it off."

She nodded, moved her soft lips in what looked like a feeble effort at a smile. He hurried, cleared his plate so they could go. He had a feeling that the longer they waited, the more anxious she was going to become.

* * * * *

Dani waited while Brand disengaged the car's alarm system, unlocked the passenger door and started to open it. Instead, he turned to her, caught her in his muscular arms and pressed her back against the cold metal of the car. Before she could protest, he took her mouth and tasted her, cautiously at first. Then he deepened the kiss, tangling their tongues. Possessing her mouth the way she still wanted him to possess her body.

His kiss reminded her of the sweet young love they'd shared, yet it sizzled with a new intensity. He'd obviously developed his seductive skills since they'd been apart. When he raised his head and stepped back from their embrace, he was breathing hard. He wasn't the only one. Dani found herself gasping for air.

When Brand opened the door and held it open, she sank onto the pale gray leather seat. Damn it, she didn't want to want him. She didn't welcome the heat that had spread like wildfire through her body the minute their lips had touched. She was nuts to have let that kiss go on. Crazy to have let it happen in the first place, because she and Brand had no future now any more than they'd had one when they were kids. Pity her damp, swollen pussy didn't realize that kiss meant nothing more than an unwise rekindling of youthful lust.

Her cheeks hot with embarrassment, she glanced toward the driver's seat. Her whole body sizzled when she saw him tugging at the fly of his khaki pants. "See what you still do to me?" Apparently he wasn't the least bit self-conscious that he'd developed a noticeable erection. "Which way?" he asked when they got to the exit from the parking lot.

She gave him quick directions to the Seminole Heights neighborhood where she and Dave lived. "Brand, we mustn't do that again."

"Why not? It felt damn good to me. You liked it, too. I felt your nipples dig into my chest, and I know you felt my cock straining to get inside you." He paused, his expression changing from warm to icy cold. "Do you have a lover?"

"No. I haven't wanted anyone, not like I wanted you when we were kids. I don't want to want anybody like that, ever again."

"Why?"

She shrugged, trying to lighten the mood. "I don't know, I guess Brand Carendon's a hard act to follow." She interlaced her fingers to keep her hands from shaking.

Oh God, I never should have said that. It was enough *she* knew no one else but him had ever been able to make her pussy burn this way by giving her no more than a heated look. Her heart still beat double-time when he was around. She might know it, but no way should she have given him that kind of power over her. Not now, when he already had enough ammunition to wreck her life if that was what he wanted to do.

"I'm glad you think so." His grin told her he hadn't missed the implication of what she just said. Handling the car with one hand, he looped his other arm around her shoulder and pulled her across the mahogany console until her head rested on his broad chest. His heartbeat resounded in her ear.

Memories came back, bittersweet but poignant. The night when he'd taken her virginity on the backseat of his silver Camaro. Other sweet, long-ago times when they'd shared young love and not given a thought to the fact it had been doomed from the start. When she looked up at him, she noticed his facial muscles had tightened. Was he remembering those days, too?

"How will we tell Dave?" she asked, her voice muffled by the soft material of his shirt.

He ruffled her hair. "As casually as possible. We'll have plenty of time to try to justify why we haven't made a home together for him."

"He'll be so angry at me." Dani felt certain, whatever her son's other reactions might be, he'd resent her for keeping Brand ignorant of his existence.

"Not any madder than he'll be at me, I don't imagine. Dave will just have to accept that we've made mistakes and want to make up for them."

She raised her head in time to point out the final turn to her house. When he wheeled onto her street, she mentally compared this block of older homes that had seen better days with the neighborhood of impressive mini-mansions where Brand had grown up.

"Which house?" he asked as he slowed the car to an idle.

"Third one on the right. You'd better pull in the driveway. The teenagers will be all over this fancy car if you park it on the street." She could imagine the kind of attention the Ferrari would draw in this modest neighborhood.

"It's insured."

"Still..." For a moment she regretted renting her little house in this changing neighborhood when she could have chosen a much fancier apartment somewhere she wouldn't have worried so much about what might happen to Brand's expensive car. Still, a yard, a nearby school, families and friends meant more to her son than a fancy address.

The last thing she imagined was on Brand's mind right now was the safety of his exotic toy. She watched him pull the key from the ignition, slide out of the car. He still moved with fluid grace, the way she remembered. When he opened her door and reached inside to help her out, she couldn't help wanting to reach out and stroke his powerfully muscled arm.

"Shall we go get Dave?" he asked, dropping his hand quickly to his side.

She nodded. Lost in her fear that she'd soon lose her son as completely as she'd lost his father long ago, Dani began to walk down the street toward the Johnsons' house. Toward their son.

* * * * *

Callie Johnson looked the same as she had when Brand last saw her. A tall black woman, more handsome than pretty, she welcomed him and Dani with a smile.

"Y'all come in. Roger and Dave are having a good time playing games on Roger's new Xbox 360." She gave Brand the once-over, obviously not recognizing him in the dim yellow glow from the porch light. Then she turned to Dani. "I'm glad you're finally getting out, having some fun for yourself. Who's this handsome hunk?"

"Callie, this is Brand Carendon. Brand, Callie Johnson." Dani spoke so softly, Brand could barely hear her.

"Hi. It's good to see you again, Callie."

Callie's expression registered pleasant surprise when she heard Brand's name. That didn't surprise him, because their paths hadn't crossed since Speed had left the Marlins and pro football following the injury that had brought his career to a premature end. "Nice to see you, too. Roger and Dave sure had a good time watching the Marlins work out today." She turned to Dani. "You could've dropped me over with a feather. I didn't have any idea you knew the Counselor." Suddenly, Callie's smile faded.

Brand sensed her sudden change of mood. "What's wrong, Callie?"

"Where's your wife?"

"What? I don't have a wife. Oh, you mean Marilee?" Callie's protective posture amused Brand. "We split up a long time ago, the year after Speed got hurt."

Her expression softened. Motioning for them to come inside, Callie followed them into the living room. Brand noticed she'd made this modest house welcoming, much as she'd done with the high-end suburban home Speed had bought after he'd made the cut and joined the Marlins midway through Brand's rookie year. He had to admire her, sticking around after they'd lost everything along with Speed's future as a pro ball player. Not every wife did. "Would you two like a glass of iced tea?" she asked, standing and moving toward the door Brand imagined led to the kitchen.

"No thanks. We just finished eating," Dani replied. "We'd better collect Dave before he gets too wrapped up in Roger's new game."

"You're right about that." Callie moved across the room and called out into the hallway. "Roger, you and Dave come on out here now. Dave's mom's ready for him to go home."

"Hi, Mom." Dave bounded into the room, Roger at his heels. "Mr. Carendon," he added, a puzzled expression on his face.

After a few minutes' conversation, they left. Brand sensed questions churning silently in his son's head. The half-block walk to Dani's house stretched out as though the distance were measured in miles, not yards.

"You said you'd come, but I didn't think it'd be so soon." Dave looked up at Brand when they stopped on the porch. "Did you have to wait long for my mom?"

"Your mother and I had dinner together." Dani had to be scared stiff. Her nervousness showed in the way her hands trembled while she worked the key in the lock. "We've known each other for a long time," he added, trying to soften the shock they were about to give their son.

"You have? Did you know my dad, too?"

"Yeah, I know him."

"Come on in. Dave, take Brand in the living room. I'll fix us something to drink."

Dani was having trouble keeping her voice steady. Guessing she needed a few minutes to herself, Brand followed his son into a small, simply furnished room, sank down onto the sagging sofa and stretched his legs out under a scarred wooden coffee table.

"Do you really know my dad?"

"Yes. Dave, let's wait for your mother."

"She won't talk about him. You promised, Mr. Carendon."

"Yes, she will. We both will."

Brand ran his hand through his hair. When he studied Dave, he saw a lot of himself in his son. Fatherly pride yielded to fury when he thought of the years they'd lost, years they couldn't reclaim. Brand had to struggle, force himself to sit still. He had an insane urge to plow his fists into something.

One glance at Dani, and he realized her emotions were at least as frayed as his. He shot her what he hoped was a reassuring smile as she paused in the doorway. Her hands trembled, he could tell by watching the level of liquid shift in the pitcher at the center of a small tray.

He couldn't help noticing, when she set the tray down and joined him on the sofa, she put as much distance as possible between them. As if she had nothing particular on her mind, she took her time pouring tea over the ice in each of three tall glasses. Only the tremor in her hands revealed the turmoil that must have been tearing her apart inside.

"I hope tea's all right." The brief touch of her fingers on his when she handed him the glass sent a searing jolt of sexual energy straight to his cock.

"Tea's fine." How was it that he could despise her for keeping his child from him yet still want to protect her, wrap her in the safety of his arms and kiss away her worries?

Dave took the drink his mother offered, looking expectantly from her to Brand. While Dani held her tea glass with both hands as if she were afraid she'd drop it, Brand rubbed his palm across his brow, certain he'd find sweat preparing to run down into his eyes. The silence was charged, as though each of them was holding back, waiting for someone else to break the tension.

"Dave, *Brand* is your father," Dani blurted out.

Chapter Three

When Brand met Dave's startled gaze, he felt the boy's tension ease then intensify. "My birth certificate says my father is *David* Carendon." Obviously confused, Dave looked first at his mother, then back at Brand.

Brand cleared his throat. "My first name is David. Brand's a shortened version of Brandon, my middle name."

Dave's mouth dropped open. Dani stared blindly at the glass she clutched between white-knuckled fingers. Brand felt the walls of Dani's tiny living room beginning to close in on him. On all of them. His chest tightened and he gasped for breath.

Like a coiled spring suddenly let loose, Dave came out of his chair and launched himself at Brand. Instinctively Brand blocked the boy's churning fists, grabbed his wrists and forced him to his knees. "Damn you! You walked out on Mom. How could I ever have thought you were some kind of hero?" Dave's tears did nothing to lighten the hatred Brand read in his eyes.

Dani moved closer and rested a hand tentatively on Brand's knee. "Don't blame your dad. I'm the one who walked out on him."

Dave looked at Dani then turned back to Brand. "Is she telling the truth, *Daddy*?"

He'd never realized a kid could express such sarcasm with just one word. If his son hadn't deserved an honest answer, Brand might just have called time out.

What should he say? Before he'd talked with Dani, his answer would have been a simple yes. Now, though, his perception of Dani's desertion had faded from black and white to a muddy gray. "It's not that simple, son," he finally said, hating to waffle but—

"Did Mom leave you or not?" Dave sounded choked up. Tears streamed down his flushed cheeks.

"Yes. But she had her reasons. We were kids, not too much older than you are now." *You were old enough to make a baby, asshole.* Frustrated, Brand looked to Dani for help.

She reached out for Dave, but he ducked away. "Please." Her plea, uttered as if she had been choking on it, tore at Brand's gut. "I left Brand. I thought I had good reasons."

"What reasons?" Dave sounded cold, too cold to be just eleven years old.

"I left because I had reason to believe your father wanted me to leave. That was not the truth. He didn't. But I thought he did. I thought I wasn't good enough for him. I was very young, and I was frightened. I made a mistake, but I didn't leave because I wanted to."

Dave stood, his chest heaving as though he'd just finished a grueling run. His face was a mask of hurt and anger when he looked at his mother.

"I don't understand. Why would *you* walk out on *him*? You're nobody. He's one of the best quarterbacks in pro football. What were you? Nuts?" When he took a step toward the door, Brand blocked his way. "Let me go," he spat out, scorching Brand with his anger.

Brand searched for words that would calm his son as he countered Dave's retreat. Shifting his position by a few steps, he blocked the only door Dave could have used to escape. His gaze locked on his son. He felt rather than saw Dani move next to him and take his hand.

"Brand didn't know about you until you came to see him today," she said, her tone as gentle as her touch.

Dave didn't move but his gaze shifted to meet Brand's. "You didn't?"

"No. Sit down, Dave. Now."

The boy hesitated, as if torn between bolting and obeying Brand's order. Finally he flopped down on the chair and stared at Dani. "Why? Why didn't you tell me? Why didn't you tell *him*? I thought my dad might be a criminal or something."

Brand cringed at having caused his son such pain. By forcing this confrontation he'd hurt Dani again, too. Her sobs damn near tore him apart.

He'd been so sure Dave would have taken this well. He should have listened to Dani, believed her when she'd predicted how their son would react. "Your mother did what she thought was best. Don't lay blame on her."

"How could *you* not have known about me?"

"I knew your mother was expecting my baby, but I didn't know until today that you'd been born." Keeping his gaze on the boy, Brand moved back onto the sofa and pulled Dani down beside him.

"That sounds dumb. Didn't you figure I'd be born sooner or later?" Dave glared at Brand.

Brand wasn't about to mention that his mother had told him Dani was going to have an abortion. He chose his words carefully. "I should have, but I didn't. Your mother thought I didn't want her or you, so she went away. I saw her today for the first time in more than twelve years."

Dave leaned back against the back of the chair, a puzzled look on his face. His gaze shifted from Brand to Dani. Needing to feel her warmth, Brand pulled Dani closer, sandwiched her hand between his calloused palms. "Are you mad at me for looking for you?"

"Mad? I'm sorry it took eleven years for me to meet you. I'm thrilled to have a son, that your mom has done such a fine job of taking care of you for all this time." Brand felt dampness in his own eyes. Instead of fighting the tears, he let them roll down his cheeks.

"Brand wants to spend time with you, get to know you," Dani said quietly. "I'm sorry, Dave. I was wrong to keep you apart. I didn't realize that because I never talked about your father you might think he was someone to be ashamed of. I hope you'll forgive me."

"Of course he will." Brand wrapped his arm around Dani's slender shoulders. "There's nothing to forgive. You didn't have any idea I'd want to know our son. You were only trying to protect him from being hurt." Silence hung in the room. Brand tried to sort out questions that remained unasked and unanswered, and he imagined Dani and Dave were doing the same. He felt as though a dozen hammers were beating inside his skull, each one pounding a conflicting emotion into his throbbing brain. He dared not let the feelings out, clue his son in to the anger, the confusion, the sense of betrayal—or the lust toward Dani that still lay beneath the surface of all the other feelings. Finally, feeling like the world's biggest coward, he decided it was time to beat a retreat. Standing, he held out his hand to Dani.

"I've got to go. There's a meeting at nine o'clock with the other quarterbacks to go over next season's playbook." Never mind that nothing would have happened to him if he missed that informal gathering. He turned to Dave. "Would you like to spend the day at camp tomorrow?" Brand held his breath, afraid the boy would refuse.

"Can I, Mom?" Dave sounded uncertain, as though part of him wanted to tell Brand to go to hell while another voice urged him to go.

"I guess so." When Dani looked up at him, Brand watched a solitary tear make its way down her cheek. It was all he could do to keep his hands at his sides. He wanted to brush that tear away. Allay the fear she conveyed with those three simple words. It made no sense that he still wanted to strangle her for keeping his son from him, while at the same time he had this irrational need to soothe her fears. Protect her from not only their son's wrath but his own.

He had to struggle to keep his tone matter-of-fact when he spoke to her. "I'll come over about seven in the morning and pick him up, then. Dave and I will pick you up when you get off from work. We can all go out and eat."

Dani looked doubtful. "I don't know if that would be a good idea. Wouldn't you rather take Dave out to eat before you drop him off at home? I can take the bus, like always."

"We'll pick you up. See you in the morning, buddy." He had to have a few minutes alone with Dani. Time to resolve some of the feelings that had his ears ringing a lot like they did just after he'd taken a hard hit from an opposing linebacker." He turned to her, lowered his voice so only she would hear. "Walk me out to the car."

"All right." She stepped off the porch, headed for his car. "What did you want?" She sounded hesitant…as confused as he felt.

He wished to hell he knew the answer to that, but he didn't. All he knew was that he wasn't ready to let her go. Not yet. Not until… Fuck, he couldn't put a time line on when he'd walk away. When his anger would get the better of those other softer feelings toward her that apparently hadn't ever completely died.

He brought her hand to his chest so she could feel his heart pounding. When he spoke, the words came out sounding harsher than he intended. "I've hated you for twelve years for walking out on me. I don't believe you ever would have come to me on your own and told me about my son. I don't trust you. So why is it my cock's burning from wanting you?" He tried without success to squelch the succinct oath that followed. "Does it make you feel good to know how hard I get for you, how you take my breath away?"

"No. Yes. Brand, I don't know." For a minute he thought she was going to pull away. She was probably smart to back off, because in his present mood he might have hurt her emotionally if not physically.

"Damn you. I hope you're remembering how you used to fall apart when we made love. How sweetly you submitted, how you screamed every time you came. I thought I'd put those times out of my mind but apparently I haven't."

A shudder passed through her as she wrapped her arms around his waist. Blood instantly slammed into his cock. No doubt about it, she still turned him on the same as always, as though they'd never parted.

Brand bent and kissed Dani, drowned in the soft warmth of her mouth. Gently he traced over her soft, slender curves. His hands seemed to have memories of their own. So did his cock. He'd never gotten so hard, so fast, with any other woman. He cupped her rounded ass cheeks and lifted her against him. When he ground his hips against her, her legs parted, cradled his erection. Just like old times.

Seconds, moments, long lonely years passed through his mind. He wallowed in desire that was new and fresh, yet laced with memories. "My God, you still turn me on the way nobody else ever has." He set her away from him, held both her hands.

"You want me, too." He needed her to acknowledge the passionate response that made her breathing ragged, her dark eyes glow. "Say it, Dani."

"I-I can't. You'd better go. I don't know what came over me." She stepped back, putting distance between them. She might have been afraid to say it, but she wasn't able to hide the fierce desire that had her shaking all over. Even in the moonlight Brand saw the flush of passion in her cheeks.

Fear grabbed at his gut. Realizing she still had the power to get him instantly hard and ready, that the years he'd spent smarting at her rejection hadn't taught him caution, didn't make Brand happy. But he couldn't have denied his reaction even if he wanted to. Dani still attracted him the way flame enticed a moth. If he let her, she could burn him again as surely as she had twelve years ago.

He wouldn't. This time around, he'd call the plays. And this time there'd be no referees to call him out of bounds.

He tucked a silky strand of dark hair behind her ear. "This isn't over by a long shot, but you're off the hook for tonight. See you and Dave in the morning." He bent and brushed his lips over hers.

* * * * *

Brand gunned the Ferrari up the entrance ramp to the Interstate. He clenched his teeth and clutched the steering wheel so hard his knuckles turned white, but he couldn't hold in his anger. Right now he wanted to strangle his mother. Pushing a button on the dash to activate the car phone, he spoke the familiar numbers. Then, realizing how late it was, he said, "Cancel the call."

He had to get hold of himself. Taking a deep breath, he tried to clear his mind of the whole bizarre situation and the part Eleanor, his snobbish mother, had played in keeping him in the dark for nearly twelve years. He turned on the radio, scanned for a local station.

In clear, crisp stereo, a man sang of making love, of having more than just an affair. Brand swore out loud, a long string of the most inventive epithets he'd heard and used in the locker room after infuriating losses. None too gently, he shoved a CD into the stereo, shutting off the singer with new Marlins play sequences he needed to memorize. Not two minutes later, he ejected the CD and shut off the radio.

Silence was no better than sound, for he still couldn't clear his head. He kept picturing Dani all alone, having his son and struggling to raise him alone. A haunting pride in the girl who'd taught him the meaning of desire sneaked into his mind, stilled some of his resentment. He could only imagine how hard it had been for her, taking care of Dave when she hadn't even finished high school before he was born.

Brand shoved those tender, sympathetic feelings into a far corner of his mind. He could want her 'til hell froze over, but wanting her wouldn't make up for her having cheated him out of eleven years with his child—his only son.

He couldn't deny the special chemistry between them. Hell, that electric feeling had been there years ago, the first time he'd laid eyes on Dani. He'd gotten that same jolt of instant lust today. Damn it, he'd have her again, keep her as long as it took to sate his need and hers. Unless he missed a guess, putting out the fire would take a long time—maybe even a lifetime.

The last time they'd had sex the night before she'd left, he'd felt youthful love and trust, and a childish anticipation of a future with her and the baby they'd made. Then, that child had been a hazy concept in his adolescent mind. Now, Dave was very real. His son added another dimension to Brand's thoughts and feelings, to the reality of his life.

He recalled the pride he'd felt in his damnable virility the night Dani had told him she was pregnant. Taking one hand off the leather-covered steering wheel, he brushed his hair off his brow. Hell, what seventeen-year-old boy wouldn't have felt a rush when he found out he'd impregnated his girl the one time they'd made love without protection, the night he'd taken her virginity on the backseat of his Camaro?

Yeah, he'd been scared stiff, too, but he brushed that memory aside. Back at the team's hotel barely in time for curfew, Brand slid his car into its parking slot and hurried to his room.

* * * * *

"Brand, where in hell have you been?" Josh Shearer asked, looking up from the playbook on his lap. "You'll be half dead by the time you finish the workout in the morning."

"Tampa. You feel like talking?" Brand lay down across his bed and looked over at his roommate.

"Sure. What's up?"

"I just met my son."

"What the hell?" Josh got up and stretched out on his own bed, apparently no longer interested in the playbook.

"It's a long story." Sorting out some of his thoughts as he talked, Brand told Josh about meeting Dave and seeing Dani again.

"So, that's why you ran off after practice. Here I'd hoped you'd decided it was time for you to retire." Josh, Brand's backup, continually groused in a good-natured way about Brand's eventual retirement, but his grin faded when he looked Brand in the eye. "What's she like? Dani, I mean. Fuck, I can't imagine seeing an old flame after so long a time, let alone finding out I had a kid I'd never heard about."

"Dani's still Dani, twelve years older but otherwise pretty much as I remembered her. Dark-haired, tiny, pretty, soft-spoken. Quiet. She hit me like a three-hundred-pound tackle when I was a kid. Seeing her again today did the same thing."

Brand stared at the ceiling, wondering what their lives would have been like if he'd had brains enough to doubt his mother's lies, gone after Dani when she'd walked out and brought her home. "I guess I never did get her completely out of my system."

"So, what now? Both of you are single, right? Do you get together, pretend the last however many years never happened and live happily ever after?"

"You must be crazy. Could you pretend it didn't matter that the woman you loved more than anything didn't trust you enough to wait, to ask you to your face if what your mother had told her was true? Could you forgive this woman for keeping you from knowing you had a kid for eleven goddamn years?"

Josh rubbed his chin. "So what made her decide to tell you now?"

"She didn't. Dave did. Dani would have damn well waited 'til hell froze over before she'd have let me know my son."

"I've met your mother. She's one formidable lady. Can you really blame the girl for breaking under her intimidation?"

"Hell. I don't know. But damn it, she could have called me. Given me the chance to know my son. Let me help support him. She wouldn't have had to brave Mother's wrath. I haven't lived at home since the weekend Dani and I got married."

"Did Dani know that?"

"Yes…no…how in hell should I know? She could have found out what I was doing easily enough if she'd wanted to. She knew I'd married Marilee. Damn it, I can't trust her, but I want her now just as much as I did when we were kids, even knowing she cost me eleven years of sharing my son's life."

Josh shook his head. "I'd say you've got one hell of a problem, Counselor."

"Well, is that all you can say now that you've heard the mixed-up tale of my misguided youth?" Brand raked his hand across his brow.

"It's sure some story. Just how old *were* you when all this happened? Sixteen, seventeen?"

"Seventeen—two months shy of not needing the phony IDs I bought before we got married. My dad had the marriage annulled after Dani left."

"So, both of you are old enough now. Other than the lurking thoughts you can't trust her now, what's stopping you from getting it together? You admit you still have the hots for the lady. And you do want your kid, right?"

For a long time Brand considered what Josh said. When he spoke, his throat felt tight. "We're worlds apart. Neither of us, especially Dani, is likely to forget that." Suddenly exhausted, he rubbed at his eyes.

"So what *are* you going to do?"

"Have it out with my mother, for starters." She was supposed to love him, for God's sake. He intended to know how the fuck she'd managed to live with herself all these years, thinking she'd talked Dani into destroying her own grandchild. How in God's name had she thought Dani would survive on her own, sixteen years old, with not even a high school diploma to her credit?

Josh cleared his throat, brought Brand back to the here and now. "When this gets out, the reporters are going to have a field day. Or do you mean to keep your son and his mom under wraps?"

Brand sat up, met Josh's gaze. "Of course I intend to acknowledge them. Immediately." He shuddered when he pictured how the press would crucify them, considered and discarded possible ways to head the vultures off. "We've got to get married," he muttered, more to himself than to his friend.

"Get married?"

Brand nodded. "There's no way I want Dave and Dani to see their names plastered all over the tabloid papers. No way I'll subject them to reading the half-truths, innuendoes, and downright lies reporters would take delight in putting out to sell more of their filth." What he imagined they'd write about his high-school girlfriend and the child he'd neglected for eleven years wasn't pretty.

"I see you remember that girl you never met. The one who decided to sue you for paternity a few years back. That story made the front-page headlines on half the rags in the country."

Brand's headache suddenly took on the proportions of an atomic blast. "Must you remind me?"

"Good luck," Josh said, grinning.

It had been hard to persuade Dani to marry him twelve years ago. He doubted that doing it now would be any easier. It would probably be damn near impossible. But he'd manage, wear her down. Hell, his tenacity had done as much as his talent toward driving him to the top in his profession. If all else failed, he could threaten her with taking their son away.

He hoped he wouldn't have to do that. He wanted to protect Dani, not intimidate her. The only way he saw to do that was to persuade her they needed to get married. Strange, the idea of tying himself to her didn't seem as distasteful as it should, considering the resentment and lack of trust that remained from the past. Brand felt better, in fact, as if a weight had lifted from his chest.

He glanced at Josh, grinned. "You realize, don't you, that my marrying Dani might encourage me to keep playing football as long as I can? I can pretty much guarantee she won't be anxious for me to retire and practice law full time back in the old home town."

Josh laughed out loud. "No problem. Bad as it may be to admit, I don't mind too much standing on the sidelines with the clipboard. It's not all bad, collecting my four hundred grand a year while you go out and get creamed every Sunday. Go to sleep, Counselor, or neither of us will pass muster in the morning." He reached over, snapped off the bedside lamp.

Chapter Four

೫

Dreading what her son would say to her now that they were alone, Dani took her time getting back inside. Ever since he'd gotten old enough to watch football on TV, Dave had idolized Brand Carendon, the all-pro quarterback. It stood to reason he'd quickly come to revere Brand Carendon, his father, even more.

She'd certainly loved Brand, even though their child had been the only lasting joy loving him had brought her. No doubt she'd suffer more now that father and son had discovered one another, but she couldn't deny Dave the dad he'd gone to so much effort to find. Dreading a confrontation, she quit stalling and went back in the house.

"Mom, I can't believe it. My dad's Brand Carendon. I can't wait to see the looks on my friends' faces when I tell them. Hey, I'll bet they won't believe me. Do you think he'd come with me, let me introduce him to the guys at the park?"

Dani sighed. It was starting already, the hero worship she expected would get worse as time went on. "I'm sure he will. Dave, one reason I never told you about your dad was that he's so well known. I thought, if he hadn't wanted to see you, you'd have even felt worse than you did not knowing who he was."

"What made you think he wouldn't want me?"

Dani wanted to blurt out the story of how Brand's mother had deceived Brand as well as her. But a voice in her head whispered that she mustn't malign Dave's grandmother. "Your dad and I were very young. I believed Brand didn't want the responsibility for taking care of a family, so I went away.

"I was wrong. If I'd given him the chance, he'd have loved you, wanted you. I'm sorry." She reached out, pulled him to her. When she hugged him, he didn't hug her back, but at least he stayed there, his chin almost resting on her shoulder while she patted the back of his tousled hair. "Think about it. Now you've got your dad, and we're both going to be here for you from now on."

Dave pulled back a little, met her gaze with what seemed almost like a smile. "Okay, Mom."

"Okay to you, too." He looked so much like Brand, it was scary. Funny how she'd never let herself dwell on the resemblance before, but now she did. It was almost as though letting go the secret had freed her to see so much she'd tried so hard to bury in the depths of her mind. "Go on to bed now. If you don't, you'll never be able to get up and be ready when your dad comes for you in the morning." She hugged her son, and while he didn't hug her back, he didn't pull away. That encouraged her.

As emotionally drained as she felt, Dani expected she'd sleep like a rock the minute her head hit the pillow. For a long time, though, she tossed restlessly. Dave, Brand, the past and the present tumbled through her mind, blurred together. Distorted images full of joy and sorrow. Finally she fell into an exhausted sleep.

In her dream, she lay secure in Brand's arms. Then a terrifying, relentless force tugged her away, transported her, alone and lonely, to a spot that reminded her of Carendon, Georgia, her childhood home. Waking up suddenly, she sat up in bed, her body drenched in cold sweat, her mind twelve years in the past.

She hadn't wanted to fall in love with him. David Brandon Carendon was old Georgia aristocracy. His father's Atlanta law firm was one of the biggest in the state, a legacy from past generations. The only connection anybody in her family had ever had with the legal system had involved law enforcement officers, not lawyers.

For God's sake, Brand's home town and his last name were the same. How much more out of her league could he have been? He might play with her, she'd thought when he first asked her out, but someday he'd marry a girl from his own world. Every day of their short, idyllic romance, Dani had reminded herself Brand Carendon was not for the likes of her. Her heart had refused to listen.

He'd been so good, so supportive when she told him she was pregnant. He'd been so sure his parents would stand behind them, uphold their decision to marry and keep their child. And he'd known as well as she did that her drunken mother wouldn't care what they decided to do. Brand's optimistic if misplaced logic had won Dani over despite her fears.

She should have told him no, but she hadn't. They'd decided their marriage should be presented to their families as a done deal. She had gone with Brand across the state line to Tennessee, where he'd heard they could find a justice of the peace who wouldn't scrutinize the fake IDs he'd bought. The wedding had been quick and simple. No flowers, no music, no friends murmuring congratulations. Still, she'd never been able to forget the vows they'd made late one night in front of the snaggle-toothed official and his sleepy wife. She'd always wished she had a picture of them that day.

She'd never forget the way he had looked, lanky and tall, a good-hearted kid trying very hard to shoulder his responsibilities like a man. His expression, scared but filled with tenderness, would stay in her memories forever. Dani touched her naked ring finger, recalling the narrow, etched gold band Brand had put there so long ago.

With the confidence of youth, they'd begun their life together in a rustic hunting cabin Brand's grandfather had left to him. For just over a week, they'd laughed, made love, daydreamed about the future they'd share.

Those dreams had shattered like iced tea glasses hitting a concrete deck. A sound she'd always associate with the awful scene that had begun the minute Brand's mother had gotten her alone. Dani had thought time had erased the love as well as the hurt. But both emotions had come back, strong and conflicting, the moment she'd seen Brand again.

She willed herself to think rationally. She should run, not walk, away from him, save herself from certain heartbreak. As she stared out the window at a crescent moon, she tried in vain to squelch the lust and love his touch still evoked.

She wasn't going to walk away this time. She couldn't deny Dave his father. Besides, she wouldn't kid herself. She could no more resist Brand now than she'd been able to twelve years ago. What hurt was knowing it could never be the way it used to be between them, before reality had intruded and destroyed their perfect world.

Burying her head in her pillow, she cried. The innocent love they'd shared as children was dead. All that was left of it was a fierce sexual chemistry, precious little to hold onto—and a shared love for one eleven-year-old boy.

* * * * *

Brand hadn't slept much. It was all he could do to force a pleasant grin for the reporter who accosted him at six a.m. in the hotel parking lot. All the way across the bridge he scanned the rearview mirror. Good. He didn't notice anybody following him.

Fifteen minutes later he pulled up in front of Dani's place. It looked older and more worn in the light of day than it had last night. Hopefully the press would never have reason to go looking into how Dani and Dave had lived since she left him.

Sure, and pigs fly, too. Brand made a mental note to think up a plausible explanation for his former wife and son's having existed on the fringes of poverty while he pulled down millions every year. So far as he was concerned, his profession made him fair game for the carrion of the press. He'd be damned, though, if he intended to let them drag his family through the mud.

"Dave just got up. He's getting dressed," Dani said when she opened the front door. "Come on into the kitchen. I've got coffee made."

Brand followed her to the kitchen. Damn, but she had a great ass. He imagined taking those rounded cheeks in his hands, holding onto them while he fucked her from behind.

"Would you like some coffee?" She lifted a battered percolator off one of the stove's burners, reminding him of their poverty, steeling him to push her for marriage.

He came up close behind her, splayed his fingers across her soft, flat belly. Her backside felt firm yet giving against his groin. Bending his head, turning hers to give him access, he kissed his way from her flushed cheeks to her lush pink mouth.

When she set the coffeepot down, he loosened his hold, turned her to face him. This time he caught her open mouth and forced his tongue inside, teasing them both with the thrusting rhythm that mimicked fucking.

When her arms tightened around his shoulders he cupped her ass cheeks and pressed her against his raging hard-on. Her unguarded response threatened his control, boggled his mind. Finally, while he still could, he broke the kiss.

He still held her, but at arm's length. "I don't just want my son. I want you, Dani." Golden shards lit her dark gaze as he dragged her hand to his groin, closed it around his swollen cock. For a moment she hesitated, but then her fingers tightened around him ever-so gently.

He damn near came from that slight contact. Wanting her as hot as she'd gotten him, he slipped his hand inside her robe and found the soft round globe of her breast. When he rubbed his palm across the pebbled nipple she let out a little whimper.

"You want this, too." It didn't take a rocket scientist to figure that out. He could tell by the way her body reacted when he touched her. He loved the feel of her skin, all hot and tantalizing, smooth as silk.

"It's been so long, too long." She sounded mindless with need. He knew damn well he was about to burst, but it wasn't the time or place to haul her off to bed.

He tried to back off, burying his face in her hair, nuzzling the sensitive spots on her throat. "It's been a long time for me, too, honey."

"You're awfully sure of yourself." She sounded annoyed, but he wasn't about to forget she'd admitted last night that she'd never found a lover to take his place. He guessed he should be grateful for her change in mood, though, for it broke the sexual tension.

"You told me yourself. Remember? Last night you said I'm a hard act to follow." He released her and sat on one of the wooden kitchen chairs. "I'll have that coffee now, unless you're willing to help me relieve this painful condition."

She blushed when he caught her sneaking a glance at his lap. "You can't let Dave see you like that," she blurted out. As if suddenly self-conscious, she adjusted her ratty terry cloth robe, tightening the belt like armor around her waist.

"The way I'm feeling now, I imagine you could take care of the problem in about thirty seconds."

"Brand."

"Well, you could." He laughed out loud when she shot him a disapproving look over the top of the coffeepot.

Dani set the coffee on the table, along with a spoon and a half-gallon carton of milk. "Sugar's in the bowl. Dave's coming. For God's sake, Brand, sit behind the table or something."

He moved the chair so the table covered the lower part of his anatomy. When his son joined them, he managed a smile and a greeting.

"Sorry I wasn't ready." Dave poured some milk from the carton, offered it to Brand. "Morning, Mom."

"Good morning."

Part of Brand was glad the boy had finally come to breakfast. He'd been about to make a total fool of himself over Dani. His aching cock would rather have had Dave stay in bed.

"Brand, have you had breakfast?" Dani asked.

"No. I could use some." Especially if she were serving pussy, but that was too much to expect. He ran his hand over his stubble-roughened face, remembered he hadn't taken time to shave. He glanced at Dani, felt a twinge of remorse when he saw his beard had scraped her sensitive skin.

Dani dipped slices of bread into beaten eggs and fried them in a big cast iron skillet. Her robe cupped her rounded ass when she stretched to reach for plates in the cabinet beside the stove. God but he loved that little ass. Soon he'd be holding that rounded flesh, steadying her while he pounded his cock into her tight, wet cunt. Or feeling that flesh against his belly while he fucked her in the ass, where he'd bet no man had ever been.

When she moved to set the table, he noticed chipped, mismatched dishes, silverware that was flimsy and bent with age. Guilt distracted Brand from his sexual fantasy. Then fury took over. The vultures in the press were going to have a field day, crucify him for having let his son and Dani live like this. Hell, he felt like crucifying himself, even though he hadn't known.

He shouldn't have listened to his mother. Shouldn't have let Dani go. He deserved whatever the bastards might say about him. But Dani and Dave didn't need to be skewered for his mistakes.

"Do you like peaches?" Dani set a bottle of syrup and a stick of margarine on the table.

His emotions too raw to speak, Brand nodded. While she dumped the contents of a good-sized can into a bowl, he tried to figure out the best way to ensure she'd accept the proposal he had to make.

When she slid French toast onto his plate and sat down, Brand shoved his frustration aside, determined to eat and be sociable.

"Don't you have to change clothes before you go to work?" Dani asked, after he had told Dave they would be going directly to the Marlins' practice field.

"I'm a football player, remember? Unless we're practicing in pads, this is what I wear to work out." Not quite true, he admitted silently, cringing at the thought of stuffing the hard-on that wouldn't go away inside a jock strap.

"Yesterday you had on socks and cleats," Dave pointed out.

Brand laughed. "You're right. I'll put them on in the locker room. "Ready, Dave?"

"Sure." Dave stood, watched Brand bend down, brush his lips casually across Dani's cheek. "Do I need to take any money? Or a sandwich for lunch?" he asked.

"No. I'll feed you." Brand lowered his voice and spoke into Dani's ear. "We have to get married. We'll talk about it more tonight."

With that, he straightened up and followed his son outside. He noted with wry amusement how Dani's mouth had dropped open as if she couldn't believe what he had said.

* * * * *

Married?

We have to get married?

Brand might as well have said they had to jump off a cliff. Dani rested her head on the table after he and Dave had left. She didn't know if she should laugh or cry.

Right now she didn't have time to do either. It was getting late, and she had to get to work. As she put on her

Tuesday outfit, she cursed Brand for taunting her with such a cruel joke.

Get married indeed! They'd been there, done that, and all she'd gotten from it had been a broken heart. She wasn't Cinderella, and Brand Carendon damn sure wasn't Prince Charming. Even if he had been, their story didn't fit in with the fairytale. It had been Cinderella, not Prince Charming, who'd had a witch for a mother!

Dani got her work done, but fortunately none of it had involved a lot of thinking. She'd thought of nothing all day except Brand's cryptic parting words. He had to have been joking. Their marriage hadn't stood a chance twelve years ago, and it wouldn't stand one now. Too nervous to stay at her desk a moment longer, she grabbed her purse and went downstairs the minute the clock on her computer indicated it was quitting time.

Outside on the patio, she sat on a bench and tried to sort out all that had happened. Caught up in her thoughts, she didn't notice the woman with the camera until the light from a flashbulb made her blink.

Dani hardly had time to note the woman's hard, brittle stare before she found a slick business card in her hand. *Ellen Harris. Celebrity Tattler.* "What do you want?" she asked as the woman sat down beside her.

"I want to know all about you and Brand Carendon." The woman's voice was as mellow as her expression was harsh. "I know you had dinner with him last night at Tonelli's."

Suddenly Dani felt violated. Exposed. "Why does it matter to you?"

"Your boyfriend's news, honey. Big news. Come on, tell me. How'd you meet him?"

Recalling some of the weird headlines she'd seen on tabloid papers while waiting to pay for her groceries, Dani shuddered at the thought she—or God forbid Dave—might become the subject of a sensationalized story in—she glanced at the card—the *Celebrity Tattler*. "I have nothing to say."

"I'll make it worth your while." Ellen opened a purse Dani thought would make an adequate briefcase and fished out a handful of money. "How much?"

Dani couldn't help gaping at what she figured had to be several hundred dollars in crisp, new twenties. Her hand went out reflexively, but she pulled it back. "I won't talk to you." Vicious stories like the ones they printed in those rag sheets could destroy Dave.

"Good girl." Brand grinned at Dani, but his blue eyes looked nearly black when he riddled the reporter with a look that could have killed. "Sifting for more dirt, Ellen?" he asked, his tone silky.

"What's up with you and this lady?"

"Nothing that concerns you. Go crawl back into whatever hole you're inhabiting these days. Come on, Dani."

Brand wasn't particularly gentle when he stood and snatched her up by one hand. Dani felt his tension as she tried to match his long, quick strides away from this woman reporter he apparently had run into before.

"I left Dave with Callie and his buddy Roger," he told her as he practically dragged her to his car. "He's fine."

Dani tried not to pant with the exertion it took to keep up with him. After they fastened their seat belts and Brand started the engine, she told him the reporter had snapped her picture.

"Damn. That woman has a nose like a bloodhound."

"Why would she care who has dinner with you?" Dani tried to recall who she had seen featured on the covers of the *Tattler*. "Isn't that paper mostly about movie and TV stars?"

"Mostly. Ellen has a thing about athletes, though. Once in a while she sniffs out some dirt about one of us that the publisher thinks is depraved enough to sell. You were smart not to talk to her."

"Then she won't write anything? I'd be embarrassed to death to get written up in one of those...those—"

"They're smut rags. All of them. Don't count on not finding your name smeared all over the *Tattler*. What people don't tell Ellen, she makes up. If it's lurid enough, the *Tattler* will print it." Brand's knuckles turned white as he held the steering wheel in a death grip.

Dani imagined the way the tabloid might report her leaving Brand, keeping his son from him. She shuddered. They wouldn't hurt an innocent child. Or would they? "Brand, would they write about us? About Dave?"

"In a New York minute, if they thought it would make them money."

Suddenly Dani wanted to find Ellen Harris, scratch out those icy green eyes that she'd felt staring right through her. "You've got to stop them," she said as he pulled into the driveway at her house.

Chapter Five

Brand had never felt more culpable in his life. He stared across the room at Dani, whose shoulders slumped as she looked out the window at God only knew what.

"We've got to talk." Deliberately, he repeated the words he'd left her with earlier. "We have to get married."

She whirled to face him as if she thought he'd lost his mind. "You said that before. What does our getting married have to do with stopping people from writing awful things about you and me. About Dave?"

"It won't stop the vultures from gossiping, but it at least will take the edge off what they say. We'll present a united front, convince them we're happy we've found each other, that I've found my son." Brand softened his voice to little more than a whisper, moved closer. He rested his hands on Dani's shoulders. "Let me take care of you, the way I should have for the past twelve years."

"Brand, your mother hates me."

"I won't let her hurt you again. You have my word. I wouldn't have given her the chance to years ago if I'd realized how cruel she could be." He moved closer still, until her quick, shallow breaths tickled his chest. With one finger beneath her chin he tilted her head back, forced her to look him in the eye.

She blinked back tears. Her throat tightened visibly when she swallowed. "I don't belong in your world. Your mother was right about that. I'm just as afraid of vicious reporters now as I was of the good people of Carendon twelve years ago. I'll never forget the way they tortured me. I won't let Dave be hurt that way."

Brand remembered how frightened she'd been years ago, when he'd insisted they get married. He felt like a first-class bastard this time, but he had no choice if he was going to protect his son. "How have you survived?" It had to have been hell, trying to support their child with no money and little education. She hadn't had family to fall back on, not with her mother thinking supporting herself meant turning enough tricks to keep herself in cheap booze.

Dani squared her shoulders, looked him in the eye. "I waited tables at a cafe in Atlanta until we moved to Tampa. For a little while, I took welfare so I could get my GED and take some secretarial classes. Until I got hired at the brokerage two years ago, I worked two jobs."

Brand's heart constricted in his chest. "Quit working. Let me take care of you and Dave."

"He's my son. I chose to have him. I'll take care of him."

"Damn it, Dani. I'm glad you had him. I didn't forget you when you left. I had nightmares about the baby I thought you'd aborted. I don't know how many times I cried for what I thought was the loss of that little life. Dave is my son, too. I'm going to take care of both of you from here on out."

"I don't know. If you come into his life, I'll lose him. He's all I have. Can't you understand?" More tears spilled over onto Dani's flushed cheeks.

"I understand trusting me doesn't come easy for you," he spat out. She'd had little enough faith in him when she'd believed his mother's lying words. "It took me twelve years and the intervention of the son you never let me know I had, just to get you to listen. You'd never have come to me, not even if Dave had been starving." He rubbed his brow, raked his hand through his hair.

"I'd never let my son go hungry." Her dark eyes blazed with apparent fury. "I'm sorry I never told you about Dave. But what your mother said made sense to me. How could you have wanted to marry anyone then, much less me? You'd have been tied down when you needed to be having fun, going to school without the burden of a wife you could never feel comfortable with."

"You could have waited an hour or so and asked *me* how I felt. You might even have ignored my mother and believed I'd been truthful when I told you how much you meant to me. Even if you couldn't have brought yourself to trust me, you damn well could have let me know when my son was born."

"I wanted to, but you were in college. I didn't know how to reach you. After you married Marilee, I brought Dave here to Tampa."

"Bull. My name was in the Atlanta papers all the damn time. I imagine I even got mentioned occasionally in the papers here, especially when the Marlins played the Bucs or made the playoffs. Hell, Dani, even perfect strangers can track me down without a whole lot of effort, just by reading the sports pages. Don't tell me you couldn't have found me if you'd wanted to."

She looked up at him, tears sparkling in dark eyes that looked as though they could see right through his anger. Her hesitation palpable, she finally squared her shoulders. When she spoke, her tone rang with righteous indignation. "If you'd wanted to, you could have come after me. For weeks I hoped you would. Finally I gave up and accepted that I'd never see you again." She looked away and trembled, grasping his arms as though she was afraid she might fall. Then she looked at him again. "I didn't contact you later because I was afraid. Afraid you'd take my son away from me," she said so softly he couldn't have heard if he hadn't been watching her lips move.

He crossed his arms, covered her small hands with his own, sensed the effort it had cost her to admit the fear that had driven her so long ago. That apparently still drove her now. "I will have Dave, but I want you too. Take a chance. Come to Milwaukee with my son and me. Marry me."

"Are you talking about a real marriage?" She pulled away, wiped tears from her stricken face.

Hell, yes, he intended to have sex with her, and from the way she reacted at the most casual of touches he knew she wanted him too. No way was he going to give her any distance. Deliberately he reached out, dragged her against him, stroked up and down the delicate curve of her back. Gentling her the way he might calm a nervous animal. Though she still shook a little, she didn't resist but looked up at him, laying her hands submissively against his chest. "Do you seriously think we could live in the same house and not have sex?"

"I—I guess not." She stayed very still, her trembling subsiding under his controlling touch.

Sensing she needed to hear the words, he drew her closer, bent and whispered in her ear. "We'll have a marriage in every sense of the word. Once you get off this notion that I'm trying to take our son from you, I imagine you'll make the perfect little sub."

"Sub?" She looked confused.

Her obvious innocence brought out every protective instinct he possessed. The same instincts he'd had toward her when they were kids…yet honed by his own years of sexual experience and experimentation. "Submissive. As in BDSM."

"BDSM?"

"Bondage, discipline and sado-masochism, although I've never gotten much into the S&M part. I'm big on control, though, and all my instincts tell me you want to be controlled in bed as much now as you did when you were sixteen and didn't have a clue what sex was all about. I want to make you let go, give you pleasure like you've never experienced before." He drew her closer, cupped her buttocks, lifted her until his hard-on pressed against her mound.

She let out a little yelp but didn't pull away. When she wrapped her arms around his neck he pushed her hair out of the way and nibbled on her inviting earlobe. "Tell me about this control you think I want," she said, her voice breathy...arousing almost as much as the feel of her soft and giving in his arms.

"You want domination." He gave her ear a quick, hard bite. "As in me telling you what to do, you doing it, and us both enjoying the hell out of each other that way. Baby, you're a sexual submissive if I ever saw one. That's good, because in twelve years I've learned I'm a Dom."

"I-I'm not sure." She bit her lower lip as though the idea scared her.

Brand couldn't help grinning. "I am. You'll like BDSM play, honey. I guarantee my major goal will be to give you pleasure." He liked the way she blushed. But alarms went off in his head when she pulled away abruptly and moved out of his reach.

"I-I meant, what if I don't want to marry you?" From the firm set of her mouth, he gathered she wasn't at all certain she wanted to jump headlong into a BDSM lifestyle at odds with the deeply held conviction she'd always had that someday the crones who'd ridiculed her would come to believe she was a lady.

Fuck. He should have thought twice about mentioning BDSM. He gave himself a mental kick in the ass for not having remembered how it had hurt her when people had ridiculed her mother because of her varied sexual encounters, some of which had qualified as kinky enough to have created a prime source of gossip in their small town.

He shot her his most persuasive smile. "You act as though I'm suggesting we flaunt our private bedroom games for everybody to see. I'm not. Whenever we're out for folks to be watching us, we'll seem as staid and conservative as all those old crones you once wanted to show you some respect."

She didn't look as though she believed him, so he tried another tack. "Honey, you're nothing like your mother. You never were. Come on, there's no reason we shouldn't get married, and I can think of several compelling reasons why we should." Drawing her back into his arms, he ran his hands up and down along her slender, trembling curves. "Can't you?"

"I'm not sure. I mean, I understand why you're asking, but I'm not sure—"

"I'm sure enough for both of us. Besides, the way I see it, we don't have much choice. As it is, we're going to take some flak from so-called journalists like the one you met a little while ago. If we don't get married, they're going to crucify both of us. More important, they'll hurt our son."

Dani let out a sigh, as though she felt the pressure already, pressure he figured she'd go to any length to keep Dave from facing.

"Dave is eleven years old," Brand pointed out, hoping to raise the ante but feeling guilty even before he mouthed the words. "I imagine he and all his friends can read. Do you want him getting fed the crap Ellen Harris and other yellow journalists like her will make up about us?"

Dani's dark eyes grew huge. "I'd do anything to keep Dave from getting hurt, but what's to say these awful people won't write just as nasty a bunch of stories if we get married?"

"We'll beat them to the punch, give the media a story they'll eat up. Everybody loves lovers. We'll feed them a happy ending for a modern-day Romeo and Juliet. Thwarted lovers find each other again, go for happily ever after and all that."

"Is that what we are?"

Brand forced himself to meet Dani's hesitant gaze. "That's what we're going to make the vultures believe."

"But not ourselves?" Dani's gaze met his, and he felt the hope in her question.

He couldn't deceive her, but he didn't want to hurt her more. "Twelve years ago I loved you. You left me. You deliberately kept me from knowing I had a son. I don't love you now, and I can't say I trust you, either. I love Dave, though—and damn it, I want you so much I've had a constant hard-on that's driving me insane."

Dani looked down at her hands. Then she raised her head and looked him straight in the eye. "What's going to happen if I don't marry you?" she asked in a firm voice.

"Much as I'd hate to do it, I'd take Dave. And you could live your life however you see fit." Brand loosened his hold on Dani and looked around, noting the missing conveniences in her modest house and feeling even guiltier for what he was doing…what he hadn't done for them the past twelve years. "I could get custody just by proving I can give him everything he might ever need." His words came out harsher than he intended, but something made him go on, ensure she'd see the necessity of them putting Dave's welfare ahead of whatever doubts they might harbor about the arrangement he proposed. "Things you couldn't possibly give him. I could point out that I've never been on welfare."

She jerked away, her expression bleak. "Neither have I, since Dave was too little to remember."

"The fact you were at one time will be on record. Besides, even if you hadn't been, that wouldn't matter to a judge. Not if I told him I'd gladly have supported my son if his mother had simply informed me of his existence." Brand wanted to take her, hold her, chase her miseries away. He'd do it too, as soon as she gave in and said she'd marry him again, whatever the reason that made her do it.

"So what kind of a marriage would we have, with you hating me like you do?" Dani asked, her tone belligerent though her expression had changed to one of resignation.

Her question stung, though he realized he'd goaded her into asking it. Gently he reached out, tangled his fingers in her soft dark hair, tilting her head back so she had to meet his gaze. "I don't hate you. I distrust you, and I resent like hell the fact you kept our son your own selfish secret. But never fear, Dani. I want to tie you to my bed and fuck you until I can't fuck you anymore. I want my cock in your cunt. Your mouth and your pretty ass too. From the way you're breathing hard and blushing, it's obvious you want me too. Lots of marriages have started off with less going for them than a healthy dose of mutual lust. Besides, we both love our son." There was more to it than simple lust and the desire to make up for the years he'd lost with Dave. Brand knew that, yet he hadn't yet come to a conclusion what that something more might be.

"I can't go back to Carendon, face all the people who remember my mom, who've always thought I was trash." Dani shuddered. "There's no way I'd subject Dave to their taunts and slurs. And I couldn't face your mother…"

She was tearing his heart out, reminding him of the Dani he once loved so much. And he was being an asshole, playing on the insecurities he once understood better than anyone. He'd hurt her, and he had to make up for that at least a little, so he put his arms around her, held her firm when she tried to pull away. "I'm sorry, baby. I wouldn't take Dave away from you. But would being married to me be all that bad?"

"Your mother would make Dave's life miserable. Either that, or she'd welcome him and turn him against me."

Brand wouldn't let her get away with excuses as flimsy as that, not when he intended to set his mother straight, along with anybody else back home who thought they were better than his woman. "Don't you know me well enough to believe I'll stand up to her, tell her to keep her nose out of our affairs?"

"Yes," she said in a small voice, as if she wanted to believe. As if she knew and trusted the boy he'd been but wasn't certain she could count on the man he'd become.

He lifted her chin until her glistening, tear-filled gaze met his, made the promise he hadn't kept twelve years ago. "Believe me on this. I'll take care of my mother and any other narrow-minded old bitches where we grew up. I won't let her hurt Dave, or you."

"You told me that before."

"I know, but I'm no kid now. I'm not afraid of Mother or anybody else. And I won't allow you now to let your fears rule you."

"I'm sure your mother still thinks I'm worse than garbage, Brand."

He hesitated. He didn't want to scare her off, nor did he want to cut his strong, lifelong ties to Carendon and Atlanta. It had taken him six off-seasons to finish law school, two more to carve out a place for himself in his family's law firm, but he'd done it. When he thought of home, he pictured the house he and Dani had planned so long ago, the home he suddenly realized was much like the one his contractor friend would complete by the end of the coming season. Then he remembered something Josh had said about distance. "What my mother thinks has little or no bearing on our lives. We'll be living in Milwaukee. That's a long way away from Georgia."

"For how long? You may play football up north, but your home is in Carendon."

"We can live in Milwaukee year-round if you want. I have to spend better than half the year there, anyhow." With a finger he wiped a tear off Dani's cheek. "We can put Carendon, Georgia on hold until you feel ready to go home. Okay?"

He cupped her chin, tilted her head back. In her mesmerizing dark gaze he saw need and hope, as well as the fear she couldn't hide. When she didn't reply, he took her silence as consent, bent to taste her lips.

Her arms tightened around his neck about the same time blood slammed into his cock. "God, Dani, I want you." He nuzzled at the velvety lobe of her ear. "Let me show you how much."

When she stood on tiptoe and brushed against him, he tightened his arms around her waist. Feeling her strain against him made him crazy. She had to be feeling it, too. He knew from the way she writhed in his arms, as if she wanted to push under his skin. He felt her pounding heartbeat, the welcoming heat of her. Her soft, subtle scent filled his nostrils as he nibbled at her honeyed lips.

Yes. She was ready and they were alone. He cupped her bottom and lifted her until his throbbing cock nestled in the heat between her thighs. He pushed away her dark curls and nipped at the sensitive skin just below her hairline.

"I'm going to fuck you now. I can tell you want it." He shifted one hand to pull up her skirt. With feathery touches to her inner thighs and the warm, velvety cavern between them, he stroked her clit until she whimpered with need.

"You're wet and ready." Groaning, he tore away the silky strip that covered her pussy. "Unzip my pants. Oh, yeah. I like the way you touch me. Feel how hard you've got me." Her seeking fingers had him ready to come, as ready as he'd been when he'd been seventeen and fucking her the first time.

He couldn't wait any longer. "Wrap your legs around me. Now." He moaned when he felt the slick heat of her cunt. Mindless, he thrust upward, joining them in one smooth, powerful stroke. "Oh, yeah. Your pussy feels so damn good."

The soft sounds she made got stronger, more intense. He pumped into her slowly, then faster. Harder. Too close to climax, he clenched his teeth and held on. Had to make her come, satisfy her. Yes! Her inner muscles convulsed around him. She screamed out his name. And he let go, coming in hard bursts that left him shaking.

He sank down with her onto the sofa, his cock still hard in her warm, wet cunt. Drinking in the clean, faintly apple-blossom scent that was uniquely Dani's, he buried his face in her sable curls and cradled her in his arms. He wished he'd undressed her so he could have felt her soft breasts naked against his chest.

"Sorry, honey, I couldn't wait," he whispered apologetically. "Let me stay tonight."

He liked the way she smiled, all soft and dreamy-eyed. "You can't. You have to stay with the team, don't you?"

He did, but he couldn't care less. The thousand-dollar fine Coach would levy would be cheap at twice the price for the pleasure he anticipated having in Dani's bed. "Not if I don't mind paying. And I don't," he told her with a grin. "Getting to sleep with you would definitely be worth a grand."

Chapter Six

A thousand dollars? Dani couldn't imagine anybody being willing to lay out that kind of money if he didn't have to. She couldn't help thinking about all the wonderful things she could do if she ever had that much money to spare. "Brand, you can't! What time do you have to be back? I don't want you to have to pay a fine."

"Curfew's at midnight." Suddenly his expression turned serious. He lifted her off his lap and zipped his pants. "Dani, we need to get married right away, as soon as we can get a license."

"This is too fast. I can't think."

"What's to think about?" He took one of her hands and brushed his lips across her fingertips. "We don't have a fairytale sort of love, but I'm not convinced that exists here in the real world. We do have a son to think of, though. And we've got a hell of a lot more going for us than a lot of couples do. There's much to be said for being sexually compatible, and you can't deny we're that. You're telling me you want me again now, the way you're looking at me. And touching me."

She moved the hand she'd rested high on his inner thigh, just inches from his long, thick cock. "Yes. I want you. I may even have a little bit of love saved up for you from years ago. But, Brand, you're who you are, and I'm who I am. No matter what you say now, sooner or later you're going to have to go home."

"We will, eventually. Hey, we'll work things out. Even my mother will accept our marriage eventually. She'll have to if she wants any kind of relationship with me and her grandchildren." When he shot her that killer smile, he made her want him, want much more than he was offering. "Dani, don't you want to get married, make a real home with me for Dave? Have another baby or two?"

"What if you meet someone and fall in love?" He'd loved her once, and she couldn't believe he'd be satisfied until he found that kind of magic again.

"Love? Love's for starry-eyed kids. I'm looking for good, hot sex rolled up in a package with home, hearth and kids. You fill the bill just fine. We've already got one fine boy." As though to prove the truth of what he said, he wrapped an arm around her waist, kissed her deeply.

Dani figured she could live without love. After all, she'd done it all her life, except for that brief, magical time they'd shared twelve years ago. Brand would be good for Dave, good to her. He'd said he wanted her and Dave more than he wanted his mom, his home. She'd be greedy to expect more.

He was right. Their best choice was to marry now and give Dave his true father without her having to give up her son. Marrying would protect them as much as possible from the cruel truths the press would certainly inflict. She'd be the best, most submissive wife Brand could imagine. Her mind made up, she took a deep breath and looked into Brand's dark blue eyes. "You've persuaded me. We have more reasons than not to marry."

"Good. We'll get the license tomorrow."

"So soon?"

"The sooner the better. In more ways than one." Brand laced his fingers through her hair, bent and took her mouth with sweet, savage fury.

Dani wished she could turn off the heat that sizzled whenever he touched her. But she couldn't. After avoiding men for so long, doing everything on her own, it felt so good to be a woman, to let go and be swept up in the power of his seduction. Whatever qualms she had about marrying Brand didn't include any worries about their sexual compatibility.

"See what I mean?" When he looked at her, she got wet. Her nipples hardened against the fabric of her bra. Concentrating on those passion-darkened eyes, she barely listened as he rattled off a list of things they needed to do. "You'll need to quit your job," he concluded.

That got her attention. Suddenly this all seemed too real. Her life was about to change drastically, and she was afraid. "What if this doesn't work out?"

"It will." Brand sounded much more certain than Dani felt.

"But if it doesn't?"

"No matter what, I'll take care of you and Dave."

His innate decency and his sense of responsibility toward her and their child were not in question. He'd always been one who kept his promises. "I know you will."

"Then let's get the details ironed out as quickly as we can. I don't want to give reporters time to speculate or dig up dirt before we drop our news on them. Not to mention you turn me on so many ways I can hardly keep my hands off you."

Chuckling, Brand gave her knee a squeeze. "I want to set a good example for our son. I also want you in my bed all night, every night. The sooner I have the legal right to have you there, the less likely it is that we'll be living in sin for Dave and everyone else to see."

Brand had a point about the explosive sexual chemistry between them. "When will we tell Dave?"

"How about now? We can get him at the Johnsons' and tell him over dinner."

"I hope he'll be okay with this." Dani had no idea what their son's reaction would be.

"My guess is that he'll be happy as hell. After all, it isn't as if one of us was presenting him with a wicked stepmother, or stepfather, as the case might be. Most kids, I imagine, want their parents to be married to each other."

"I suppose you're right. Speaking of wicked stepmothers, Brand, how will your little girl feel when you suddenly pop up with a new wife?"

"Somehow I can't picture you as a wicked stepmom. You're too little and cute."

"You're evading my question."

His expression sobered. "I don't see much of LeeAnn. She'll like you, and I'm sure she'll love playing with Dave. Every time I see her, she says she wants a brother."

Dani smiled as she pictured them all together as a family. "I imagine LeeAnn has a baby brother in mind, not one that's half grown."

"If my daughter wants a baby brother, I'll be happy to oblige her, if you're willing."

"Do you ever lose an argument?"

"Not if I can help it. I want my son. I want you, too, even more now than I did when we were kids." He stroked her hair, sifted the silky strands through his long fingers. "Are you willing to have another baby, Dani? Will you stay around this time, let me watch him grow inside you? Be there for the birth? Help my son or daughter learn to walk and play ball and read?"

"Oh, my God!" Dani could hardly breathe. Just a short while ago they'd made love, and neither of them had done a thing to prevent conception. "I don't know if I'll have the choice," she said, mortified.

He had the good grace to look embarrassed. "Then it's a good thing you've agreed to marry me."

"If you've gotten me pregnant again on the first try, it will be eerily like history repeating itself. But no, I'd like another baby, as long as I don't have to raise him or her all by myself." Dani couldn't help picturing Brand holding a new baby the way he hadn't had the chance to hold Dave.

"Good. Come on, honey, let's go get our son."

After they collected Dave, Brand drove to a nearby family restaurant. Dani agonized over what her son's reaction would be to the plans they were going to reveal.

*****

Brand liked the feeling he got when he watched Dani and Dave, and realized they were soon to be a family. As he ate he thought briefly of his little girl and wondered if she would ever again be part of his life. He brushed regrets from his mind and smiled at Dani before turning to Dave.

"What would you think of us all living together?"

"You mean, like a real family? With Mom staying home?" Dave's dark eyes sparkled with excitement. "Could I watch the Marlins play?"

"Like a real family. In Milwaukee. You can go to all the home games." Brand wasn't above a little bribery if that was what it took to sway his boy.

If he hadn't known better he'd have guessed from the joy on his face that his son had just won the lottery. "Will you get Mom a car?"

Dani's cheeks turned red. "Dave, you sound greedy. Brand can afford more than I've been able to give you. But that isn't the point. What's important is that we'll all be together. You'll have both of us to love you and take care of you."

Dave shot her a sheepish look. "I didn't mean anything bad, Mom. It'd just be nice if we didn't have to ride the bus."

Brand reached over and stroked Dani's hand as he spoke to his son. "I'm thrilled to have discovered you and found your mom again. I'll probably spoil both of you rotten. We're getting married. How about coming to our wedding?"

"You're kidding! When?"

"Sometime in the next few days. First, I want to get you both moved over to the team's hotel. Then, we'll make arrangements."

"Wow!" Dave's grin widened. His gaze shifted from Brand to Dani. "Wait 'til I tell Roger! Can he and his folks come?"

Dani held up a hand, as though she thought Dave was going too far, too fast. "It's not going to be that kind of wedding," she said with what sounded to Brand like regret.

For Dani, more than to convince the press theirs was the happy ending to a thwarted teenage love affair, Brand found himself wanting their wedding to look like the real thing. "It will be small, but it will be a real wedding. We'll be sure to invite Roger and his parents."

He reached across the table and took her hand. "The first time we got married, your mom and I went to a shabby justice of the peace in a little town across the Tennessee-Georgia border. This time, we're going to do it right."

"You really were married before?"

Regret for the slights his son must have endured tore at Brand's conscience. Would he ever be able to make up for all they'd suffered because of his mother's lies? It was for damn sure, Eleanor Carendon had meddled in his life for the last time.

He met Dave's gaze. "We were married." Brand tried to explain what had happened in a way his son could understand. "Your mom and I wanted you. We wanted each other," he concluded. "We still do. That's why we've decided to remarry, make a real home together."

He glanced over at Dani, hoped he had reassured Dave without promising her more emotional commitment than he was able to give. He watched tears spill over, dampen her flushed cheeks. "Honey, don't cry," he said gruffly. It tore him up to see her sad.

"Mom, what people said didn't bother me." Dave reached for Dani's free hand. Not able to resist reaching out to touch his son, Brand took Dave's hand, completing the circle.

By the time he left them and returned to his hotel room, Brand believed the marriage he and Dani were about to enter had as good a chance as any for survival.

* * * * *

"How did the family dinner go?" Josh turned off the sound on the televised baseball game.

"Fine. Tomorrow I'm moving Dani and Dave to a suite over here." He looked over at his friend. "How would you feel about having Elaine and the boys come down? I'd like for Dani to have some company. I'd also like for Elaine to teach her how to dress."

Josh raised an eyebrow, as if surprised.

"Dani's never had a lot of money for clothes. Elaine can help her shop."

It wasn't her cheap, drab clothes that bothered him as much as her attitude. Her conviction that she wasn't good enough for him, or for his mother and her small-minded cronies.

"You're bringing them to camp? Has Coach Allen started extending wifely privileges to exes, too?"

"Not that I know of. Want to stand up with me at my wedding next Monday after practice?"

Josh stood, extended his hand. "Congratulations." Then he laughed out loud. "One hell of a honeymoon you're gonna be having, I'd say, between working out with the Marlins and having a kid with you."

His expression sobered. "You want Elaine to do a makeover on Dani while you're honeymooning?"

"Why not? Dani will need something to do, anyhow, while I'm stuck on the practice field. Don't worry about me, pal. I'll manage to squeeze in some quality time in bed with my brand-new bride. Will you bring Elaine down?"

"Sure. You afraid I'll try to take your lady as well as your job?"

Laughing, Brand looked at Josh. "Get serious. I want Dani to feel comfortable. If anyone can help her be comfortable, Elaine can."

Brand stripped and headed for the shower. A few minutes later he stretched out on the empty bed, just as Josh hung up the phone.

"Elaine's flying down in the morning. Her mom's going to keep the twins." Josh pounded his pillow into a ball and stuffed it behind his head. "G'night."

"See you in the morning." Brand flipped off the light and lay back, but sleep wouldn't come. He wished he'd ignored Dani, stayed with her. Coach Allen's fine would have been a small price to pay for the pleasure of going to sleep with Dani's soft, warm body in his arms.

* * * * *

For once Dani saw a benefit in not having a whole lot of possessions. Packing them wasn't going to take her much longer than the hour she'd spent earlier this morning, quitting her job and emptying her desk.

"Mom?"

Glancing up from the stack of sheets and towels she was packing, Dani saw Dave standing in the doorway. "What do you need?"

"I can't find my swimsuit."

A missing swimsuit hardly qualified as a major crisis. "Don't worry about it." Closing the box of linens, she smiled at Dave. She crossed the room, started pulling clothes out of dresser drawers.

"But, Mom, there's a swimming pool at the hotel. Dad said we could use it. I need my suit. Is he coming to pick this stuff up?" He gave the growing stack of boxes a doubtful look. "I don't think all of it will fit in the Ferrari."

"We're shipping most of it to his place in Milwaukee. All we're taking with us are a few of our clothes."

Caught up in mundane chores, Dani hardly had time to worry about whether she and Brand had made the right decision, or a horrendous mistake.

* * * * *

At the hotel later on, Dani found plenty of free time to fret. The minute they'd arrived, Dave had put on the swimsuit Brand bought him at a shop in the hotel lobby. He'd taken off for the pool as soon as he changed, so she didn't have him around to distract her.

She explored the two-bedroom suite, then stretched out on the king-size bed to torture herself over the decision she'd made. Before she could focus on anything except superficial problems, Brand strolled in and started to shed his clothes.

"Hi." He grinned at her as he dragged down his zipper. "I'm finished with practice for today."

"Hello to you, too." Dani decided to get one question answered before it drove her crazy. "How are we all going to ride to Milwaukee in that tiny car of yours?"

"We aren't. We'll fly. I hire someone to drive my car to Milwaukee from wherever the Marlins hold preseason camp." He grabbed the hem of his T-shirt, pulling it up slowly over clearly defined abdominal muscles, his massive chest.

She watched him, amazed at the fact just watching him do something as simple as shedding his clothes could send raw desire slamming through her. When he toed off his loafers and started to shove down his pants and underwear in one smooth motion, she practically drooled as he revealed his arousal...and heavily muscled thighs furred lightly with soft brown hair. His left knee bore a surgical scar she hadn't noticed before, and well-developed calves sported a couple of mottled bruises. Somehow those small imperfections made him seem more real. Even more desirable than when she thought of him as six feet four inches of pure hot male hunk.

The grin he shot her way when he sat beside her on the bed and pulled off his socks sent waves of desire rolling through her, made her pussy clench with anticipation. Finally naked, he lay back on the opposite side of the bed.

He was gorgeous. Nothing less. She couldn't help staring at him, watching those well-defined muscles ripple gently as he breathed. She had to touch him, run her fingers through his silky body hair. "You're beautiful." She found his flat male nipples and teased them into tiny erections. Resting her head on the hard pillow of his shoulder, she breathed in the woodsy, masculine scent of him.

He twined his fingers in her hair as though determined not to let her get away. "I'm just a big, ugly football player. You're the beauty."

Ugly? She loved every hard, masculine inch of him, his sun-streaked dark brown hair and rugged features. Brand didn't have an ugly bone in his entire body. He had a way of making her feel plain, clumsy. But wanted, so very wanted.

Eyes half closed, he looked incredibly sexy when he grabbed her, rolled her over him. His rigid cock pulsated insistently against her belly. With calloused hands, he cupped her breasts, rubbed the nipples against the hard wall of his chest. She loved the feel of him, the way she went all hot and soft against his hardness. Then he claimed her mouth, thrusting his tongue deep. He took her breath away.

She was drowning in sensation, tastes of chocolate and mint and something else that was uniquely his. The smells of him and her and sex surrounded them, made her pussy wet, her mouth dry. His hard, rough hands abraded the tender skin of her belly, and his hot, smooth shaft seared her pussy lips when she opened her thighs to let him in. She loved the contrasts, the warmth of his muscular body and the cool air against her naked breasts. The feel of him fucking her mouth with his tongue was driving her wild, and shock waves deep in her belly made her squirm. She wanted to stop this erotic torture and beg him to fuck her, make her come.

Chapter Seven

Instead she pulled back a little so she could reach down and touch him, tentatively at first until she felt him grow huge and even harder in her hand. "You like that?" she asked as she leaned over and nuzzled his hard, flat belly.

"Oh, yeah. I like it a lot. God, Dani."

His cock was hard as steel, soft as velvet. She couldn't resist stroking it with her hands and tongue, weighing his balls, tangling her fingers in the springy, soft mat of hair at his groin. When she tasted the pearl of moisture at the very tip of his shaft, it reminded her of the clean, salty fragrance of the beach outside.

She wanted more. When she took him in her mouth and began to suckle gently, he pulled away, apologizing mutely as he positioned her beneath him, thrust home, hard and deep. "Love your hot little pussy, baby. Love to fuck you."

He felt so good inside her, so long and thick and pulsing with life. Wanting it all, she shifted, wrapped her legs tightly around his waist. She clung to him, wanting release but needing to prolong the ecstasy. The feeling of completeness she'd only ever had with him.

Restless, she rose against him. As if aware of what it was she needed, he responded with wild, deep strokes, whispered words of lust that heightened her arousal.

"That's it, squeeze my cock. Oh, yeah. I want to feel your wet, hot pussy milking me. Come for me, baby. Now."

Pressure built inside her, more intense with his every long, hard thrust. Pressure intensified by him taking control, taking her higher… "Oh God, yesss." Every nerve in her body sizzled with sensation and she clamped down on his cock.

Holding him in. Wanting the feelings to go on forever. "Don't stop. Please."

"Yeah, baby. You fuck me so damn good." His words dissolved into a hoarse cry as he came in short, hard bursts while her climax kept going on, fed by his own. For a long time he held her, his cock still pulsating inside her. When he rolled over, he took her with him, cradled her on top of him.

If sexual compatibility had anything to do with successful marriages, Dani couldn't help believing they'd make it this time, the way they hadn't all those years ago. She hoped they would, that they could give their son the kind of home she'd only dreamed of when she'd been Dave's age.

* * * * *

"Honey, we've got some plans to make," Brand murmured when he finally caught his breath. Sex with Dani was dynamite, better now than he remembered from long ago. She still could sleep through a tornado, though. He nudged her awake, framed her beguiling face in both hands before giving her a quick, hard kiss. "You know, being around you makes it damn hard to think of anything except fucking you. You must be a witch."

Dani stretched, a slow, sensuous motion that made him want to take her again. Especially when she looked him over head to toe. "Yeah, my cock doesn't seem to remember we just fucked a few minutes ago," he said when she watched him getting hard again.

"I like making love with you, too, but I can think better when you have clothes on."

"Me, too. That is, I can think better when you're dressed." Brand would have liked nothing better than to stay in bed all afternoon, cuddling and fucking and sleeping. He wished he could have ignored the situation that had brought them together in the first place. But he couldn't, so he had to watch, getting horny all over again while Dani rolled out of bed and slipped into that moth-eaten robe he swore he was going to grab and toss into the nearest dumpster.

He pulled on his own clothes and padded into the sitting room. By the time Dani joined him, he had fixed mild, fruity drinks for them.

"Thanks," she said as she took her glass.

He set down the cheese and crackers he'd been putting onto a plate and forced his mind off the notion of taking Dani right back to bed. "We've got a press conference scheduled for tomorrow afternoon."

"We?" Her eyes widened.

"Yeah. We're going to tell our pretty little story and announce our wedding plans. The team's press people have set the conference up for three o'clock."

Dani looked stricken. "I can't," she croaked when she finally found her voice.

"We have to. I can do all the talking if you want me to. All you have to do is stand there and look happy and pretty."

She frowned at the word "pretty". "That may be too large an order to fill. What will I wear?"

Brand grinned. "Something new. Elaine Shearer, my roommate's wife, is all set to take you shopping in the morning. She'll help you find just the right outfit to face reporters in."

"I'll try not to embarrass you." Dani's tone had an edge, and she averted her gaze.

Brand had hoped she wouldn't get miffed because he wanted her to buy new clothes, but apparently she was even though she obviously recognized that her wardrobe might be lacking. He swore he'd never understand women. "You won't embarrass me."

Her lower lip quivered, and she focused her gaze on a section of carpet in front of her bare feet. "You don't trust me to pick out the right thing to wear."

"Hell, Dani, it's not that. Women—even some guys, Josh tells me—pay good money for what Elaine's going to help you do for free. She's an image consultant, for God's sake."

"Oh." She sounded doubtful. "Is what I look like all that important?"

"Yeah. I want you to look as if I've taken care of you, at least in a material way. It's to protect Dave, keep the vultures from getting the idea that researching our past might make for a juicy story." He paused, gauging her reaction. "Besides, I want to see my woman wearing clothes that show off her hot body, since I don't intend to let you run around naked in front of God and everybody. Is that so wrong?"

"No, it isn't wrong. Besides, I'll enjoy decking myself out in pretty things for you." She smiled, chasing away his concern that suggesting a makeover had hurt her feelings. "What about Dave? His wardrobe could use some sprucing up, too."

"I'll take him shopping, myself, as soon as I can tear him away from the pool." Brand looked forward to some time with his son, doing fatherly things like helping him pick out some new clothes.

"Dave will like that. You know, he thinks he's died and gone to heaven, having you as a dad…and us together. He won't have to talk with any reporters, will he?"

"No. He doesn't even need to be at the press conference. There's nothing in my contract that says my kid has to put up with rude reporters."

"All right. I'll let this Elaine help me find a dynamite outfit to wear."

Brand leaned against the sofa back, relieved Dani had given in gracefully about shopping for clothes. "You can take my car in the morning since I have practice. Dave can come with me on the team bus, and you can meet me at the Dome office a few minutes before three."

Dani shook her head. "I don't know how to drive."

"You would have learned if you'd have stayed with me." Why in hell did half of what this woman said drive him nuts with guilt? "Elaine can drive, then. Why don't we go down by the pool and meet her now? Dave's splashing around, probably wondering where we are. Come on, I want you to meet her and Josh."

* * * * *

Dani liked Elaine. Prepared to find the woman at least a little intimidating, she was surprised when Elaine seemed genuinely happy that she was marrying Brand.

When nagging worries about Brand's being ashamed of her popped up, Dani squelched them. She'd do whatever she had to do, to become the kind of wife Brand needed. She'd learned a lot in twelve years. She had a base to build on.

The next morning she followed Elaine into an exclusive hairstyling salon. A stylist trimmed and snipped, and when he stepped back and handed her a mirror, she smiled at her reflection. She liked the way her sable hair turned under at the shoulders, loved the wisps that framed her face and made her eyes look bigger.

Next Elaine took her to a boutique on the waterfront across from the St. Petersburg Pier. Before Dani could protest, she found herself in a spacious dressing room, trying on clothes as Elaine pulled them from the racks.

"You're lucky. A perfect size four petite." Elaine handed Dani a silvery jumpsuit. "This will be great for casual evenings when you and Brand are home alone. Do you like it?"

"It's gorgeous, but it's awfully expensive for something to wear around the house." Dani fingered the soft folds of the dusky mauve silk with silver threads running through it. The material was the most luxurious-feeling stuff she'd ever felt.

Elaine shrugged off her protests about the jumpsuit, and about the bright colors she tried to tell Elaine she'd always avoided. While it made her nervous to think of attracting so much attention to herself, Dani had to agree reds and rose tones made her look better than the drab browns and grays she usually picked out for herself.

She guessed she didn't need to hide anymore. Brand seemed to want her to shine. She thought about how Brand could have any woman he wanted and laughed out loud at her own foolishness. Even if she wanted to hide, there was no way she could escape attention as long as he was at her side. She might as well indulge herself, forget downplaying her looks, have fun. She picked up a sapphire blue dress and tried it on.

It looked good and felt good, so she decided she'd wear it for the press conference. The store manager packaged the rest of the clothes she'd chosen. As she swirled in front of the mirror, Dani marveled at the perfect way the dress fit. How different this was from shopping at discount stores, where she had to buy shirts that were much too long, dresses and pants she had to hem so much the lines were ruined.

"I like Dave. He's so like his dad," Elaine commented as she pulled out into traffic. "I'm glad Brand found you. I've never seen him as relaxed as he seemed at the pool last night."

"Do you think this dress will do for the press conference?" Dani lowered her voice, as though somebody might overhear her. "I'm so afraid he'll be ashamed of me."

"You look great. And the dress is fine. Blue's one of the Marlins' colors, after all."

Dani wondered if she'd ever be even half as put-together as Elaine. Even casually dressed as she was in pale blue crinkly cotton shorts and a matching top, the woman looked cool and sophisticated. The multicolored scarf that held back her long blonde hair, flat-heeled sandals, and a tote bag whose colors echoed those in the scarf looked as though they'd been made to go together.

Shaking her head, Dani tried and failed to picture herself ever becoming as self-assured as her new friend. Elaine had more going for her than a new hairdo and a trunk full of expensive clothes. Dani envied her what seemed a natural and unerring sense of style. Her mind wandered to her own new clothes—and the huge bill Brand would be getting for them.

She knew now why she'd stayed away from that exclusive little shop before. While it catered to young adult women whose proportions were tiny, its prices were beyond anything she could have afforded on her own.

"Brand will kill me," Dani muttered under her breath. "The clothes I just bought cost more than I make in a year."

"No, he won't kill you. I heard him tell you to buy anything you liked." Elaine smiled. "Josh would think he got off easy if I bought that little for a season's wardrobe, and Brand has to make at least four times as much as my husband does. Let's find some shoes, now. We need to get back in time for the press conference."

* * * * *

Because of the upcoming press conference, Brand shaved after practice and put on lightweight gray dress slacks instead of his usual faded jeans.

"Hey, you throw good," a rookie receiver yelled from across the room. "I'm glad they gave me a chance to catch your passes."

He looked up, letting his pale blue dress shirt dangle in his hand. He struggled to remember the name of the slightly built black player who'd been drafted in the fourth round. "Wilder," he said when he finally recalled the kid's name, "you're expected to catch passes when no one's chasing you and no one's trying to knock me on my ass. Wait and see how you do in scrimmages before you get too cocky."

"I'll do it, Counselor. Are we all supposed to dress up like that?" He watched Brand tie the knot in his gray and blue striped tie.

"Not until you have reporters breathing down your neck. You get to relax and watch old game films this afternoon. I get to go to a press conference."

Brand grinned at the rookie as he shoved his feet into black loafers. He shrugged into a navy blazer and headed toward the makeshift pressroom. This was one ordeal he'd be glad to have behind him.

"Hi." Brand bent and brushed a kiss across Dani's lips when they met outside the practice facility's main office. "You look great."

That was an understatement. She nearly took his breath away. Although he didn't detect any makeup, she had to have used some because her eyes looked bigger, almost luminous. Her face glowed. He liked the way her dark hair curled at the ends. Flyaway wisps caressed her cheeks, made him want to take his fingers to them, muss the casual arrangement and feel the silky strands.

Had she always worn those plain gold studs that winked in her ears? For some reason it bothered him that he couldn't remember. If she had, he hadn't noticed them until now.

Her bright blue dress buttoned down the front, sort of like a shirt. He liked the way her legs looked in high-heeled black shoes. She looked pretty. Ladylike. Not particularly sexy, he told himself when his cock twitched.

No matter how she wrapped the package, she turned him on.

He tried not to picture her wrapping those long, slim legs around his hips. Instead he focused as much as he could on the coming torture session they'd have to endure. "I like your dress."

"You won't like it when you get the bill." Dani frowned, but she still looked adorable. "This—and everything else we bought—was obscenely expensive."

"Don't worry, honey, I'll blame Elaine if she made you spend too much. Let's go get this over with." He took her hand then opened the door to the room full of reporters.

The reporters' chattering stopped when he and Dani walked hand in hand to the microphones set up in the front of the room.

"Okay, they're here. Brand has agreed to give you fifteen minutes to ask your questions." One of the team's public relations men—Brand couldn't recall his name—stepped away from the mike.

"Are you going to introduce your fiancée?"

"Where did you meet her?"

Brand held up a hand, the one holding Dani's. "One at a time, guys. This is Dani, and I've known her a long time. Since we were high school kids, in fact. You might say we were like Romeo and Juliet, only we didn't give up and commit suicide." He looked down at Dani when he felt the tremor in her hand, shot her an encouraging smile. "Now we've found each other again, and we're getting married."

A tabloid reporter Brand recognized from past encounters stood. "Is it true you two have a kid together?"

Brand didn't like the salacious look on the guy's face when he gave Dani the once-over. "Yes. His name's David, and he's eleven years old. He's off limits to the press, by the way."

"Dani, how did it feel to have the Marlins star quarterback bounce back into your life after so long?"

Brand tensed, was about to cut the reporter off when Dani reached for the mike. "It was a surprise," she said. "A good surprise, for both Dave and me."

"Are you a Marlins fan?" asked George Januch, an AP reporter who'd been covering sports events for years.

The way Dani smiled made her answer obvious. "Yes, I am. Don't expect me to quote statistics, though."

"She'll be able to do it by the end of preseason, George." Brand felt Dani's discomfort, even though she was obviously charming the mostly male sports reporters. Smiling down at her, he reclaimed the microphone before anybody had a chance to ask questions that would make her more uncomfortable. "Five more minutes, guys. The team's PR folks have some fact sheets they'll pass out. No need to take up time asking personal questions—the answers will be right there for you."

The rest of the press conference went well, because Brand was careful only to recognize dyed-in-the-wool sports fans among the press group—older men who couldn't care less about his personal life, so long as they got their answers about how his knee was holding up and whether off-season treatments had worked to get rid of chronic pain in the elbow of his throwing arm.

Chapter Eight

"Those folks seemed a lot nicer than the woman who tried to pay me for information the other day," Dani commented once the conference was over and they were back at the hotel changing out of their dress-up clothes.

"They were mostly sports reporters from reputable media outlets. The one who chased you down is a prime example of the carrion who like to report half-truths mixed with downright lies about anybody who's in the news." Brand pulled on a swimsuit and grabbed a hotel towel. "I'm going out to spend some time at the pool with Dave. You look like you could use some rest."

"Yes, sir. It's not every day I shop 'til I drop." As soon as Brand left, she stretched out on the bed. But her mind refused to shut down. She kept going over what they'd told those reporters, wishing the story had been more truth, less fiction.

Everything was moving too fast. Today, the press conference. Tomorrow, a trip to the courthouse for a marriage license. The wedding would be the following day at a chapel near the beach. They'd be married. Again. And it didn't matter that Brand had spun a pretty tale of timeless love to the reporters—theirs would be a marriage of convenience entered into because of a wonderful kid. And a healthy case of lust, she added, although that alone wouldn't have been enough reason to take the drastic step of marriage.

She'd known that from the get-go, but it still had stung when he'd joked that they'd be getting into a marriage of convenience after the press conference—and added that a lot of lust and the mutual love for Dave would be the cement holding it together. Though she'd told him yes when he asked if that would be enough, she couldn't help wishing he'd mentioned the romantic love he'd intimated about to the reporters. She couldn't help worrying that they'd be replaying Romeo and Juliet, with a similar sad ending.

She was scared. Scared this whole arrangement was going to backfire. But she didn't dare express her misgivings, couldn't even let herself think about them very much. If she dwelled on her worries, she'd go crazy.

Why couldn't Brand had stayed, kept her demons at bay? Immediately she scolded herself for being selfish. After all, he was making up for lost time with their son, and that's what she wanted for Dave.

It struck her that the only time she felt secure was when she was tangled in Brand's arms and they were making love. No. Not making love because they weren't in love—but having hot, passionate sex. That wasn't likely to happen now, not until after the wedding, because their son would be chaperoning them...and later after he was asleep, Brand would have to go back to his own room before the team's curfew.

* * * * *

"Brand, your mother's on the line." Josh handed over the receiver, retreated into the bathroom.

Brand knew he'd turned off his cell phone for a reason. He hadn't counted on Eleanor being resourceful enough to track him down through the hotel switchboard. He let out a loud sigh then sat on the edge of the bed and lifted the phone. "Yes, Mother."

"Brandon Carendon, you've gone completely insane this time. Do you realize your face, and that trashy girl's face, were plastered all over the Atlanta newspapers? They even played part of your press conference on television here. You must take fiendish pleasure in humiliating me."

He held the receiver away from his ear. Fuck it, he knew how his mother felt without hearing her screech her opinions through the phone lines. "I didn't know you followed sports news."

"I didn't have to. At least a dozen people have called to tell me about the stories. How do you think it makes me feel to hear you're bent on making a perfect fool of yourself, again? You didn't even have the decency to tell me, or your own daughter, before you let it be spread all over the newspapers that you actually intend to marry that little nobody. Certainly you don't have to go that far, just to get your hands on the child she tried to trap you with when you were children."

Brand counted to ten then propped the receiver between his shoulder and his chin and tried for a civil tone. "I wouldn't pursue that particular line of thought if I were you. Incidentally, I did try to call Marilee. She's out of town. I spoke to Uncle Jimmy at the office, though. I assumed he'd tell you, and you or Marilee's mother would tell LeeAnn."

"Jimmy hasn't seen fit to contact me."

The sneer in his mother's voice came through, loud and clear. "I suggest you call him, then. He can fill you in on any details you may have missed on television."

"Son, you can't do this. You can't."

Holding onto his temper was proving almost impossible. "I can and I will. I doubt I'll ever forgive you for stealing eleven years of my son's life. Or lying to Dani to get her to leave me. I won't tolerate you interfering in my life again. I'm going to hang up now before I say something no man should say to his mother no matter what the provocation." He set the phone back on the nightstand, lay back and took long, deep breaths until the blood stopped pounding in his head.

When Josh came out of the bathroom and stretched out on his bed, Brand rolled over and faced his friend. "Thanks for deserting me, pal."

"Sorry about that. Remember, my friend, I've had the dubious pleasure of meeting your mother." Josh pounded his pillow into a ball then shoved it behind his head. "Gotta get some sleep if we're gonna have decent workouts tomorrow."

"Yeah. G'night." Brand doubted sleep was going to come easy, but he flipped off the lamp and lay quietly in the dark until he heard Josh snoring. Needing to hear Dani's voice, he picked up the phone again and called her suite. She sounded sleepy when she answered. "Did I wake you?"

"It's okay. What's wrong?"

"Nothing. I just wanted to say goodnight, let you know I wish I were there with you. Do you miss me?"

"Mmm-hmmm."

"I spoke with my uncle. He's coming down here for the wedding. Do you mind?"

Silence stretched out the space of a few seconds before she replied. "No. I don't mind." Another pause. "Brand, your mother isn't coming, is she?"

"No, honey. I made it a point not to invite her. You'll like Uncle Jimmy. He's happy for us. Besides, he's my closest living male relative, except for Dave."

"I don't remember you mentioning him before." She sounded relieved.

"Uncle Jimmy stayed away from Carendon for years. After my dad died, he left his job in Chicago to come back and manage our law firm. If he'd refused to pick up Dad's workload, I wouldn't have been able to play pro ball. I'd have had to go straight through law school so I could have taken over as soon as I passed the bar."

"I'm glad I'll have the chance to meet him. It sounds like you owe him a lot."

"Yeah. I do."

"Did you talk to your little girl yet?" Dani asked quietly.

"No. Marilee took her somewhere, probably to New Orleans to see the distant cousin she's been dating. Her mother wouldn't, or couldn't, tell me where to reach them." He shifted the phone to his other hand. "How's Dave tonight, honey?" he asked, deliberately changing the subject.

"He's asleep now. He's so excited, he can hardly stand it."

"Where are you now?"

"In bed."

He pictured her there, laid out naked for his pleasure, her arms held over her head, legs spread in blatant invitation. Damn, it was torture, having to stay here listening to Josh snore when he could have been tasting her pretty cunt, fucking her until they couldn't come any more. "Touch your pussy for me, honey."

"I am." She moaned softly.

His balls ached and his cock felt as though it would burst. Certain Josh was sound asleep, Brand wrapped his fingers around his aching flesh. "I'm jerking off. It's a damn lousy excuse for fucking your pretty pussy, but tonight we've got no choice. Come on, talk to me. Help me out here."

"Mmmm. I wish you were here. I'm hot and wet. Thinking about the delicious way it feels when you hold me, wishing I could run my tongue along that vein that runs the length of your cock. I can practically taste that drop of lubrication that always beads up at the very tip."

God help him, she was about to make him come, talking sex in her soft, sweet voice. "Don't stop now. Keep on telling me what you want to do to me…what you want me to do to make you feel good. Imagine me taking you the way I want to, hard and fast, nothing between us. I want to get so deep inside you that we can't tell where I end and you begin. Fuck you all night long." When she moaned, he felt himself coming, too, and grabbed a handful of tissues from the nightstand. "Yeah, honey, you talk a good fuck," he said once his heart had quit pounding.

She sounded breathless. "So do you."

"I do it a lot better than I talk about it. After we're married I'm going to do things to you, things you've never imagined. Things beyond making slow, hot love that will make you feel real good. Things neither of us even thought of when we were kids."

Through the phone line, he heard her sudden intake of breath. "Things having to do with domination and submission?"

"Yes. I assume Elaine said something about it." Brand wished she hadn't. More important, he hoped Elaine hadn't filled Dani in on some of the scenes he'd taken part in. Surely the woman had to have figured out Dani was pretty naïve about sex. He meant to introduce her slowly to bondage games, develop her taste for the kinks he'd found added an extra, tantalizing dimension to sex. "We'll go slowly. And if there's anything you don't find arousing, we won't do it."

"I'm not afraid. To tell the truth, letting you take over responsibility is pretty appealing, and not only when it comes to our sex life. I've spent the last twelve years knowing that if I didn't do something, it wouldn't get done."

Relief swept through Brand's head at Dani's words. Apparently Elaine had possessed the good sense to realize Dani wouldn't have enjoyed hearing about dungeon scenes they'd played with Josh...or about the ménage he'd been enjoying with Vlad and Vlad's gorgeous wife when a serial killer had interrupted their fun—and caused the local media to publicize the situation if not all the titillating details. "I won't let you down again." Brand lowered his voice. "In bed or anywhere else. And I'll never intentionally do anything to hurt you. Dani, I hope that if you're not pregnant now, you'll get that way soon."

"Why?"

"Because I want to do all the things for you that I didn't get to do before Dave was born. And because I want to touch you and feel my baby moving inside you. I'll rub your back when it aches and go out in the middle of the night if you suddenly get a craving for pickles or cherry-vanilla ice cream. I want to be there all the way. See our baby the minute he's born." He choked down the anger that rose every time he thought of all he'd missed with their son. "You're not using birth control, are you?"

"No. I like to feel you inside me, without anything between us. Until the other day, I never knew how good sex could feel."

Brand groaned. "You didn't? And here I thought you'd enjoyed me as much as I enjoyed you, back when we were kids."

"I didn't mean I didn't like it. It's just…so much more intense now. So much more physical." Her soft voice, her gently sensual words sent blood straight to his groin.

"I'm coming over. I don't give a damn how much it costs me in fines."

"Please don't. I want to spend tonight dreaming about you, not worrying that your being here is going to get you in trouble with your coach."

He obviously was going to have to teach his fiancée there were pleasures worth more than the few thousand bucks she fretted about him losing if he got caught breaking Coach's rules. Reminding himself there were only a couple of days left before their wedding, Brand closed his eyes and started counting sheep in his head. They didn't look like sheep, though. They looked like a parade of petite brunettes with bright blue skirts swaying in the breeze. Enticing him into a restless, dream-filled slumber.

* * * * *

On the morning of his wedding, Brand stepped into a tiny chapel, Josh at his side. The room glowed from sunlight that filtered through stained glass windows. Rays of red, green, and gold bounced off baskets that overflowed with multicolored summer flowers. The sun's rays overshadowed the flickering glow of candles that flanked the floral arrangements. A hell of a lot nicer than the justice of the peace's shabby living room where he and Dani had first said their vows, the place thankfully reminded him even less of the huge church where he'd married Marilee in a three-ring circus orchestrated by their meddling mothers.

The chapel had a comfortable, friendly feel about it. Intimate, the way he intended to be with Dani. Did she love him? She hadn't said so, but the way her face brightened when she looked at him, the affection she showed him with every touch, each warm smile, gave him the feeling she might. That made him feel good—and guilty, because although he loved to fuck her, he didn't love her.

He nodded toward Uncle Jimmy then turned his gaze to Dave, who was squirming, kid-like, in his seat. His son. A bright, happy boy, no thanks to him. As he did every time he thought about how Dani had struggled alone, Brand vowed neither of them would ever do without again.

He was glad to see a few of his friends had come. He made eye contact with Vlad Ivanov, who was sitting next to Uncle Jimmy, his gorgeous wife Darlene at his side. When Darlene shot him a brilliant smile, he wondered if she, too, was remembering that night last year in a Detroit hotel…and whether she and Vlad might someday join him and Dani in BDSM play. Not any time soon, he imagined, since Vlad had told Brand when they spoke yesterday that he and Darlene were expecting a baby. Besides, for some reason Brand wasn't as keen on arranging a ménage a trois as he'd been before he gave serious thought to sharing Dani with another Master.

He stood up straighter when recorded music filled the chapel. Elaine walked down the aisle, looking gorgeous in something pale blue and clingy. Her flowers looked like the ones in the baskets. Brand looked past Elaine and saw his bride.

She took his breath away. A silky, dusty rose skirt swirled around her legs, teased him with its narrow panels of pale, see-through lace. The white roses in her bouquet went well with her delicate olive skin and sable hair. Brand stepped forward and took her hand. This time he wouldn't let anyone or anything disrupt their lives. Not even Dani herself.

Chapter Nine

"I thought they'd never let us get away." After they left the reception the team had set up, Brand scooped Dani into his arms, stepped inside their suite and deposited her smack in the middle of the king-size bed. "Want more champagne?"

Dani shook her head. The toasts they'd made at the reception were already making her head swim. Apparently Brand didn't want more, either, because he set the bottle back in the wine bucket and lay beside her on the bed. He lifted her left hand, held it to the light.

"Ring looks good on your finger." Brand brought her hand to his lips, kissed each finger. Curled his fingers around her palm until the light caught his plain gold band as well as her sparkling, diamond-studded ring. "I like wearing yours, too."

"I'm glad." She was glad now that she'd decided to surprise him with a wedding band.

"I've never worn a ring before, but it feels right."

"Really?"

"Yeah, really. Makes me feel as if I belong to you now. You know I'll have to take it off when I play ball."

"I figured that. I didn't know if you'd want to wear one at all, but I wanted to give it to you."

She looked down at the icy brilliance of the diamonds on her finger, and for a moment she wished she had asked him to use the same narrow band he'd given her before. She still had it, buried deep in the corner of her jewelry box. She could have handed it to him and said she wanted to wear it again. But she hadn't. It wouldn't have been right. That wedding so long ago had been the culmination of love. The ceremony they'd shared today legalized their parenthood and legitimized the satisfaction of their mutual desires.

"Do you like yours? If you don't, I can get you another one," Brand said, nibbling at Dani's fingers.

"It's beautiful." She couldn't help wishing he'd given it along with his love. "It was nice of your uncle to come. He seemed to like Dave. Laura, his secretary, was sweet, too."

He sucked her ring finger, sending a little shock wave through her. "Yeah. I was glad they came." He eased his long legs onto the bed and stretched out beside her. "Laura's not just Uncle Jimmy's secretary. They've been lovers since I was a kid, although I didn't know it until I started working at the office during off-seasons. Just thought you ought to know. We don't mention Laura around Mother."

"Oh."

"Not 'Oh'. Uncle Jimmy would marry Laura in a minute if he could. Her husband's still alive, if you can call it that. He's been in a nursing home, in a coma, for nearly twenty years. No one except my mother would fault Laura for finding some happiness with Uncle Jimmy."

"I imagine your mother would object. She's so proper. Background, education, culture, plenty of money. That huge, beautiful house where you grew up."

"My parents didn't have quite everything, no matter how they may have made it seem. They could barely stand each other."

"I never would have guessed."

He laughed. "You didn't live in the same house with them for nearly eighteen years. How did you like Vlad and Darlene?"

"I liked them. Have you known them long?" The blond, Slavic-looking lawyer had an accent that placed him from somewhere other than the South, even though his striking black wife spoke with a cultured, southern drawl.

"I started law school with Vlad, but he finished several years before I did since I only attended classes half the year. He joined the FBI right after graduation. We met again last winter while he was working on a case. He was damn near killed solving the groupie serial murders. After that he married Darlene, and they decided they didn't want him risking his neck any more. I suggested he talk to Uncle Jimmy about joining our firm, and he's now developing a criminal defense practice there. If we go back to Atlanta, we'll be seeing a lot of them."

Dani remembered seeing that news on TV—and the fact Brand had been there and avoided injury while the action had gone down. "Now I know where I'd heard Vlad's name before. I'm glad that awful man's dead," she said, laying a hand on Brand's chest, feeling his heart beating beneath his clothes. "You were in a hotel room with him and his wife when the killer came bursting in, right?"

"Right." He rolled onto his side, traced a line around her throat with one calloused finger. "Vlad and I share a taste for sexual dominance. Maybe someday the four of us can—"

"What? Elaine told me you sometimes like a little kink with your sex, but…" She couldn't go on, couldn't imagine him asking her to take part in—in what? A foursome?

He stroked her bare arm, his touch sensuous, almost as arousing as if he'd been playing with her nipples. "How much do you know about BDSM?"

"Not much." Somehow, with him touching her this way, with his midnight-blue gaze searing her with its intensity, she wanted to know more. "To be honest I can't imagine us wearing black leather stuff with brass studs, or you getting any sexual pleasure out of whipping me. I assume there's more to it than what I've seen on TV."

"Yeah, honey, there's more. A lot more. I'm not particular about black leather myself, and the only reason I'd ever use a whip—the little ones are called floggers—on you would be to enhance your pleasure." He traced the length of her arm then moved to encircle her throat with a gentle hand. "BDSM is all about control. And trust. You said the other night that you were looking forward to handing over control, that you'd had to make all the decisions for too long. I want you to trust me to always give you pleasure."

"You mean it's not that you want me to give you the pleasure?" She covered his hand, lifted it to her lips.

"A sexual dominant gets pleasure by giving it. By making his lover come on command. Taking her higher than she's ever been before. Doing whatever it takes to make her feel good." *Everything, maybe, except sharing you with Vlad or another Dom.* Brand had never felt so possessive before, but he shoved aside that thought. Later would be time enough to analyze those unfamiliar feelings.

"Mmmm. I like the sound of that." The light puffs of her breath against his knuckles aroused him almost as much as her willingness to try the sexual lifestyle he'd practiced for years. "Let's play," she said, shooting him an impish grin as she pretended to grip the faux rails on the headboard.

His gaze darkened. "You're sure?"

"Oh, yes." The menacing tone of his voice made Dani tingle with anticipation. Anticipation tinged with a titillating dash of fear. She grew wet, and her heart pounded in her chest.

"All right. I want you to get up now. Take your clothes off. Do it slow and sexy. Get me hot."

"Yes, sir." His glittering midnight-blue gaze as she stripped for him made heat spread all over her body like flames licking, teasing, burning with their intensity. "I don't remember your being so bossy when we were kids," she said, needing to slow the burn.

He grinned. "I was too damn scared. I was a virgin, too."

She'd thought so at the time, but then she'd been so green she wouldn't have known the difference. "You're not scared now, though." Or indifferent. Though he was still wearing suit pants, his erection was obvious.

"No. I'm not scared. I know you want me to fuck you as much as I want to get my cock into your hot, wet pussy. And I've got the feeling you want me to make you forget all your inhibitions and make you scream with pleasure."

"You didn't talk like that back then." Naked now, she lay back down, raising her arms again and clasping her hands together.

"No. But you like sex talk. I can tell."

She nodded. There was something about the needy look in his eyes, the stark sexuality of how he looked at her, the raw sound of words she doubted he'd ever use with a woman except during sex. Something that had her skin tingling, her nipples beading into tiny points of sensation…her—her pussy—wet and swollen, emanating the scent of desire. Of blatant invitation to her mate.

"Oh, yeah. You like it. So do I." Never taking his gaze off her, he got up. Clothes flew in all directions, and he stood there naked, his cock rigid and pulsating against his flat belly, a perfect specimen of bone, skin, and blood, muscle and sinew nicked here and there by scars that made him no less perfect in her eyes. A big man intent on claiming her.

Her tongue darted out, wet her lips. She trembled, ached to taste that gleaming drop of lubrication at the very tip of his cock. Her fingers itched to tangle in the thatch of pubic curls that cushioned his ball sac. She wanted him to take her, pin her beneath his weight, hold her helpless while he pounded into her wet, swollen pussy.

His eyes dark with passion, he watched her. His gaze, hot and needy, made her want to scream for him to fuck her now, fill the empty place deep inside her.

"Fuck if you're not everything I ever dreamed of." In one smooth motion he came onto the bed, stretched his long body over her. Intense heat surrounded him, scalded her, made her want…

"Please show me. Show me how to please you."

"Later, honey. Right now I can't wait another minute to fuck you."

Breathing hard, he nudged her legs apart, held himself rigidly above her, as though waiting for her permission. Silently she gave it, arching her body and wrapping her legs around his waist. "Oh, yesss," she whispered when he began to move.

He sank into her over and over, loving the tight wet feel of her cunt, the slapping sounds that went with every downward thrust. He'd fought from the first plunge to keep from coming, make this as good for her as it was for him. When she shifted restlessly against him, he grasped both her wrists in one hand, holding her immobile…helpless.

"Please," she begged.

No way was he going to last long. Not tonight. Not as long as she seemed as eager as he to rush to climax, as anxious to submit as he was to conquer and claim her.

He shifted, used his free hand to cup her breast, his fingers working the nipple. God but she was the most responsive woman he'd ever fucked, and her ecstatic whimpers at every hard thrust into her had him close to the edge. He wanted to consume her, place his mark on her so indelibly there'd be no room for any other man. Yet he felt protective, too, determined to remember she was fragile, not only in body but because he'd given her no choices.

"Yesss. Oh, yes." Her tiny body shuddered beneath him. Her cunt gripped his cock as though it would never let him go. She strained to take him deeper, locked her legs around his waist. Panted. He tasted the salt of her sweat when he took her mouth.

"Let it out, baby. Keep on coming. Oh, yeah. Milk my cock. That's the way." His balls tightened. The pressure built.

Her whimper when he nearly withdrew took him over the edge. He tightened his grip on her hands. Took her mouth once more to taste her honey. And came in hot, staccato bursts that left him drained.

Spent, he rolled to his side and drew her close, absorbing the aftershocks that still shook her from head to toe. When the cool air in the room made her start to shiver, he drew up a blanket to cover their sweaty bodies.

He couldn't remember when he'd felt so damn contented.

* * * * *

When Dani woke, Brand lay beside her, one arm casually draped over her naked hip. She still had trouble believing this golden hero actually wanted her as well as their son to share his enchanted life. Tears came to her eyes as she stared at the large, powerful hand that so gently imprisoned her and the plain gold band that symbolized her claim on him.

He looked so handsome. So peaceful now as he slept. Love bubbled up inside her. She stared at his heavily muscled chest and arms, at the soft, light brown mat of hair that tickled her nipples so delightfully, at powerful thighs and calves. At his big cock, gently curved now against his thigh, its base resting in a nest of crisp, dark brown pubic curls. The boy she remembered had been hot, but the man he'd become was absolutely breathtaking. Not only to her, she thought with the tiniest bit of resentment, but to an army of females who liked the way he tossed a football and the sexy way he smiled at them from the pages of magazines and newspapers.

"Morning, baby. You like what you see?" When he grinned, she felt her cheeks grow warm.

"I like. I'll bet every woman in the country likes, too." She shouldn't have said that, damn it, but she wasn't able to squelch the fit of jealousy that had reared its ugly head as she inventoried her new husband's considerable assets.

"Everyone can like all they want, honey, but you're the only one who can touch."

"It's not a teasing matter." She couldn't help it. Couldn't cope with the sudden fear she'd lose him to one or more of his beautiful fans.

His expression turned serious. "Whatever else I may be, I'm no cheat. I promised to be faithful and I meant it."

"It's all right. I'm sorry I..." She couldn't say it, wouldn't admit she worried that she wouldn't be enough woman to hold him. She couldn't set aside her fear, either.

"Come here." He pulled her over on top of him, wrapped his arms around her. "It's time for you to take a ride." He lifted his hips, rubbed his hot, hard cock against her clit.

"Oh." Her pussy muscles clenched at the contact. She straddled him, eager but not quite certain what he meant. "Please, Brand."

"Touch me. Put my cock in your cunt where it belongs." He lifted her, raised her hips. When she grasped him and guided him to her aching center he lowered her, impaling her. She closed her eyes, concentrated on the feeling, the motion.

"That's right, baby. Squeeze me. I wish there were three of me so I could fuck all your delicious holes at once." He paused, drew her down and tongue-fucked her mouth. "Yeah. Does that feel good?"

"Mmm." She should have been shocked, but having him fuck her and kiss her at the same time got her hot. So hot she couldn't imagine not liking him to do anything he wished with her body. Her pussy twitched. Her clit rubbed against his pelvis each time she lowered herself on his cock. She wanted to take his tongue down her throat, suck it.

Intense. When he ringed her asshole with a searching finger shock waves radiated. Surely he didn't mean... But what he was doing to her felt good, made her want more. She rubbed her nipples against his hard chest, desperate to ease the pressure inside her, but it only strengthened. Ripples of sensation surged through her. "Stop. No. Don't stop." She bent, took his lips again as the bubble burst and she came.

"I didn't give you permission to come," he growled, but she barely registered the admonishment because he grasped her hips and turned her over, thrust inside her all the way to her cervix and flooded her womb with his hot semen. "I can see I need to go buy us some toys," he told her as they lay together in the aftermath and he stroked the wet, swollen places between her legs, delving his fingers not only into her pussy but her ass. "You may as well know now, I'm going to claim this hole, too. Not now, and not right away. But when I do, you'll like it. I promise."

He didn't ask. He demanded. God help her, she loved him even if he didn't feel the same.

During the days that followed, they spent Brand's free time with their son. But at night, cloaked in darkness, they found the private time they needed. Time for exploring both feelings and sensations, for getting to know each other again. By the time they left Florida, Dani had found she liked the Master in her husband…and she'd made peace with her inner submissive.

She looked forward to making a home in Milwaukee—and to exploring the BDSM lifestyle further. Maybe not dungeons—she didn't think she was quite that adventurous, but she was eager to explore the locked closet full of toys that Brand had mentioned he'd equipped in the master bedroom.

Chapter Ten

"Will you teach me how to ski, Dad?" Dave sprawled on one section of the big, pearl gray leather conversation pit in Brand's Milwaukee condo, his attention focused on a slick magazine that detailed local attractions. "Boy, I can't wait for it to snow, I'll bet it's neat." He set down the magazine and stared out through the bank of windows against one wall. "Hey, look at how tall those big blue-green pine trees are!"

Brand followed Dave's gaze. The panorama of hills and northern spruce that were so familiar to him were new sights for his son. The boy had missed out on too damn much! Neither he nor Dani had guessed the prospect of winter sports and snow would excite Dave more than any other facet of their move, but apparently it did.

"Will you?"

Brand shook his head. "I've never skied. You can take lessons from a pro, though. There's a ski resort on the other side of the lake."

"Will you learn with me?"

"I can't. My contract doesn't allow me to ski, sky dive, or do anything else the Marlins think might put me out of commission." Silently, Brand thanked the team's super-cautious lawyer who'd insisted on that clause. "How do you like your room?"

"It's super! I never had a TV of my own before, much less my own VCR and computer."

Brand smiled. He hadn't been off the mark when he'd guessed the high-tech electronic stuff he'd told the decorator to get would please his son. "Did I forget anything?"

Dave shot him a grin. "A stereo?"

"There's the master system. You program it over there to play whatever you want to hear in your room." He indicated the huge component stereo system built into the inside wall of the family room. "If you want music when you're away from the house, you can use the iPod I got you down in Florida." Brand stood and stretched his legs. "Why don't you relax and watch the boats? I'm going to go find your mom." He took the curved, wrought iron stairs two at the time to the upper level that held nothing except the private master suite, his mind on fulfilling a promise he'd made Dani an hour earlier.

Finish undressing and put on that sexy thing I laid out on the bed. I'll be back soon to take care of you. Relax while I see what our son is up to.

* * * * *

Dani wasn't in bed as he'd assumed she'd be. He found her on their balcony, staring pensively through branches of dense, blue spruce trees at the crystal-clear lake beyond. Brand stretched out beside her on a candy-striped lounger. At least she'd put on the black satin slip sort of thing that clung to every inch of her tiny frame and had him itching to take it off.

"Tired, honey?" He brushed a dark strand of hair off her cheek, felt her tense at his touch.

"Not really. Don't you think you overdid it a little on Dave's room?" Her expression pained, she met his gaze.

"I got the things I thought a kid his age would like. What don't you approve of?"

"How about that big flat-screen TV? And the computer with more features than any I've ever seen before, even at work."

"I thought he'd like them. He does."

She shook her head. "Of course he likes all that stuff. Who wouldn't? Was the red hot tub already in his bathroom, or did you have it put in just for him?"

Brand couldn't help grinning. Dani was cute when she got steamed. "Not guilty on that. It came with the condo."

"That's good." Her tone implied just the opposite.

"Come on. Out with whatever it is that's really bugging you."

She met his gaze then looked away. "No eleven-year-old kid needs all those things. I think you deliberately went all out just to show our son how disadvantaged he's been up until now."

That struck a sore spot. "Well, if I've deprived my son, it's because you chose to keep me from knowing he existed. I want to make up for those years."

"I didn't tell you because I had no reason to think you'd want to know. Dave never went hungry, no matter what you think." Dani tried to fight the guilt she felt every time Brand reminded her she'd robbed him of years with his son.

"Not hungry, maybe, but don't try to tell me you and he both didn't have to do without things you really needed." The dangerously low pitch of his voice projected guilt and frustration of his own.

But she wasn't ready to let it go. "That's no excuse for spoiling him rotten now."

"No? I think Dave needs a little spoiling, and I know you do." If his words hadn't told her in no uncertain terms that this conversation was over, his action did. Looking her in the eye, he stood and scooped her up in his arms. Once in the bedroom he set her in the center of the white duvet cover on the biggest bed she'd ever seen. "You're not complaining about this bedroom, are you? Everything in it is new, too."

"No." The closet he'd just opened revealed a paradise of luxurious, sensual treasures meant to add excitement to their sex life. The suite was perfect. Perfect, now that she knew it contained no ghosts of other lovers he might have brought here in the past. She couldn't help the small smile that flickered on her lips when she saw his eyes had darkened with passion.

"Don't resent what I want for you or Dave." He joined her on the bed, traced a pattern with one finger along her jaw, her throat. "Raise your arms."

Her heart skipped a beat when she looked up at him, saw the raw hunger in his expression. He was going to restrain her now, the way he'd talked about doing at the hotel in Florida. When padded handcuffs clicked closed around each wrist, fear warred with hot anticipation.

He bent, sucked first one nipple then the other through the thin silk of the nightgown he'd laid out for her to wear. Shards of sensation cut through the fear, made her squirm restlessly against the knee he'd slid between her legs. "Oh, yesss. Fuck me, please."

"Not yet, baby." He rose, his gaze searing her skin as he undressed. "I'm going to play with you first, and you're going to love it. Spread your legs."

The motion when she complied made the ben-wa balls he'd inserted earlier shift in her pussy. Her juices flowed, tickling as they made their way along her slit and pooled around her anus. When she felt padded straps enclose each ankle and realized he'd made her helpless, her whole body sizzled with sexual anticipation.

"Brand?" He'd smeared something cold and wet around her anus, and now he was working a finger in. No, not a finger, but something bigger. She tensed when she remembered him saying he was going to fuck her there, too.

"Easy. This is a butt plug, the smallest of three. We're going to play with them every day until you can take the biggest one. Until we've stretched this tight little hole enough to take my cock."

She couldn't help it. The plug made the ben-wa balls shift. Got her so hot, she tried to raise her hips. "Please. I want your cock in my pussy now."

He laughed as he straddled her face. "Impatient, aren't you? Here, suck my cock. I want to eat your pussy." Bending, he closed his lips over her clit, flicked it over and over with his tongue. His big cock stretched her lips, made her swallow convulsively when she deep-throated him until his pubic hair tickled her chin and his balls bounced against her nose.

The sensations were too much, but she couldn't move, couldn't escape the triple onslaught that had her juices gushing now. He lapped her greedily, his tongue satin-smooth as he pushed it into her pussy. The sucking motion had her squirming against his mouth, wanting... *Oh God. Oh yesss. Don't. Don't stop.* She couldn't talk around his huge, pulsating cock but somehow she knew he knew. Shock waves rolled through her, each one stronger than the last.

She sucked him harder, felt his balls tighten, his muscles tense. He pulled out the ben-wa balls and she came again. Out of control now, he fucked her mouth, pulling out then going deep, deeper. "God baby, I'm coming. Take it all. Swallow it."

The vibration of his words against her spasming pussy started another wave of sensation coursing through her. She sucked him harder as he began to come in short hard bursts. Bursts that matched the rhythm of her own climax. Made it better.

She liked being restrained, helpless to whatever sexual stimulation he subjected her to. Strangely, her bonds freed her from guilt, gave her body permission to feel, her mind freedom from long-held inhibitions. After all, he was in total control. Control that gave him the power to do as he would, to force dark, delicious sensations she'd never have dared to reach for on her own.

"Brand?"

"Yeah, honey." He finished untying her and was soothing the chafed skin beneath the cuffs with his lips and tongue. When he finished, he lay beside her, holding her close, as if he didn't want to give up the physical contact just yet.

She traced a lazy figure-eight around his flat brown nipples. "I think I'm going to like this Master/slave thing."

He cupped her ass cheeks, jiggling the butt plug that no longer hurt but served as a reminder that it was there to ready her to take him there. "You're my perfect little sub. And I'm always going to take care of you."

* * * * *

Their first week in Milwaukee was busy. Brand had registered Dave at the exclusive boys' academy across the lake from their condo, and Dani had to call around to find the books and uniforms their son would need before school would start the following week.

On Labor Day, Brand barbecued steaks at the lakeside dock. They were becoming a real family, Dani thought as she watched her husband and son cavort in the lake water that had felt too icy cold when she tested it with her toes.

The next day Dani decided to try her hand in the big, cheery kitchen. She looked up from the biscuit dough she'd been rolling out, smiled when she saw Brand. "Hi. You're home from practice early."

He grinned then bent and brushed his lips across hers, setting off a chain reaction that had her pussy creaming. "I missed you, baby. How did Dave like his first day at school?"

She'd missed Brand, too, wanted nothing more than for him to take her here and now. That wasn't about to happen, though, not with the housekeeper still finishing up her chores. "He likes the kids. Hates wearing the uniform. He's still at school, trying out for the middle-school football team. He'd probably like it if you'd go pick him up."

"Okay, I will. What's cooking?" Brand uncovered the pots, sniffed the country-fried steak and southern-style green beans. "Where's Mrs. Blair?"

Dani wished he wasn't insisting on keeping the housekeeper who'd worked for him since he'd bought the condo. "She's in Dave's room, straightening up after him. I chased her out of here because I felt like cooking tonight." She floured a round cutter, cut two dozen biscuits from the dough she'd rolled.

"It smells great. What time does Dave finish with tryouts?"

"In about half an hour. Elaine called earlier. She wanted to know if we could come over tomorrow night for a cookout."

"Sure. Josh told me we'd be invited. Elaine always has a cookout the Friday before the first home game of the season. Did you tell her we'd come?" He nuzzled her neck and sent shivers all the way down her spine.

"I told her I'd ask you and let her know. I'll call her back now. I'm sure Dave would be thrilled if you got to school early enough to watch him try out for the team."

She smiled. Brand looked big and gorgeous and terribly impressive. She imagined Dave would practically burst with pride when his dad showed up in the distinctive bright-blue Marlins sweats.

"I'm going. I'd rather stay here and look at you, you know." His dark blue eyes sparkled with apparent amusement as he watched Dani watch him. "What I'd really like to do right now is take you upstairs, tie you down and fuck you until you scream for mercy."

"Later."

He cupped her bottom with both hands, dragged her against his half-hard cock. "Are you ready for this, baby?"

"I-I think so." The idea of him taking her there excited her, but it embarrassed her to admit it. "I'm wet for you."

"Good. I like to keep you that way. Wet and eager. Keep thinking about this—" he nudged her with his erection—"and it'll be bedtime before we know it." Moving one hand to her cheek, he lowered his head and kissed her long and deep.

Heat bubbled inside her, the way it always did when he touched her. It amazed her that he could turn her on with words—sometimes with just his presence in the room. She guessed her hormones had been deprived too long and now were making up for lost time. "Go on, get Dave," she said, pretending to shove him through the kitchen door.

When Brand had left, Dani checked the progress of her steaks and laid out the biscuits on a shiny cookie sheet. Then she poured some coffee and sat down to call Elaine. As they talked, she looked out the window in front of the kitchen table. She loved the quiet, the beauty, the crisp clean colors of the trees and lake. Maple, elm, and oak trees were just beginning to show their brilliant fall colors, in contrast to the tall, blue spruce.

The lake was magnificent, not the reddish brown of Georgia lakes or the opaque green of ponds in Florida. Lake Marion was crystal clear, almost transparent. She wished the water were warm enough to enjoy swimming, then chided herself for being too greedy. She could swim in Brand's indoor lap pool anytime she wanted.

She loved living here, living with him. In only two weeks, she'd managed to learn where things were. She'd started to feel as if she belonged. Comfortable except for the fact her son idolized his father while he ignored her. Logically, she knew her resentment was unfair, that Dave was bound to want to do boy-things with his dad. But it was hard to be taken for granted when before she'd been the center of Dave's life.

You've got almost everything you ever dreamed of. Don't expect to have it all. Determined not to feel left out, she got up to finish dinner. It was a pleasure cooking with every possible convenience. When she looked over at the pizza oven built into a stone wall next to two regular ovens and a ceramic range top, she recalled how much Brand had liked pizza when they were kids. She'd have to make one for him—but she doubted his taste ran to the frozen ones she used to fix for Dave.

Brand had given her all these luxuries she'd never dreamed of until a few months ago. She had it good. Very good. A sexy, attentive husband. A bright, happy son. A beautiful home. A closet full of every piece of clothing she might need.

She'd finished putting the steaks onto a platter and sliding the tray of biscuits into the oven when she heard the distinctive roar of Brand's Ferrari. She set the table and put out condiments, vegetables and a fruit salad she'd made earlier. By the time the biscuits were ready, Brand and Dave were waiting at the table.

"Mom, you should have seen Dad throw the ball!" Dave exclaimed, his eyes bright with admiration. "He was showing us how to pass without messing up our arms."

"Did you make the team?" Dani tried not to think about the fact that Dave's interest in playing football would give him one more reason to worship his dad.

"Sure. Coach said that with a dad like mine, I couldn't help being great." Dave stuffed a bite of steak into his mouth. "Hey, Mom, this tastes good," he said, following up the steak with a bite from a gravy-drenched biscuit.

"Don't talk with your mouth full, son. Like my mother used to say, the food's not going anywhere. It'll still be there if you take your time and mind your manners."

Dave looked, shamefaced, at the fork full of green beans he'd been about to shovel into his mouth. "Sorry, Dad. I'm not used to having to watch my table manners."

Dani bristled. "You are, too. Dave, I've told you ever since you were little not to mess around at the table." She'd been pretty casual about their meals, but she couldn't let Brand think she hadn't taught their son how to eat right.

"Aw, Mom, you weren't ever so strict." Dave tried to con her with the grin that mirrored his dad's.

"Maybe not about using the right forks, or things like that, but I certainly have tried to teach you basic good manners." Dani recalled the scene two nights ago when Brand had noticed Dave buttering his bread with his table knife instead of the fancy spreader Mrs. Blair had set beside his bread plate. Since she'd done the same thing, it had embarrassed her when Brand had shown Dave what the little spreader was for.

"Dave, drop it," Brand said. It was obvious he didn't want to spend another hour or so, soothing her ruffled feathers the way he had the night of the butter spreader incident. He shot a look of silent warning at Dave before turning to her. "Dani, did you take your driving lesson this morning?"

"Yes. Mr. Phillips actually let me drive all the way around the lake. It's not hard, especially with an automatic shift." Dani had made one futile attempt in St. Petersburg to let Brand teach her to drive the Ferrari. It had not been pretty, and she'd vowed never again to touch it or any similar vehicle. Brand had bought her a silver Mercedes the second day they'd been in Milwaukee. The next day, he'd arranged for a professional to teach her how to drive it. Dani wanted to learn, if for nothing else than to please Brand. "Tomorrow, I'm going to try the Interstate." With luck she wouldn't make a horrible mess of the lesson.

"Good. You'll soon be zipping around everywhere. You need to go to the Wives' Association meeting next week. I left the notice about the damn thing out in the car." Brand finished his steak and took another piece from the platter. "Dinner's delicious. You'll have to cook more often."

"Thanks. We don't really need Mrs. Blair. I can keep up with the house, I'm sure." The housekeeper was nice, and Dani supposed she was good at what she did. It made her nervous, though, having a housekeeper she was supposed to tell what to do when Dani felt as if Mrs. Blair should be directing her. "I don't need to take driving lessons every day or go to every meeting I'm invited to, do I?"

"Mrs. Blair's gone with this place ever since the first owners built it. She needs the job, and the home," Brand murmured. "Don't you like her?"

"Yes. I'm not used to sitting around doing nothing, that's all." Dani would have hated to put the woman out of a job for no reason other than her own discomfort. "I can learn to enjoy my leisure, though, I'm sure. I made peach cobbler for dessert. Would you like some?"

Father and son grinned, their faces mirror images of delight. Dani enjoyed watching them eat the rich, cream-garnished dessert, hearing them groan in unison when the last crumbs were gone.

Chapter Eleven

ം

"Did you help Dave finish his homework?" Dani called from the bathroom when she heard Brand open the door to their suite.

"Yeah. I'm surprised he didn't already know how to multiply and divide fractions. He should have learned that last year." Brand came in, shrugged out of his sweats and stepped into the hot tub. The water rippled, lapped at his chest. When he adjusted the jacuzzi jets, it turned to a sea of bursting bubbles that made her skin tingle, her muscles relax.

When she looked at Brand, though, she realized something was bothering him. Dave's lack of knowledge, she guessed. "Dave was in a different school last year. Maybe they didn't teach things the same." Dave's difficulties more likely lay with his being placed in that exclusive, all-boys' school across the lake. A school Brand had said reminded him of the one he'd attended, not at all like the mediocre public school where Dave had gone in Tampa.

Brand shifted, sank deeper in the tub and let the jets pound at the muscles in his upper back. "Could be. I'll try to spend more time, help him more. You might want to give him a hand, too. Can't have him getting behind so early in the year."

"I will."

"Good girl. Come here." Before she could comply, he'd grabbed her at the waist and set her on his lap. "Hand me the soap."

His big hands warmed her as he lathered her from neck to toes. By the time he finished, he'd sensitized every place he'd touched. His erection throbbed against her hip, inviting… She shifted in the water, straddled his lap. Her pussy twitched at the intimate contact.

"Bad girl. I guess I'm going to have to punish you," he said, his tone so menacing she was half-afraid in spite of the twinkle that lit his eyes. "Want this?" He raised his hips, poked her with his hard-on.

"Oh, yes."

"Then I want you to shave your pussy for me."

The idea excited her—made her feel a little naughty, as though she were the star of that triple-X DVD Brand had rented and played on the DVD player one night while they'd still been in Florida. "Why?" She'd never thought a bare pussy might turn a man on until she saw that flick.

"Because I want to eat you without your little muff getting in my way. And I want my balls rubbing baby-soft skin when we're fucking. You'll like how it feels."

"I will?" She knew she'd like it. Her pussy was already wet, swollen, ready to take him any way he wanted her.

He slid one hand up her body, his calloused fingertips abrading her skin, heightening her anticipation. "Yeah, baby. You'll like it. And so will I."

"Do you want me to do it now?" She hoped not. As hot as she was, she'd probably shake so much she'd slice herself up…

"No. Get it waxed at a salon tomorrow. I don't want to risk you getting my playtoys cut. Besides, I'm going to fuck you now." He lifted her, impaled her, took her mouth. He plucked at her nipples with strong, capable fingers. Slowly, then faster, he fucked her, his cock pounding her cervix with every thrust. The water lapped at her skin, heightened her response. She shuddered, felt her inner muscles clench around him, shared his shout of triumph.

Grinning, he splashed water on her neck, then gave her ass cheeks a playful squeeze before nudging her rear entrance. "How's this going?"

"Fine. I kept the plug in for two hours this afternoon. Pretty soon—"

"Pretty soon you'll be ready to let me claim this tight little hole. Won't you, baby?"

"Hmmm. As soon as you decide you want to take it." As long as he held the reins of control, she'd be ready for every sort of sexual pleasure he wanted to dish out. "Come on, let's go to bed. You have a heavy workout tomorrow, don't you?"

"Yeah." With fluid grace, he stood, stepped out of the hot tub and held a warmed towel out for her. When they'd dried off, he lay across the bed, watched her search through a drawer.

She found the rose silk nightie she wanted, dropped it over her head, enjoyed the feel of the slick material slithering down her warm, damp skin. When she lay down, he cradled her head against his chest. For a long time she listened to the steady beat of his heart, counted herself lucky to be his wife.

* * * * *

The next afternoon Brand stormed into the recreation room and slammed a stack of papers on the coffee table. "Sit down," he snapped when Dani got up from the desk where she'd been looking for information on the computer.

He'd never sounded so angry, even when he'd confronted her about having kept Dave's existence a secret. "What's wrong?"

"Didn't you have any notion our son wasn't getting the proper education? I've just come from school. They're going to have to move Dave down into fifth grade, or we're going to have to have him tutored. He's not prepared to handle sixth grade work."

Dani couldn't believe her ears. "Dave's always made straight A's. He was in the gifted program in Tampa. Maybe this school's too hard for him."

Brand slammed his fist into the back of a leather-upholstered chair. "Dave's IQ is a hundred forty. According to the headmaster, that's higher than most of the kids at Eastover have. His problem is that he hasn't been taught what he should have been, not that he has trouble learning."

Dani hadn't liked the idea of Dave going to school with a bunch of snobbish rich kids. "Why don't we let him go to public school? I don't want him humiliated. He doesn't need to repeat fifth grade."

"That's not an option. Security isn't good enough."

"Security?"

Brand quit pacing, sat across from Dani, rubbed a hand through his windblown hair. "For God's sake, Dani. Think. It's not as if I were some anonymous executive. My contract's a matter of public information. Dave's a prime target for kidnappers."

"I never thought about that. Can't we get a tutor for him, help him catch up?"

"Yes. Dave's math teacher has agreed to tutor him on Saturdays at school, but you'll have to take him there, go back and pick him up. I have pre-game sessions every Saturday before home games. If we're playing away, I'll already have left town. Can you handle that?" He smoothed an errant wisp of hair off her forehead, his touch gentle yet incredibly arousing.

"I think so. I passed the test for my driver's license this morning."

"Congratulations. Didn't I tell you learning how to drive would be a snap?" He pulled her onto his lap and kissed her playfully. "What was that you were looking at so seriously that you didn't notice me when I walked in?"

She smiled. "An online site about etiquette. I was reading about how to send and reply to invitations."

"I can't imagine that being all that interesting."

"Actually, it's confusing. You can only ask people over for really casual things on the phone. Otherwise, you write out invitations, and the way you write them tells the person you're inviting just how dressy the party's going to be. If it's real formal, you write the invitation like someone else was writing it, and that's the way the people you send it to are supposed to respond. I've never gotten a written invitation to anything."

He tried to smother his laughter in her soft dark hair. Dani was a delight. He loved that she always tried to do the best she could, whatever the situation. That had included the way she'd taken care of Dave before he came on the scene. Yes, it disturbed him to know Dave would need help to meet his new, harder academic challenges, but Brand couldn't fault Dani because she'd lived in a place without exceptional public schools and hadn't had the money to send Dave to a decent prep school.

He also couldn't remember a time in his life when he'd been happier than he was now. "You're priceless, you know. Only you would voluntarily sit and read things most people's mothers have to tie them down to make them learn."

She smiled. "My mom never taught me anything. I want to learn so I can tie Dave down, pound it into his head."

"I don't know if I want to let you torture him like that, but we can talk about it later. Come on, I'm hungry." He didn't know what it was about her, but he could easily have spent all day, every day, making her scream with pleasure. He stood, holding her securely to his chest. And he took the stairs two at the time.

"You know, you turn me into a satyr," he whispered against her cheek as he used a foot to shove the door open. "All I have to do is look at you, and my cock's rock hard and ready."

"Whatever you want. I did as you said and had your pussy waxed this morning. It made me hot, imagining what you're going to do to all that bare flesh."

"Oh, fuck yes." He slid his hand between her legs. She felt smooth even through her damp panties, and her swollen clit poked impudently at his seeking fingers. "I'm gonna strip you naked and fuck you until neither one of us can stand up another minute."

He pressed her to the innocent-looking set of crossbeams against one wall and secured her arms to it with Velcro straps then ripped off the satin bikini pants that covered her silky cunt. "Spread those legs for me."

"Like this?"

Oh, yeah, he thought, wrapping the restraining straps around each leg and tilting the crossbeams to position her just as he wanted her. Not bothering to remove the dress he'd shoved up around her waist or shed his own sweatshirt, he shoved down his sweatpants.

God but she had a fuckable cunt. He bent, tongued her, loved the way she squirmed and whimpered when he inserted two fingers in her virgin ass. His cock was throbbing, his balls already drawn high and tight, but when he felt the satiny smoothness of her bare cunt lips he nearly came on the spot. "You're already wet. And soft as silk. Lie back and let me make you feel real good."

"Oh, yesss."

He sank into her hard and fast, matching the thrusts of his hips with the movement of his fingers in her ass. "Someday maybe I'll share you with another Dom. Let you feel two hot cocks inside you, two sets of balls slapping at your smooth, wet cunt lips. You know, that's one of the ways the cross can be used."

She was breathing hard, almost as hard as he was, obviously trying to wait for him to give her permission to come. He bent, took a pebbled nipple in his mouth and sucked it hard.

"Fuck me harder. Please," she said, her hips straining to take him deeper, harder.

"My pleasure, baby." Standing straight, his gaze locked with hers, he pounded into her cunt, his balls slapping her wet, swollen pussy lips as he slipped a third finger up her ass. "Come for me. You're so goddamn beautiful when you come, it drives me crazy."

"I'm coming. Don't…don't stop." Her cunt clenched around his cock like a hot, wet glove. He held back as long as he could, milking her pleasure until her screams morphed to tiny moans.

"One more time, come for me one more time," he ground out. "God yes." He'd have said more but his entire being centered on his cock, on her hot flesh constricting around him…on the steaming bursts of semen that left him drained.

And satisfied. Every time they made love it only made him want her more. He rained gentle kisses over her thighs, her belly, her glistening pussy as he freed her from the cross and finished undressing them both. He doubted he'd ever get enough of her.

* * * * *

When Dave came home from football practice that afternoon, he headed straight for his room, almost as if he wanted to avoid his parents. Brand caught him just as he shed the last of his clothes, climbed into the red whirlpool tub Dani had thought was more than a little too much for a kid Dave's age. Brand sat down on the bench beside the tub, looked Dave in the eye.

"Hi, Dad. Hey, you should have seen me throw the ball today. I think Coach is going to let me play quarterback, 'specially if you can help me some more after practice."

"You aren't going to be playing ball at all unless you get your grades up. I talked with the headmaster today. You're going to have to spend your Saturdays being tutored." He hated to be the bad guy, but he supposed it went with fatherhood.

"Aw, Dad. I always made A's in school before. I just don't know how to do some of the stuff they want me to do at Eastover. Can't you help me? I've gotta play ball." Dave sounded appalled at the idea of giving up his place on the middle school football team.

"I'll help. So will your mom. But the tutor can help you more, and faster. Your mom will drive you there, come back and pick you up every Saturday."

Dave looked pained. "How long do I have to do this?"

"Until your teachers think you can handle the work by yourself." Brand stood, stretched. "Hurry up and change," he said. "We'll toss a football around for a little while after we eat. Then I'll help you with your math."

* * * * *

Between Dave's math and getting ready for the season's opening game, the week zoomed by. Dani had enjoyed the Shearer's barbecue, an event that had set an expectant mood for the game that was about to start in a few minutes. Dani watched Dave trade stories with some of the other Marlin players' sons, visited with Elaine and some of the other wives in the mid-field box seat area reserved for them.

When the Marlins trotted onto the field, Dani strained her eyes, looking for Brand. She'd enjoyed watching him, Josh and Tom, the third string quarterback, warming up earlier with the receivers and running backs. Now, she was eager to see her husband play a real game.

"There they are!"

A booming voice over the public address system carried over the noise from thousands of fans who had come out on the brisk, fall day to see their team battle the Memphis Gamblers. The din continued while the Gambler starters were introduced, settled to a low roar when the Marlins jogged to the middle of the field.

The microphone crackled. "On offense today. At quarterback, number eleven, Brand Carendon, all-pro, two time All American out of Emory, six-four, two hundred twenty-five pounds, in his eighth season with the Marlins!"

The crowd roared. Dani stood up and cheered with them. In pads Brand looked huge, invincible. Her mouth dropped open when she noticed the Gamblers player Brand stood next to. The man made Brand look like a little boy.

"That guy is a monster. He must be half again as big as Brand." She couldn't take her eyes off her husband and his gigantic adversary.

Elaine laughed. "That's Bruiser Smith. He's about six feet eight and must weigh nearly four hundred pounds. I think he's the biggest linebacker in the league. Josh says we're going to put two offensive linemen on him today."

"That man could hurt somebody." Dani hadn't considered before that there might be anyone big enough to pose a threat to her big, brawny husband. "Don't linebackers try to keep quarterbacks from passing the ball?" Her concern grew as she tried to remember a few rudimentary facts about the game.

"Yes. They also try to knock out runners and blockers. All the offensive linemen try to keep the defense away from the quarterback and running backs. The backfield defensive players go after the pass receivers. Haven't you watched a football game before?"

"Just on TV. And Brand played some tapes for me. This is the first time I've been to a game." Dani noticed the Marlins had won the toss and elected to start out on offense.

"Did he show you the tape of the last game we played against the Gamblers?"

Dani shook her head, glanced at the players lining up on the field.

Elaine laughed. "I didn't think Brand would have showed you that one. He and Josh shared a hospital room for nearly two weeks after that game, thanks to Bruiser."

"Oh, no." A chill ran up Dani's spine.

"Oh, yes. The rookie who went in after they both got hurt has never played again. Look, Dani, the game's about to start."

* * * * *

Brand took a deep breath, went over the opening play again in the huddle. "Walzak, Monk, keep that goddamn monster out of my face. I can't throw if I'm buried under six feet of turf. Put it this way, guys. My wife and kid haven't seen the tape of our last game with the Gamblers, and I don't want them seeing a live repeat, today."

He remembered having spent two painful weeks in traction and playing the last six games of the season wrapped in tape, held together with various metal braces. The icing had been the off-season surgery he'd had to have on the knee Bruiser had collided with.

The first play was a long completion down the middle, called back for holding against Monk Davis. Backed up fifteen yards on third down, Brand threw again, this time for a touchdown. The Gamblers' pass defense seemed to be concentrated mostly on keeping the ball from being passed, instead of defending their goal when passes were completed. This time, Brand thought with a sigh of relief, the officials hadn't seen Walzak holding onto Bruiser. It had helped that Monk and two other Marlin linemen had piled on top of the big linebacker and his ball-and-chain.

At halftime, the Marlins were up by fourteen, and Brand had only been sacked once, not by Bruiser but by a Gamblers safety who had moved through the line while Bruiser fought off three burly tacklers. Walzak, though, was out for the day with a dislocated shoulder. With the burly Pole out of business, prospects didn't seem so bright for the second half.

The Gamblers drove for a field goal, and the Marlins' lead was cut to eleven. Brand threw for another touchdown just as Bruiser hurled him to the ground. He saw double, felt bones crack. Had to get up, couldn't let Dani watch him getting carried off the field. Fuck, it hurt too much to move. He gave up, closed his eyes and waited for the trainers to come with a stretcher.

"Elaine, he's hurt."

"It may not be so bad. Bruiser probably just knocked the wind out of him."

Dani watched Brand clutch at his rib cage, figured a few cracked ribs were more likely. "Can I go down there?"

"No. They'll send someone for you if it's serious enough to take him to the hospital."

"Well, Josh will get some playing time." Dani tried to smile. The Marlins kicked their extra point then stopped a Gamblers drive at mid-field. Brand was still somewhere in the bowels of the stadium. Josh consulted with Coach Allen, then buckled his helmet and trotted onto the field.

Dani saw Elaine trembling. Her eyes were glued on the bright blue number fourteen on her husband's back when he bent over to take the snap.

Dave came back from the concession stand with popcorn, sat down next to Dani. "Hey, that's Mr. Shearer playing." He looked at Dani. "Dad got hurt?"

She nodded. "They took him to the locker room." Dani watched Josh drop back for a pass. A hulking, burgundy-clad figure came into her line of vision, followed by several smaller ones in blue. Josh got off his pass before Bruiser Smith slammed into him.

Elaine screamed. The crowd roared when a Marlin receiver caught the pass in the end zone. Dave tried to distract Josh's twin boys. Numb, Dani watched trainers, stretchers and physicians converge at Josh's side.

Chapter Twelve

Brand heard the crowd roar, sensed something was wrong when the noise level dropped to a dull roar. Naked from the waist up, he sat still while a trainer wrapped roll after roll of tape around him, from just below his armpits to an inch above his navel.

He glanced at the closed circuit television screen, grinned at the Marlins receiver's playful antics in the end zone. Good. Bruiser's knocking him out of the game hadn't helped the Gamblers' chances of winning. Then the picture shifted. Josh lay on the field, much like Brand had a few minutes earlier.

"Have you still got that straitjacket you tried to get me to wear last season?" Brand hated the high impact plastic and metal contraption the team doctor had designed last year to protect his cracked ribs. Still, he had no desire for Bruiser to push a rib into his lung.

"You ain't playing any more today. Doc's orders." The trainer continued taping Brand's rib cage.

"Get the goddamn thing. Didn't you see, Josh is hurt, too."

"Let 'em kill the kid. He's expendable."

"Tom's got potential. Would you want to play your first pro game against Bruiser?" Brand remembered Randy Jones, the cocky black rookie of two years ago, whose hopes of playing ball had been shattered in just one encounter with the monster linebacker.

"They ain't gonna let you play. This is a waste of your time and mine." The trainer strapped the miserably uncomfortable protective equipment on, adjusted it. Trying to fight down the nausea that threatened every time he moved, Brand let the trainer secure his shoulder pads again.

"Get a clean jersey out of my locker." Feeling as though he'd been run over by a steamroller, he didn't want to expend unnecessary motion. It hurt like hell when he held up his arms so the man could wrestle the shirt over his head.

A few minutes later he passed the stretcher carrying Josh through the tunnel. Good, from the way he looked, Josh probably hadn't suffered any season-ending injuries, either.

Brand rejoined his teammates, waved at Dani. He figured the Marlins' eighteen-point lead would have to hold for the last quarter. Running the clock as much as possible, he kept the ball on the ground, relying on the Marlins' defense to stop the Gamblers' drives. He hated playing that way, but he hadn't enjoyed that hospital stay Bruiser had caused him two years ago.

When it was over, they'd won by fifteen, Brand was still alive, and the fans were happy.

Dani was waiting outside in the Mercedes with Dave and the Shearer twins. Brand sank wearily into the passenger seat, asked Dani to show him her new driving skills. He was damn glad he hadn't insisted on driving to the game in the Ferrari. There was no way he could have handled the stick shift, not with three cracked ribs on his right side.

"Elaine asked us to take them. She wanted to wait until the doctors finish with Josh," Dani explained as she pulled out onto the crowded expressway. "I hope you don't mind. Dave said he'd like for the boys to sleep over, keep him company while we go to that party tonight."

Brand groaned. He'd completely forgotten about the team owners' annual first of the season bash. He'd been looking forward to a long, solitary soak in the hot tub, followed by at least twenty-four hours' unbroken bed rest. He muttered a vicious expletive.

"Brand, the children." Her rebuke, like everything she did was gentle. Except when he got her wild and hot in bed. For once, the thought of getting Dani into bed didn't make him instantly hard.

"Sorry. How much time do we have before we have to be at the party?"

"About four hours. It's at nine o'clock."

"Then I can spend three hours in the Jacuzzi." He sat very still, breathed carefully. When Dani stopped the car in the garage, he could barely manage to crawl out.

* * * * *

Dani took Dave and the Shearer twins into the kitchen, put out some grapes and apples for them to eat while she grilled ham and cheese sandwiches for their supper. She hated to bother Mrs. Blair, especially when the housekeeper would be babysitting for two extra children later. When the boys had finished eating, Dave took them to his room to play computer games while Dani went upstairs.

"Come here and help me unwind this tape. I feel like a fucking mummy." Brand sounded like a petulant little boy trying to get sympathy for his aches and pains. He stood in front of the bathroom mirror, naked except for the white tape around his torso.

Steam rose from the hot tub, water spurting from all ten of the Jacuzzi jets. Brand had removed a lot of tape already, or so it appeared from the stuff he'd strewn all over the floor.

"Are your ribs broken?" Dani unwrapped the rest of the bandaging and breathed in Brand's unique masculine scent, mixed tonight with the strong smell of liniment.

"Cracked." He sounded as though he was in pain.

"Should we be taking the tape off?"

"You'll have to tape me back up when I get out of the tub." Brand shuddered when the last layer of tape came off.

"They shaved your chest." Dani liked the soft, furry, light brown pelt that tickled her breasts so delightfully. She'd miss it. "Oh, no. You're all bruised." Very lightly, she brushed her fingers over a huge, discolored spot on Brand's right side.

Brand grinned, stepped into the hot tub. "Want to join me?"

She pulled her sweatshirt over her head. "Do you always get banged up like this in games?" The assortment of cuts, lacerations and bruises that marred his body made him look as if he'd been in a gang fight.

"I hope not." Brand lay back against the jets, watched her shimmy out of her jeans and bikini panties. "Come here, babe."

She hoped the swirling water would soothe his aches and pains. Carefully, for she didn't want to hurt him more, she curled up against Brand's more or less undamaged left side. "Want a massage when you get done here?" she asked, wondering if he had some kind of liniment that would relieve the soreness.

"The hot tub does the most good." He toyed with her breast with his uninjured left hand. "If you want any action for the next few days, though, you'll have to do most of the work."

When she imagined being the aggressor, having him in her power, Dani's pulse quickened. She could pet him, tease him the way he sometimes teased her. Ride him, make him wait, savor every sensation until she couldn't hold back any longer.

"I'm glad you didn't get hurt here." With one hand, she encircled his cock under the swirling water. "Or here." She dropped a kiss on his nipple, just above the water line. It hardened instantly under her exploring tongue.

"Stop. You're torturing me. There's no way in hell I can move right now." He lay back, let the jets pound into his back and shoulders, not moving until he had to get up and change for the party.

Dani managed to tape Brand's ribs and help him into his tux. For the first time, she felt as though he needed her. She even had to fasten the black onyx studs in his shirt, put his tie on for him. He sat, looking as pained as she was sure he must feel, and watched her wiggle into a strapless sheath made out of rose-colored sequins. When they were ready to go, she had to kick off her shoes and stand on the bed to help him put on his jacket.

Brand had flinched when she helped him get his right arm into the fitted jacket of his tux. "Wouldn't they understand if we didn't go? They know you're hurt."

"No. I'm not hurt enough to weasel out of this. The only way we could get out of going would be for me to be in the hospital. Epps likes to show off all his human animals to his friends. Damn, I must be hurt. You look good enough to eat in that outfit, and I haven't even got a hard on."

"Mr. Epps owns the team?" Dani asked.

"Along with a few minor investors. He has his lawyer put into every contract that attendance at this little gathering is required just as much as at the practice sessions and games." Brand stuffed a money clip into his inside jacket pocket, motioned for Dani to join him.

Dani hadn't driven at night before, but she didn't want Brand to hurt himself further, so she slipped under the wheel of her car. Brand belonged at home in bed, not at this party. His bosses must be heartless, making hurt players attend their party unless they were hospitalized. Would Josh and Elaine be there? She hoped so, and not only because if he was, Josh wouldn't have been hurt as badly as Elaine had thought. Josh and Elaine helped her feel comfortable.

It hurt her to watch Brand, knowing he was hurting. He should have taken some medication, but she hadn't been able to persuade him to take anything. "I'm not about to get hooked on drugs," he'd said through gritted teeth before explaining that football players always had some kind of injury pain pills could be prescribed for.

When Dani relinquished the Mercedes to the hotel doorman, Brand stifled a groan, hauled himself out of the car and escorted her inside.

* * * * *

Neither Josh nor Elaine was there. Dani glanced around the room, saw the long, intimidating reception line she and Brand would have to suffer through before they could find a table and sit down. Taking a deep breath to steady her nerves, she gripped Brand's elbow, followed his lead.

Coach Allen looked more at home in sweats than in his tux. He and his wife stood beside the team owners, greeting each of the Marlin players by name. That way, Dani guessed, the owners wouldn't be embarrassed if they didn't recognize all their employees. It wasn't necessary for Coach Allen to murmur Brand's name, she noticed with pride. Everyone knew Brand Carendon.

Brand avoided having his shoulders pounded in congratulation for winning the game by reminding the team owner about his injury. The man, who said he'd watched the game from his penthouse box, should have remembered. "Dani, meet Mr. and Mrs. Epps and their daughter, Nancy."

"I'm glad to meet you." Dani didn't like the way Nancy looked at Brand. The tall, elegantly garbed redhead had a predatory way about her and eyed Brand as if he were a prime morsel.

Almost too quickly, he steered Dani away from the reception line, found them a spot at a table with Monk and Walzak, who didn't appear to be slowed down too much by his injured shoulder. Dani had met the tackles' wives at Josh's party, felt comfortable with them because, unlike many of the players' wives and girlfriends, they seemed more interested in their families than their favorite hairdressers and clothing stores. She and Brand soon found out Josh was spending the night at University Hospital because of a mild concussion.

"Sorry I can't dance with you tonight," Brand apologized after their table mates had gone to gyrate to the band's pulsing beat.

"I don't mind. The place is pretty."

"Yeah. I wonder when we can cut out of here. My side's killing me." Brand tried to grin, figured he probably achieved a grimace.

She looked up at him, her expression serious. "I could pretend to be sick."

She didn't look sick. She looked gorgeous. If Brand hadn't seen the transformation for himself, he'd have never believed a good haircut and a few new clothes could have gilded the lily. His wife was a knockout. Every man in the room had stared, made him proud and more than a little jealous when they'd come into the ballroom.

"Brand, aren't you even going to dance with me?" Nancy Epps practically purred, dropped a nonchalant kiss on his cheek while bending over, giving him a close-up view of her impressive cleavage.

"I can't even dance with my wife." Brand didn't even try to stand. "Dani, I believe you met Nancy earlier."

"Miss Epps." Dani smiled. Nancy slithered onto the chair Walzak had vacated next to Brand. The musky smell of her perfume hung in the air like a cloud.

"Brand, come on. You can dance with me, just once, for old times' sake." Nancy tossed her auburn hair, turned to Dani. "I was crushed when Daddy told me Brand had gotten married. We've been so close, I thought he'd have let me know first."

Dani wished she dared say something rude, but she didn't so she looked at Brand instead. He shook his head apologetically then turned back to the team owner's predatory daughter. "Come on, Nancy. Why would I have told you anything about my plans? I never made a point of letting you know about anything going on in my personal life."

"Well, I thought you'd tell me if there was ever anything personal to tell. After all, we—"

"Nancy, why don't you go dance with your fiancé? If you had any sense, you'd be embarrassed." He toyed with the idea of getting up and walking away. He would have, if that wouldn't have left Dani in the woman's clutches.

Nancy shut up but made no effort to leave. Dani looked piqued. Brand felt like a piece of meat being fought over by two hungry tigers. When he stood and moved behind Dani's chair, his ribs paid him back for jarring them with a sharp jab of pain.

"Let's dance," Not giving Dani a chance to refuse, he lifted her at the waist, drew her into his arms. It hurt like hell to move, but he managed to shuffle around the dance floor with her until the song was finished.

He couldn't take any more. Not tonight. "Let's go home," he told her when they got back to their table.

* * * * *

Dani was happy enough that Brand had wanted to leave the party early. She'd felt ill at ease among so many elegantly dressed strangers, and more than a little threatened by Nancy Epps. The woman had given the impression she thought she *owned* Brand.

She thought about his ribs, the bruise on his side. He had to be hurting. Extra carefully, so as not to hit a bump and jar his battered bones, she drove home. She didn't trust herself to talk and drive, but she couldn't help wondering what Nancy had done with Brand—and for how long.

Funny, she hadn't considered before what he'd done with women after his divorce. It had been bad enough, picturing him married to Marilee Sheridan, the girl she'd envied most when they'd been teenagers. Imagining him with Nancy Epps and others like her amplified Dani's insecurities.

At home, she checked on Dave and the Shearer twins. Then she climbed the stairs to their suite and found Brand struggling to get his jacket off. She didn't say a word, just helped him undress and laid back the covers so he could stretch out on the bed. By the time she got out of her own party clothes, he'd gone to sleep. When she pulled the comforter up to his waist, she couldn't help noticing how the white tape around his chest stood out against his tanned skin and the midnight blue bedding.

* * * * *

The next morning Brand woke up late, alone. When he tried to move, his bruises protested, so he lay back against the pillows and bellowed for Dani. She appeared as if by magic, a vision in white velour sweats.

"What time is it?" Still half-asleep, he sniffed the coffee on a tray in her hand, tried for a smile.

"Almost noon. Josh and Elaine just came over and picked up their boys. The doctors let him out of the hospital this morning."

She set the tray down on the bedside table, moved quickly in front of the curtained windows, turned and met his gaze. "Brand, how many other women like Nancy Epps am I going to run into?"

So his wife had a jealous streak? He found that endearing. "I don't think there are any other women like Nancy."

She scowled. "Let me rephrase my question. How many women am I going to run into who have the idea they're an important part of your life?"

Brand rubbed his hand across his brow, grimaced at the pain when the motion disturbed his injured side. "My God, Dani. I promised to be faithful to you, and I have been. I always will be. I was selective. I was careful. I can't say I lived like a monk while we were apart. Other than Marilee, there's never been anyone but you who had a claim on me."

"I understand Marilee. She was your wife. But that woman last night implied pretty strongly you'd had something serious going with her. All I want to know is how many others I'm likely to meet."

Why couldn't Dani develop self-confidence as fast as she'd learned how to maximize her petite, dark beauty? Brand sat up, met her gaze, chose his words carefully. "Nancy had her father practically order me to escort her to functions once in a while over the past few years. I occasionally asked her out myself. I slept with her a few times. I was single, so was she. It was never serious. For God's sake, it couldn't have been. She's always known she'd eventually marry Maury Burns, one of the other owners."

From the tight expression on Dani's face, Brand figured he hadn't gotten off the hook quite yet. "I knew Marilee when we were kids. She was beautiful, smart, knew what to do and say. Nancy Epps is all that and more. You don't deny you've had other women, too. Do you know how that makes me feel?"

"You should feel damn good. I've never wanted another woman as much as I've always wanted you. The satisfaction I got from fucking them was nothing more than scratching the sort of itch every healthy human feels. It's different with you. With you I want to make you come more than I want to get myself off."

The corners of her mouth turned up as if she wanted to smile. "That's sweet. But sometimes I get scared. I can't help being afraid you'll get tired of me, that you'll want a woman your friends won't laugh about. One who can give fancy parties, impress people with her background and the way she talks and dresses."

"Come here." Ignoring the pain, he stood and held out both arms. With more satisfaction than discomfort, he moaned when she walked into his embrace. He withdrew when he felt her relax.

"You'd better eat your breakfast," she reminded him.

He grinned, nuzzled her neck, then sat back down on the edge of the bed. "Come sit by me?"

"Want me to feed you?"

"Would you? It hurts like hell to move my arms."

She nodded, took the tray onto her lap. After she fed him the pancakes and link sausages, she poured him some coffee, handed it to him.

Dani was the only woman alive he'd let baby him this way. Marilee had never tried, and no one else who'd made the effort had succeeded in doing more than annoying him. Brand guessed he was basically a one-woman man. He didn't understand precisely why, but Dani had a talent he'd never discovered in any other woman, some quality that made him want to commit himself, make a home, build a family. She'd had it when they were kids, and she had it now. He wasn't about to complain.

Chapter Thirteen

Dani didn't have much time during the following weeks to brood about her place in Brand's life. Between his practices, weekend games, and therapy sessions with the trainers, his days were full. Dani found herself driving most of the time, playing chauffeur to Dave, running around town, doing things with others of the Marlins' wives. When she had a spare minute, she made small changes around the condo, took care of little details Brand apparently hadn't cared about when he'd lived there alone.

After the third regular season game, Dani and Brand had filmed a commercial together. It was fun. They paid her, real money. That made her feel good, even though she'd already spent most of her check buying some of the stuff they paid Brand and her to endorse.

She hadn't been able to resist after getting a look at him stretched out naked over a patterned sheet, one of the coordinating towels draped artfully across his lower torso. Those sheets and towels ought to sell like hot cakes when the ads hit national TV.

All she'd had to do was walk onto the set wearing a modest, satin robe in a color chosen to coordinate with the bedding. Then she sat beside Brand and laid a hand on his washboard abs. She'd been shocked when, a week after they'd filmed the ad, Brand's agent had called her and asked if she'd be willing to appear in another ad with Brand.

This Friday morning, she was feeling lazy. Brand had left this morning for the airport. He wouldn't be home until late Sunday night, after a game with the Rangers out in Los Angeles. Already she missed him. She wandered outside, crunched through a carpet of fallen leaves as she walked toward the lake. Birds chirped from trees that still held autumn leaves. A strong, clean breeze tossed her hair, pushed water gently against the dock.

Dani loved it here. Loved Milwaukee. She was getting acquainted with Brand's teammates and their families, growing more confident every day. Dave was happy with his school, in spite of the tutoring the headmaster had just told them he still needed. Dani wished they could live here permanently, the way Josh and Elaine did.

The idea of going back to Georgia, spending the off-season so close to her and Brand's home town, still gave her occasional nightmares. Brand had promised they would live out in the country, not right in Carendon. They wouldn't go at all, he'd said, until she felt ready to face the past. Although she told herself she had no reason at all to worry and reminded herself she'd vowed to overcome the pangs of insecurity, worry still plagued her.

"Mrs. Carendon. Phone for you."

Dani got up, came back inside. Anxious to hear Brand's voice, she hurried to take the phone from Mrs. Blair.

"It's Mr. Carendon's mother." The housekeeper looked frazzled. "She asked to speak to you when I said he wasn't here."

Dani stared at the phone. The innocuous pale gray instrument took on fearsome characteristics. Forcing her hand to stop shaking, she took the phone, brought it to her ear. She wouldn't let the woman intimidate her anymore. Steeling herself, she murmured an appropriate greeting.

"You. I wanted to speak to my son. When will he be home?" Eleanor Carendon's soft drawl grated on Dani's ears, brought back memories of that painful conversation they'd had so long ago.

"Sunday night, late. He's in Los Angeles for a game." Dani pictured her mother-in-law's condescending sneer without the slightest trouble. Although she'd only met the woman once, they'd met frequently in her nightmares.

Eleanor sniffed. "You may tell Brandon he absolutely *must* have that awful advertisement withdrawn. The one where he's lying in a bed, stark naked. I'm sure you know what advertisement I'm referring to, since you were in it, too."

"Brand wasn't naked. He had on a swimsuit. I didn't realize the advertisement was already being shown on TV." Dani held the phone a little bit away from her ear.

"If it weren't being shown, how would I know about it? At least ten of my friends have called me to say they've seen it. If you had any upbringing at all, you would realize how humiliating it is to me for my son, my only child, to expose himself on national television. It's hard enough for me to hold my head up as it is, with him humiliating me by playing that barbaric game. Marrying you," Eleanor added, as if that last sin was the worst.

Dani wanted to scream at Eleanor. Swear. Hang up the phone. Dissolve in tears. But she didn't. She'd promised Brand she wouldn't let his mother get to her, and she wouldn't. No matter what. Biting her lip, she said nothing, let Eleanor finish her vicious diatribe.

"If that football team doesn't pay Brandon enough to live on, he should come home, do honest work. There wouldn't be enough money on earth to persuade any decent couple to film that advertisement, let alone let it be publicly displayed." Eleanor finally paused.

"I'm sorry you're upset," Dani said, although she wasn't. "There's nothing Brand can do about the ad, though. He signed a release for the advertisement to be run on TV. I know, because they had me sign one, too."

"Just have my son call me. I assume you can contact him, wherever he is. Do so, and tell him I expect to hear from him immediately. Marilee would never have allowed Brandon to film that advertisement, much less encouraged him by being part of it. *She* is a lady." Eleanor slammed the phone down.

Dani's ear rang with the bad vibrations she'd felt across the phone wires. She checked the time, set down the phone when she realized Brand wouldn't be back at his hotel room for several hours. She wouldn't bother to call him on his cell phone while he was having dinner with the Rangers quarterback, Casey Weldon, and his wife. Eleanor Carendon could damn well stew awhile, vent her venom on somebody else.

Brand's mother had done her evil best to make Dani feel like dirt. It took Dani a few minutes, recalling the conversation, to realize she wasn't sobbing. Her eyes were dry. She hadn't knuckled under, begged forgiveness for whatever she might ever have done to make the woman hate her. She'd stood up for herself and Brand.

And she was still in one piece. Not a tremor in her hands or a tear in her eyes. Dani headed to the kitchen, feeling good about herself.

"Could I fix you something to drink?" Mrs. Blair asked when she sat down at the breakfast bar.

"Thanks. A raspberry seltzer?"

The housekeeper filled a glass with ice, set it and the seltzer bottle on the bar. Dani picked it up, toyed with the frost on the rim of the glass before taking a sip.

"Mrs. Carendon, you mustn't let her upset you. She's been calling, giving him what for about something or other every once in awhile since I've been keeping house for him."

"I'm trying not to, but she hates me." Dani swirled the seltzer around in her glass. "Right now she's furious about that linens ad Brand and I did."

"Don't worry about her. Your husband's crazy about you. That should be what you're thinking about. I've never seen him as happy as he's been this season. You make him that way, you and that fine boy of yours."

"Thanks. It would be a lot easier, though, if Brand's mother would accept me."

Dani wasn't at all sure Mrs. Blair, no matter how friendly she was, wouldn't share Eleanor's hatred for her if she told the sordid story of her childhood. While Dani was certain the housekeeper could tell she hadn't been brought up to the luxury she now lived with, she didn't think Mrs. Blair could guess her family had been so awful that everyone in Carendon had considered her trash. Dani didn't want anyone to know that, or that Brand had married her solely because of their child. And because for some reason she kept him with a perpetual hard-on.

Dani set aside her drink and excused herself. She needed some quiet time outside the house. Slipping a red fleece-lined coat over her turtleneck sweater and wool slacks, she collected her purse and car keys. She'd pick Dave up from school. If she got there too early, she'd sit and wait.

* * * * *

Dani took in the venerable buildings that made up Eastover School. The campus smacked of pure, old, aristocratic money, like the fancy prep school Brand had attended in Atlanta.

Surely Brand cared for her, at least a little. Here she sat in a new Mercedes, wearing clothes that had cost more than she'd spent on her entire wardrobe in years gone by. The car was worth more than the weather-beaten shack where she'd grown up. She looked at her wedding band, smiled. It probably had cost more than that sorry house and the worn-out, red clay lot where it sat.

Dani had known folks whose homes weren't a whole lot fancier than the one where she grew up, but who'd worked hard and earned the respect of their neighbors in Carendon. Her mother, though, had taken up with an itinerant salesman who'd left her and moved on to greener pastures. She'd been the town's best known drunk.

Dani couldn't remember a day when her mom, or her grandfather when he was alive, hadn't ended up slobbering drunk before noon. Many nights, she'd had to drag one or both of them off to bed after coming home from work at the Dairy King. She really couldn't blame the good folks of Carendon for labeling them trash.

Dani sighed. Until Brand had come back into her life, she'd always worked. At first, having a job set her apart, at least in her own mind, from her mother, who'd supplemented her welfare checks by selling her body to anyone willing to buy. Later, working had enabled Dani to take care of Dave. She recalled the sense of accomplishment she'd felt when she was finally able to stand on her own two feet, support her son without taking charity or welfare from anyone.

If she were to be honest with herself, Dani would have to admit Eleanor Carendon had good reasons for sending her away. As a mother, Dani would discourage Dave from forming a friendship with anyone whose family was as despicable as hers had been. Would Brand's mother ever be able to accept her as a worthwhile person? She didn't know.

Finally. There was Dave, coming down the steps of an ivy-covered classroom building. She welcomed his excited chatter about a project he'd finished for his science class as the much-needed distraction it was.

* * * * *

When Brand called, Dani and Dave were having pizza. She let Dave speak with his dad while she went to their bedroom so she could talk privately with him. After giving them a few minutes to chat, she picked up the phone, told Dave to tell his dad goodnight and hang up.

"Hey, honey. I saw a little doll on TV this afternoon while I was visiting with Casey Weldon and his wife. She turned me on something fierce," Brand said, his tone husky, teasing. "Would you believe, the guy with her looked a lot like me?"

"Your mother wants you to call her. She saw the ad, too."

"Oh Jesus, I'm sorry. Was she awful to you?"

"She wasn't very nice." Dani cradled the phone on her shoulder, recalled Eleanor's caustic words.

"I bet that's the world's biggest understatement. Don't let her get to you. Hey, I wish I were home, or you were here with me."

"I miss you, too. Will you call your mother?" If he didn't, Eleanor would probably accuse her of not having delivered the message.

He groaned. "Yeah. Just what I need, to listen to her litany of complaints before a game. Does she have LeeAnn with her?"

"She didn't mention LeeAnn. Just the ad. And the fact Marilee wouldn't have let you do it, far less pose for it with you."

"Mother can be a real bitch. She didn't say anything about Uncle Jimmy, did she?"

"No. He called you after last week's game, didn't he?"

"Yes. I just thought Mother might have heard from him since then. You remember I told you they expect Laura's husband to die any time. I'll ask when I call her." He paused, let out a sigh. "I want you to remember, my mother's thoughts aren't mine. I miss you. Can't wait to get home. Tape the game, will you?"

"Sure. Dave and I are going to watch it over at Elaine's. I'll set the DVD recorder up before we go over there. I love you, Brand." Dani hung up.

It was moments later when she realized she'd said those three words aloud, words she doubted she'd ever hear him return.

* * * * *

Brand lay back on the bed, replaying their conversation in his head. Dani had sounded controlled, rational. He hadn't heard even a hint of a sob, a tremor of fear in her soft, calm voice. She'd come a long way in the few months they'd been married, worked through most of the insecurities that had limited her before.

He didn't harbor any illusion that Eleanor might have gone easy on Dani—that wasn't her style. Furious when he imagined how she must have sniped at Dani, tested her self-confidence, he lifted the phone again. It was a fucking pity he couldn't wring his mother's neck when they were three thousand miles apart. Taking out his frustration on his cell phone, he punched in her number hard, let his fury build while he waited for her to pick up.

"You wanted to speak to me, Mother?" he asked crisply when she finally answered. He imagined her the way he'd seen her so many times, curling her lips in distaste as she sat at her antique desk in a sitting room no one could enjoy actually sitting in.

Eleanor repeated the complaints she'd doubtless heaped on Dani. While she did, Brand held the phone away from his ear, fumed in silence until she concluded her tirade with the usual question. "Why do you do this to me?"

"Mother, I do commercials because, first, it's extremely profitable considering how little time and effort it requires. Second, it's good publicity for the team. I do not do obscene advertisements. No TV station would air them if I did. I don't appreciate your berating Dani, and I'm not thrilled to have you sticking your nose into my business. I'm thirty years old, damn it."

"You have the mind of a teenager. Despite the fact your insane obsession with football killed your father, you persist in playing that barbaric child's game. Now, you think nothing of humiliating me by letting your pictures be smeared all over television screens, practically naked, for everyone to see and talk about. If that's not enough, you flaunt your common little trollop on national TV."

"Your opinion of professional football has always been crystal clear, as have your feelings about Dani. In spite of your best efforts, she's my wife, and I won't listen to you insult her. While I'm at it, I won't put up with your poisoning my daughter's mind against me anymore, either."

"That, you won't have to worry about. Neither Marge Sheridan nor I will continue assuming responsibility for that child, since you and Marilee have both gone off and ruined your lives separately. I sent LeeAnn to her mother, where she'll stay, unless you personally want to exercise your visitation privileges. I doubt you'll bother, since you're so enamored of that woman and her child."

Brand slammed his fist into an unsuspecting pillow. "Her name is Dani, and Dave is my son, too. Dani's a loving, decent woman. If not for her and Dave, I probably would have stopped trying to have a relationship with my daughter. A daughter who, thanks in part to you, dislikes everything I do and hates to be around me."

"You've never wanted to spend time with LeeAnn."

"I couldn't stand living with her mother any more than Marilee could tolerate being married to me. I never missed a visit with LeeAnn until she started kicking and screaming in protest every time I came to see her." Bitter, he'd pretty much given up trying to build a relationship with his daughter—although he realized his attitude toward her prissy manners and the frilly stuff she always wore might have had something to do with LeeAnn's dislike of him. "Where are LeeAnn and Marilee?"

"They're in Houston, with that crippled cousin of Marilee's."

"Phil Sheridan?"

"Yes. Do you want his phone number?"

Brand muttered under his breath as he wrote down the number. "I'll call LeeAnn when I get home." He stretched out, tried to relax after telling his mother goodbye.

So, he thought, Marilee was trying again to get Phil. They'd been an item since high school, had broken up Brand's senior year in college soon after the accident that had left Sheridan wheelchair-bound. Brand had understood Phil's reasoning. Brand wouldn't have wanted to saddle any woman he cared for with a cripple.

Marilee had been decimated. Her love for Phil hadn't died, and she'd tried for months to persuade him she wanted him, no matter what his condition. Finally, she'd given up. A few months later, she'd allowed her mother to badger her into marrying Brand. They'd spoiled a wonderful friendship by trying to force a different, special kind of love.

Brand recalled the early days of his and Marilee's ill-fated marriage. They'd tried to be content, settling for less than either of them had hoped for in a relationship. Marilee had cringed every time he'd fucked her, broken into heartbroken sobs sometimes when she looked at his healthy, unbroken body, mourned her loss of Phil.

He hadn't been blameless, either. He'd mocked Marilee for her quiet, artistic temperament, exaggerated his own arrogant, blatantly masculine personality just to irritate her. He'd made fun of her dainty social graces, deliberately acted the coarse, crude jock. If he hadn't gotten her pregnant one of the infrequent times they'd quit fighting long enough to get it on, they wouldn't have stayed together as long as they had.

LeeAnn. Brand tried to remember what his daughter looked like. Having Dani and Dave made him feel guilty about the little girl who was almost a stranger. She was pretty, like Marilee. He'd never seen much of himself in her, except that she'd always been awfully tall for her age and sex. Her grandmothers constantly lamented that, blamed him for providing the genes that caused his daughter's supposedly unfortunate height.

Brand switched off the lamp, forced himself to rest. The game tomorrow would be rough, and he needed to be ready.

Chapter Fourteen

୬

The game was over. The Marlins had won. The steaks Elaine had barbecued had taken care of Sunday night dinner. Dani leaned back in the car seat, thought how she'd greet Brand when he got home. He'd missed her, wanted her. She repeated his words in her head for the thousandth time. If only Brand could love her.

"It must be fun to be a twin," Dave said. "Josh and Jake always have someone to play with."

Dani smiled. She was glad Dave had enjoyed himself, popping corn and roasting marshmallows in the fireplace with the lively seven-year-olds while she and Elaine watched the Marlins game on a projection TV.

Brand had played the whole game, which meant Josh had sat on the bench the whole time. She'd felt bad for Elaine, happy and relieved that Brand had avoided being hurt.

"You don't mind playing with younger kids?" she asked as she pulled her car into the garage.

"Josh and Jake are fun. I think I'd like a little brother." Dave slid out of the car, opened the back door to retrieve the big bag of popcorn Elaine had insisted he bring home. "Dad had a great game today."

"Yes, he did."

Dani went upstairs, leaving the recreation room to Dave and his popcorn. He was a good kid. If he really wanted a sibling, he'd be pleased if her suspicions were on target. She had her doubts. Dave would be a very mature twelve by the time his brother or sister arrived.

She wasn't seventeen anymore, either, she thought ruefully as she stripped off her clothes. Tired, she stretched out in the Jacuzzi. For the last few weeks, she'd seemed exhausted too much of the time. A trip to Elaine's gynecologist was in order, just as soon as she could get an appointment.

The phone rang, and Dani grinned. Despite the fact she teased Brand about his penchant for having a phone in every room, she was glad he'd had one put in on the wall by the hot tub. Stretching lazily, she answered the call. She thought it would have been Brand, calling from the airport before the Marlins' chartered plane took off from Los Angeles.

"Dani?" The cultured, feminine drawl didn't sound familiar.

"Who is it?"

"Marilee Sheridan. How are you?" She sounded hesitant, yet surprisingly friendly.

"I'm fine. Brand isn't back from Los Angeles yet."

"I know. I wanted to talk to you."

"Why?" Dani didn't know if she'd recognize Brand's exwife now, even though they'd gone to the same school for several years. Years changed people.

"To see if you'd be willing to have LeeAnn visit for awhile. Brand hasn't had her stay with him for ages."

Dani couldn't have been any more surprised. Brand hadn't actually said a lot, but she'd gotten the impression Marilee did her best to keep him from seeing his little girl. He'd be delighted, she was sure.

"I'd love to have LeeAnn. I thought—well, actually, Brand thought—LeeAnn might be staying with his mother." Dani felt bad because Marilee thought she'd need Dani's permission to send Brand's child for a visit.

"LeeAnn's with me. I'm in Houston with my fiancé. Her grandmothers decided they didn't want to be responsible for her, so they packed her up and sent her to me."

"Brand can't take time off now to come get LeeAnn." Shocked to learn the little girl had traveled alone from Atlanta to Houston, Dani wasn't about to suggest Marilee allow her to come to Milwaukee without an adult.

"If you don't mind her staying with you, Phil and I will fly to Milwaukee with her. We have to go to New York, anyway, to leave on our cruise. We've planned the cruise, and our wedding aboard ship, for months. I'd thought my mother would keep LeeAnn, but I was mistaken."

Dani's heart went out to Brand's daughter. The child didn't seem wanted very much by anybody, even her own mother. But from what Brand had told her, his mother and Marilee's had always taken care of her in the past, while Marilee and Brand pretty much did their own separate things.

"When will you be coming?" Dani asked. She'd love taking care of Brand's little girl. She couldn't imagine Brand objecting to her visit.

"Tomorrow morning, ten-fifty, Northwest Airlines Flight 479. If you'll give me your address, we'll take a limo from the airport. Phil and I won't leave Milwaukee until the next day. We'll get a room near the airport."

"You don't need to do that. We have plenty of room. You're welcome to stay with us." Dani gave Marilee their address, felt vaguely happy to learn Marilee hadn't lived here with him. "LeeAnn will probably be more comfortable if you stay here for the night," she added.

"That's awfully nice of you, Dani. We'd love to stay. Phil's in a wheelchair, though. Will that be a problem?"

"We have a guest room on the ground floor. There are a couple of steps up into the house, but I'm sure we can manage something." Dani figured Brand could probably pick up Marilee's fiancé and carry him up the steps, then decided to see about rigging up a makeshift ramp. The poor man would probably be mortified, being carried around by Marilee's former husband.

After a few casual pleasantries, they hung up. Dani stepped out of the tub, hugged her flat, slender belly. She pictured the tiny life she hoped was growing inside. Even though she knew Brand wouldn't be home for hours, she dabbed the apple blossom fragrance he loved so much between her breasts before sliding, naked, between the sheets.

* * * * *

The team's elation at having won a crucial game rubbed off on Brand. By the time their plane landed in Milwaukee, he felt great. Laughing, he fielded an off-color suggestion from Walzak as he slung his travel bag across his shoulder. He ignored the small crowd of fans who had gathered on the tarmac, hurried to the parking lot. Eager to get to Dani, he broke the speed limits getting home. It amazed him just how much he could miss her in just two and a half days.

The sight of her sleeping in his bed never failed to prime his cock for action. Quietly, so as not to disturb her, he stripped off his clothes, slid across the bed and braced himself on his elbows. She purred like a kitten when he rubbed himself gently against her rounded bottom.

She never failed to excite him. Her instant awakening warmed his heart, and her soft, sensual touches heated him to a fever pitch. Groaning, he rolled to his side, brought her with him. She'd waited for him naked.

She felt like satin, smooth against his rougher skin. The smell of apple blossoms filled his nostrils. Her taut nipples grazed his chest, her legs opened, made room to let him in. He kissed her, their tongues fencing until he couldn't resist the temptation of her gorgeous breasts.

He shuddered when she squeezed his cock between her thighs. He couldn't wait to tease and caress her. Not tonight. Her warm pussy, instantly wet to his intimate touch, told him she wanted him just as much. With one quick move, he turned her to her back and joined them fully. It took only a few wild, fast thrusts for him to feel her come. With one more deep, final plunge, he found his own fulfillment.

"You please me, so damn much." He held her, stroking the length of her back, glad as hell to be home. It struck him that he didn't have to tie her down, didn't need the extra stimulation of toys and such. All he needed was to let her know he wanted her, and to bury his cock in her hot, wet cunt. Hell, he'd even passed on the chance to join in a ménage with his good friend Casey Weldon and Casey's wife—something he'd never have done before Dani.

* * * * *

The next morning Dani watched Brand sleeping, wished she didn't have to wake him. If she could have, she'd have rigged a wheelchair ramp herself—but she couldn't, so she bent and woke him with a kiss.

He opened one eye then closed it again. "I don't have practice this morning."

"I know. We have company coming. Your daughter."

"What? How? Do you have any idea what you're letting us in for?" Brand became alert instantly. Dani didn't need him to put in words that he was none too thrilled with her news.

"Marilee's bringing her this morning. She called last night, late, to ask if we'd mind keeping LeeAnn while she and her fiancé get married and take a honeymoon. Brand, I couldn't refuse."

"I could have. I would have. My daughter hates my guts. She's a tiny carbon copy of my dear, sweet mother and Marge Sheridan, rolled into one." He rubbed his hand across his brow, cursed under his breath. "How long do Marilee and Phil plan to take for this honeymoon?"

"She didn't say, or if she did, I don't remember. It can't be too long. She mentioned something about a cruise." Dani had read ads about weekend and week-long cruise ships that sailed from the Port of Tampa.

"I've never spent even twenty-four hours at a stretch with my daughter. It doesn't take nearly that long for her to make me wonder why I ever laid a hand on her mother."

"Brand! I don't believe you. You're wonderful with Dave."

"Dave's a wonderful kid. Thanks to her grandmothers, LeeAnn is a little monster." Brand got up, shot Dani a disgruntled look. "Do I have to pick her up at the airport?"

"Marilee and her fiancé are going to bring her here. They'll be staying overnight, so LeeAnn won't be so uncomfortable being left in a strange place."

Dani followed Brand into the bathroom, watched him lather his face. He didn't look anywhere near as cheerful as he did when he was pushing the shaving cream on TV. She sighed, left him to dress in peace.

Brand fumed. He disliked being angry with Dani, but he was, even though he knew he shouldn't feel such downright terror at the idea of having to endure lengthy contact with a child who'd learned to disparage him and everything he did.

He'd tried to be a good absentee dad, but he'd given up rather than make the kid angry, downright belligerent, every time he came near her. Marilee had witnessed how their daughter reacted to him. She'd seen how LeeAnn had tried to hide, then struck out at him, every time he'd come to take her for a visit. "Fuck it all anyhow."

He'd like nothing better than to wring his exwife's neck for conning Dani into inviting LeeAnn to stay here. It was bad enough the kid would make him miserable, but he had a good idea the unhappy little girl would make life hell on earth for Dani, maybe Dave, too.

Dave. The thought of his son made him smile. He was proving with Dave he could be a decent parent. Unlike LeeAnn's grandmothers, Dani hadn't poisoned Dave's mind toward him.

Brand rummaged in his closet, grinned when he found a shapeless, hole-infested gray sweat suit. He'd enjoy watching Marilee's horrified expression, hearing prissy little LeeAnn ask him if he dressed like this all the time.

Then he remembered how pretty Dani looked in her dark blue and rose plaid jumper. She'd dressed up for their guests, and he figured playing the uncouth jock would insult her, not Marilee. He put the old sweats away, selected charcoal gray, pleated slacks to wear with an Irish fisherman's knit sweater. Feeling guilty, he even tossed his Nikes back into the closet and shoved his feet into soft, Italian loafers.

By the time he came downstairs, Dave had left for school. Brand hated missing breakfast with his son, but he'd not been fit company for anyone since he'd found out LeeAnn was coming. Dani brought his breakfast into the recreation room so Mrs. Blair could finish setting the dining room table for lunch.

"Do you have any wood we could use to make a ramp?"

Brand thought a minute. Why on earth would Dani think she needed to make a ramp? Then it came to him. Phil and his chair. "I can wrestle Phil and his chair up those few stairs outside. If for some reason I can't, I can always pick him up and carry him, set him down somewhere and go back and get his chair."

He set down his empty coffee cup, forced a smile. "I've got to call my accountant before we get tied up with visitors. Come get me when they arrive." He got up, headed for the office next to their bedroom where he took care of their personal business matters.

* * * * *

Dani scurried around downstairs, checking to make sure the smaller bedroom next to Dave's was ready for LeeAnn. She'd set out white eyelet-trimmed, pale pink sheets and pillowcases, a quilted comforter in a pastel floral design. They looked pretty on the brass double bed, although she imagined

Brand's little girl would like Disney prints, or maybe dinosaurs, better. She'd go shopping tomorrow. Maybe LeeAnn would like to go with her. They could have lunch at one of the restaurants near the mall.

Dani picked up the *Sports Illustrated* and *Southern Living* magazines Mrs. Blair must have set on the night table. They made the room look lived in, but she doubted a six-year-old would find them very interesting. She sat on the white, leather contemporary chair beside the room's narrow, floor-to-ceiling window, pondered the absence in her husband's home of anything his daughter might have left behind. Then she realized LeeAnn had never been here.

As soon as they'd agreed to get married, Brand had set plans in motion to make Dave's room a young boy's dream come true, ordered everything he'd thought his son might possibly want. He'd done it all long-distance and hadn't missed a single detail.

He'd never pictured his daughter being here, or he'd have fixed up a room for her, too. What had happened to alienate them? Dani's heart went out to Brand, made her want to find him, hug away the sadness he had to be holding deep inside. It didn't matter that LeeAnn wasn't hers. She'd love her anyhow, and somehow she'd find a way to mend whatever had happened to keep her husband from his little girl.

Dani got up slowly, crossed the hall to the seldom-used guest room Mrs. Blair had spruced up for Phil and Marilee. Did they sleep together? She guessed they did but wasn't sure. To be safe, she found Mrs. Blair, asked her to put fresh linens on the bed in the last, small bedroom, in case Marilee wanted a separate room.

Everything was ready. Checking the time, she hurried upstairs to freshen her hair and makeup. She'd show Marilee she was worthy of Brand's love, that she wasn't the same naïve girl Brand had once dragged home the way he might have adopted an orphan pup.

She brushed her hair until it crackled, confined it with a stretchy headband that matched her jumper. With a light touch, she added the tiniest bit of mascara to her lashes, a hint of rosy blush to her cheeks. She smiled at her reflection as she inserted the small ruby earrings Brand had bought for her a few weeks earlier.

"You look good enough to eat." Brand bent, nibbled playfully on Dani's earlobe. "These look nice with your jumper." He flicked his tongue over the twinkling ruby.

"You look fantastic, too. Are we dressy enough?" she asked seriously.

"We're in our home. We'd be dressy enough if we decided to wear jeans or sweats. I would have, you know, if I hadn't noticed the pains you took this morning to look especially nice. Hey, it's not every woman who could shame me into wearing this when I'd have been much more comfy in my broken-in running shoes and an old sweat suit." He pulled Dani into his arms, stroked her cheek with a gentle finger.

"I hope you aren't mad. I mean, about me saying it was all right for LeeAnn to stay with us."

He cupped her chin, made her meet his gaze. "I'm not mad at you. But I'm damn furious at Marilee for timing her request when she knew I wouldn't be here to deny it."

"You don't like LeeAnn, do you?" Dani looked up into Brand's stern face, wrapped her arms around his neck.

He lifted Dani, sat down and settled her on his lap in a big leather lounge chair. "LeeAnn hates me. There's not a milder word that would describe the way she feels. My mother and Marilee's have made damn sure they've painted me the villain to my child, since long before she was old enough to understand."

"Brand, how on earth could you have let anyone poison your own child's mind against you?" As soon as the words came out, Dani wished she could have snatched them back, erased the wounded look on her husband's face. She reached up, caressed his smooth-shaven cheek.

"I don't know." Twisting a lock of Dani's hair idly between his calloused fingers, as though he was struggling to discover the truth, he sat silently for the longest time.

Chapter Fifteen

When he'd sorted out the thoughts bombarding his mind, Brand met her gaze, cleared his throat. "After you left me, I changed. Mother didn't like who I'd become, and she made no bones about it. In spite of the fact I'd talked about wanting to play pro football as far back as high school, I'd known deep down I wouldn't. I'd have played college ball, then let the dream go. I'd have gone to law school and taken my place in the family firm, the way Dad and Mother expected."

"What changed your mind? I always wondered, after I read you'd signed with the Marlins."

It felt natural to tell Dani things he'd never told another soul, thoughts he'd shoved to the deepest corner of his mind. Over the past few months she'd become his best friend as well as the best lover he'd ever had. Brand shifted, held her a little tighter, cleared his throat.

"When they treated you the way they did, they showed me they didn't give a damn for what I wanted or how I felt. I guess on some level I blamed them, especially Mother, for your having left the way you did. When I made all-American my junior year in college, I realized a pro career wasn't just a boy's idle pipe dream. It was within my reach. I wanted it, and I decided to hell with my parents' plans for my future. Mother was horrified. Dad didn't like it any more than she did, but at least he wasn't quite so vocal about his objections.

"After the pro draft the next year, I called home. The Marlins had picked me in the first round. I wanted my parents to be happy, respect the choice I'd made. Or maybe I wanted to rub it in their faces. I'm not sure. Mother went ballistic, insisted they drive to Atlanta, find me, talk me out of signing the contract the team had offered.

"It was foggy, wet. Dad collided with a semi on the old road from Carendon to Atlanta. He died at the scene." Brand paused, drew Dani closer, let her warmth dispel the feeling of senseless loss that hadn't gone away with time.

"Mother walked away with a few bruises. I felt so guilty, I almost changed my mind about playing ball, until Uncle Jimmy came and encouraged me to follow my dream."

Her touch gentle, Dani stroked his cheek, conveyed without speaking that she understood, accepted him. More important, in the time they'd been back together she'd helped him accept himself, own his choices, good or bad.

What he'd done was finally clear in his mind. As a spoiled teenager denied what he'd wanted most, he'd deliberately taken a path his mother hated. He'd played ball, made all-pro, become a household word because of his passing prowess and the endorsements that had made him even richer than his seven-figure annual contracts with the Marlins. He'd set himself on the path at least in part because he'd known subconsciously that his disapproving family had a lot to do with Dani's disappearance from his life.

But he had cared. On some level he'd wanted to appease his mother. So he'd married Marilee. When their marriage had ruined the friendship they'd shared, he'd blamed everybody but himself. His mother, Marilee's mother, Marilee, even the tiny, helpless baby whose appearance had delayed the divorce. He'd studied hard during six off-seasons, to earn the law degree his father had expected him to get. And he'd joined his family's firm, albeit part-time.

"How did you and Marilee happen to get together?"

"Phil—the same Phil Marilee's apparently going to marry now—had broken up with Marilee not long after my dad died. Marilee and I spent a lot of time together, crying on each other's shoulders. We let our mothers push us into getting married. All we managed to do was to prove, beyond a doubt, that friendship doesn't substitute very well for love. Or even for lust. By the time LeeAnn was born, we weren't even friends anymore."

Dani nodded, her acceptance giving him the courage to go on. "We divorced. Marilee and LeeAnn moved back home with her parents. She tried to cope for a while, but I guess LeeAnn reminded her of the miserable life we'd had together. After about six months, Marilee pretty much gave up on mothering. Her mother and mine took turns being responsible for LeeAnn."

"That poor baby. She didn't even have her mother. Couldn't you have taken her?"

Brand fought down the anger that had plagued him for years. "The courts decided I wasn't fit to be a single parent. According to the lawyer Marilee's mother hired for her, I spent half the year amusing myself by playing a child's game, the other half going to law school."

Dani's expression turned fierce. "That's not fair. Football is your career. Seems to me you have more time to spend with Dave than most fathers find for their children. You must be paid awfully well, too. Either that, or you make enough being a lawyer on the off-season that you can provide everything we could ever possibly need or want."

"You're right. I do have more free time when I'm playing ball than I do when I'm working at the firm. And I make more money in one season playing football than I'd earn in ten years or more practicing law full time. Still, since Marilee objected, the judge wouldn't give me custody. Her mother, and mine, made damn sure she fought my petition."

Brand massaged his eyes with the back of one hand, tried to squelch the thought that maybe he'd been the one to egg his mother on by rebelling so visibly and audibly against everything she thought was important. Maybe if he'd compromised —

"You tried to get custody of your daughter?" Dani sounded surprised.

"Yeah, when LeeAnn was two. She pitched a fit every time she saw me, refused to leave whichever grandmother was watching her to go somewhere with me. Didn't take me long to realize Mother and Marge Sheridan were poisoning her mind. I bought this condo and another one in Atlanta, promised to hire a nanny for her. I even fixed up a room in my Atlanta place, since I was going to be there for the next few months. Still, the judge said LeeAnn was better off in Carendon, year round, even if her mother was gone most of the time."

"So, you just gave her up?" Dani looked up at Brand, her eyes glistening with tears.

Realizing he might have averted some of the conflict that had shaped his daughter's life made him reply more sharply than he intended. "What else could I do? I tried coming more often, keeping visits short, but LeeAnn got more and more obnoxious to me every time I saw her. It was painfully obvious being around me made her miserable. Finally, it got to the point I couldn't stand the idea of making her unhappy, so I started staying away."

Dani nodded, as if she understood his jumbled feelings. "From what Marilee told me, LeeAnn's grandmothers have refused to keep her any longer. Why, when they've pretty much had her to themselves for most of her life?"

"They've always used her as a tool to try and force Marilee and me back together. When I married you and Marilee went back to Phil, I guess they finally gave up hoping we'd reconcile. It was almost as if LeeAnn lost her value, and they couldn't get rid of her fast enough. I imagine they'll try to stick their noses into her life again when she's old enough to be launched into Atlanta society." Brand didn't even try to mask the bitterness he felt.

"That poor little girl. Brand, we've got to show her we love her." Dani framed his head with both her hands, brushed her lips across his mouth. Needing her warmth, her strength, he pulled her close, held her fiercely.

They were like that, several minutes later, when Mrs. Blair's voice on the intercom warned them of their guests' arrival. Together, they went downstairs, his arm draped possessively around her shoulders. He was grateful she was there for him, to help him face the child he'd lost and then abandoned.

* * * * *

Marilee pushed Phil's wheelchair across the brick walkway. She looked happier, more relaxed than Brand had seen her since they were kids. Then he saw his daughter. LeeAnn wore the petulant expression he knew so well.

He squeezed Dani's hand, forced a smile his daughter's way as they stepped outside. He hoped to hell his mother hadn't had time to poison his daughter's mind against Dani, too. They stopped at the bottom step of the entryway.

Without a jacket, Brand shivered. When he exhaled, he saw his breath, a white trail against the bright blue sky. "Let's get inside before you southerners freeze to death."

Marilee set her handbag on Phil's lap, tried unsuccessfully to push his chair onto the first step. Always pretty with her blonde hair and china blue eyes, she looked radiant with her cheeks brightened by the cold breeze. Brand couldn't help wishing they could have salvaged their childhood friendship.

He also wished he'd done what Dani asked, found some wood and set up a makeshift ramp. "Here. Let me." Brand nudged Marilee away from Phil's wheelchair, tried to maneuver it up the first wide, deep step. The chair's motor was in the way, so he gave up. "Phil, will it hurt you if I pick you up?"

Phil shrugged then smiled. "No, it won't hurt if you pick me up. It probably wouldn't hurt if you dropped me." Brand lifted him easily, figured he couldn't weigh much more than a hundred forty. He strode into the house, paused in front of an overstuffed chair in the living room.

Damn. He wasn't certain Phil could sit up by himself, without the arms of his chair for support. "Is it okay to put you here?"

"It's fine."

Brand set Phil down, asked again if he was okay.

"I'm not going anywhere. You'd better go help Marilee and your wife with the chair. It probably weighs more than I do."

Brand brought the wheelchair inside, his gaze on LeeAnn as she preceded him into the house. The kid hadn't said a word to him, not even a sullen hello. When he'd deposited the chair in a corner, he sat beside Dani on the sofa, put his arm around her shoulder.

He gave LeeAnn an inquiring look. "Welcome to Milwaukee," he said, trying to sound enthusiastic in spite of his daughter's expression. "This is my wife, Dani." He tightened his hold on Dani, as if he could shield her from their guests. "Dani, my daughter, LeeAnn. You remember Marilee. And this is Phil Sheridan."

"May I go to my room?" LeeAnn had nodded coldly but correctly toward Brand and Dani then glared at her mother. Without waiting for a reply, she stood, looked in the direction Mrs. Blair had disappeared with her suitcase.

"Go ahead." Marilee shrugged, as if she had no control over her daughter's actions. When LeeAnn had left, she turned to Brand. "She really doesn't care much for you, does she?"

"She doesn't seem especially fond of you, either. Damn it, Marilee, you manipulated Dani. You knew as well as you know your name I'd never have agreed for LeeAnn to come here during the season." How could he have thought marrying this woman might give him the contentment he'd been looking for? The sort of contentment he'd found with Dani.

"Our respective mothers have refused to keep LeeAnn any longer. You have no idea what Phil and I have gone through to arrange this cruise. My mother certainly knew about our plans. Took pleasure, I'm certain, in undermining them."

"Don't snipe, sweetheart. It doesn't become you." Phil turned to Dani. "You have a beautiful home."

"Thank you."

Marilee stared at Brand then turned to Dani. "I must say, Dani, you've managed to make Brand dress decently, if nothing else."

"Brand always looks good, no matter what he's wearing," Dani replied, smiling.

"Did it ever occur to you I might like to look good for Dani?" Brand asked, giving his wife an affectionate hug.

"You never did for me." Marilee caught herself, laughed out loud. "Here we are, together five minutes, and already we're sniping at each other. You and I both have what we always wanted. It would seem that LeeAnn's the only problem we've ever had that we can't bury and forget."

"Marilee, LeeAnn's a child, not a problem. I'm more than willing to be her stepfather, and it seems Dani's ready to share Brand with his daughter. It looks as if you and Brand have to accept the fact you're the parents of one unhappy, difficult little girl, and figure out what it will take to make her happy."

Phil didn't have an inkling of what he was talking about—or at least Brand didn't think he did. "You're full of it, or else you have no idea what Marilee's mother and mine have done to our little girl's mind. Mother hates what I do, so she programs LeeAnn to hate it, too. Marilee's mom wants nothing except for us to get back together, so she tells LeeAnn she should hate both of us because we broke up her happy home."

Brand paused, met Phil's questioning gaze. "Yeah, I know I should have fought harder. Marilee should have stuck around more, too. But I don't think you realize, my friend, just what a hateful, sullen child you're calling 'an unhappy, difficult little girl'." Frustrated, Brand rubbed at his forehead.

"Honey, we can bring LeeAnn around. Her grandmothers aren't here now to undermine you." Gently, Dani rubbed the back of his hand. Her simple touch never failed to soothe him.

"Are you willing to have LeeAnn live with you and Phil?" Brand asked Marilee. He wished he didn't dread her answer.

"We expect LeeAnn to live with us." Phil was the one who replied. Marilee stared silently out the wide expanse of windows. "Dani, why don't you show Marilee around outside? She commented on the way here how gorgeous the lake is. Brand can stay, entertain me for a few minutes."

Dani got up, invited Marilee to join her. When they left, Brand strode over to the bar, poured drinks. He handed one to Phil, sat back down, and met the other man's gaze.

"I'm damn sorry, Brand. I didn't realize how badly LeeAnn's mind was set against you until she pitched a fit this morning about coming. We couldn't just leave her with a strange housekeeper and go off on our wedding cruise. Marilee couldn't bear postponing it. We'd take LeeAnn with us, but Marilee can't take care of both of us in a ship's stateroom." Phil sipped his drink.

"How long is this trip? Marilee neglected to mention that detail to Dani when she conned her into volunteering to take my daughter."

"Six weeks. We'll be back three weeks before Christmas."

"Shit." Brand finished his drink in one gulp, went to the bar for another.

"Hey, we can still cancel. The only thing is, Marilee's planned the wedding for the second night out."

"No. You deserve some happiness. The only thing that bothers me is Dani having to put up with a sullen, spoiled stepdaughter. We're still on our own honeymoon, so to speak."

"Marilee says you have your son with you. LeeAnn may like having a playmate."

"Dave's almost twelve years old. Somehow, I can't see him and LeeAnn being very interested in each other."

"I've heard LeeAnn say she wants a brother or sister."

"She would. Mrs. Sheridan couldn't tell her enough of how great her life would be if Mommy and Daddy got back together and gave her a baby whatever." Brand tossed the ball back in Phil's court. "Maybe you and Marilee should think about having a baby."

When Phil's eyes clouded with apparent pain, Brand wished he'd kept his mouth shut. Then the other man smiled, shrugged.

"The only way that can happen is in a doctor's office. I'm not sterile, but I am impotent. Marilee swears she doesn't miss real lovemaking, but I want to be fair to her. If things work out, we may try the procedure in a couple of years. She'll still be young enough, don't you think?"

Brand could vouch for the fact Marilee had always been a lousy mother to the child she already had, but he didn't think it would be appropriate to point that out. He dropped back, replied directly to Phil's question. "Hell. I don't know. My mother had me when she was nearly forty."

Phil cleared his throat, looked around the room. Then he met Brand's gaze. "Look. I don't want to pry, but I've always considered you a friend. You were married to Marilee for almost two years. Did you know we'd been lovers before my accident?"

"Yeah, I knew. You damn near killed her, blowing her off the way you did after you got hurt. She talked about you a lot. We were good friends until we made the mistake of getting married to each other." Where the hell was Phil headed with this conversation?

"Maybe time has done a number on my memory, but I remember Marilee as one sexy, sensual woman. Now she swears she doesn't need—God, this is hard to ask." Phil paused, downed the rest of his drink. "Do you think she can be happy without a full, normal sex life?"

Brand could vouch for the fact Marilee had preferred nearly any activity to a good, old-fashioned romp beneath the sheets, at least with him. "She may have liked having sex with you, but she certainly never liked it with me. Want another drink?"

Phil handed Brand his glass. "I assume you've left other women satisfied," he said lightly.

"A few." Uncomfortable discussing his sex life with a man who was incapable of having one, Brand handed Phil his drink then turned, stared out the window before turning back and trying to answer honestly. "I've never been into having indiscriminate sex. I believe it takes a special chemistry between lovers to make sex great. And a compatible mindset."

Phil looked as if a cloud had lifted, freed him from some inner conflict. He grinned. "I've had a hard time believing Marilee could love me the way I am. She convinced me, after all these years, when she marched in my house, tossed out my valet—a polite name for a male nurse—and proceeded to take care of all the disgusting rituals that keep what's left of me functioning." Phil went on to describe the extent of his infirmity.

Brand hadn't realized how much care Phil required, had assumed his only handicap was the visible one. Brand understood now why Phil had rejected Marilee after the accident, why he felt now that he had to ask these personal questions. "Marilee always loved you, even when she was married to me. I'm sorry I came down on her so hard for conning Dani into taking my daughter." Brand suppressed a groan as he mentally pictured the ways LeeAnn could make their lives miserable for six long weeks.

He forced a smile. "Enjoy your cruise. You two will have plenty of time with LeeAnn when you get back. Dani and I will do our best to charm some of the meanness out of her."

Chapter Sixteen

During the coming days, Brand sincerely hoped Phil and Marilee were enjoying their honeymoon. He, Dani and Dave were all going half mad trying to cope with the six-year-old tyrant. Nothing any of them did pleased LeeAnn.

Dani had it the worst. Since LeeAnn's visit was to be so short, they had decided not to enroll her in school. As a result, the girl was home all day, rejecting every effort Dani made to be her friend. Yesterday, Dani had told him sadly, LeeAnn complained of missing her grandmothers and the cultured, proper life they lived in Carendon. Resolutely, Brand sat at the dinner table, sent Mrs. Blair to fetch his recalcitrant daughter.

Like a little matriarch, LeeAnn grimaced daintily as she sat down to their informal Saturday brunch. She ate silently, correctly, until Brand told them they were going to Dave's school football game that afternoon. Her chin jutted out and she stared at Brand.

"I hate football. It's a dirty, nasty game. I want to see a new movie." LeeAnn's thin, pale face contorted in an expression of disgust.

"I'm going to be playing, LeeAnn." Dave's falsely hearty voice belied his disappointment that his mother would, again, have to miss his game to stay with his prissy half sister.

"We'll all go." Brand refused to cater for one more minute to his daughter's petulant demands. "You can see a movie another time, LeeAnn."

"I will not. I won't go to watch you play Monday night, either. Grandma Eleanor says ladies don't watch such awful, violent things." LeeAnn paused before asking with icy courtesy to be excused from the table then flounced off without waiting for permission.

Brand sensed Dani's temper was on the verge of exploding. She bit her lower lip, clenched a fist around her fork. He, too, had reached the end of his patience with his spoiled little girl. He pushed his chair back from the table and stood. "She needs a good spanking. I'll take care of that right now." Resolutely, he rose and started off after his daughter.

"Don't. Not until you try to talk to her." Dani had gotten up, too, followed close behind him.

"I've talked all I'm going to. My mother would have switched me senseless if I'd talked to her the way LeeAnn talks to us." He knocked perfunctorily, stepped into his daughter's room.

"You've got exactly five minutes to get out of that party dress and into something warm. We are all going to watch Dave's game."

"I won't. Grandma Eleanor said football's a dirty, common boys' game. She says everybody that's anybody laughs at me 'cause my daddy plays football for a living."

Brand took a menacing step toward his daughter. "Get dressed. Dani will find you something appropriate to wear." It was all he could do to speak civilly. He couldn't help knotting his fists at his sides. "Dani, find some jeans or something and get them on this child. I'll go warm up the car."

He started to leave, reconsidered. He glared at his daughter as fiercely as she was glaring at him. "Five minutes. If you're not ready to go, I'm going to take a switch to you." With that, he strode out, itching to clutch a supple poplar switch in his hand, make it sing on its way to his daughter's sassy butt.

* * * * *

"Here. Put these on." Dani laid out crisp, new jeans and a heavy pink sweatshirt on the bed. Thankfully, she'd gone shopping after Mrs. Blair had told her LeeAnn's wardrobe included nothing but the ruffled, dainty dresses she always wore.

"I hate you. I hate Daddy too. Grandma Eleanor said you've turned him into trash, just like you." LeeAnn's pale green eyes filled with tears as she pulled off her dress and struggled into the jeans. "Grandma Eleanor says jeans are trashy. Trashy, trashy, trashy," she repeated in a singsong drawl.

Dani wanted to scream, tell LeeAnn what a witch her grandma was for having poisoned the child's mind against them all. Even her own son. Instead, she held out the sweatshirt. "The jeans are warm. If you'd come with me to shop, you could have picked out the sort of winter clothes you like." Fighting to hold her temper, Dani herded LeeAnn toward the garage, paused only to collect two fur-lined parkas from hooks on the mud room wall.

Brand practically had to drag LeeAnn up on the bleachers when they got to Dave's game. If he hadn't sat her down between them, Dani didn't doubt but the girl would have bolted and run. Every time they looked over her bowed, petulant head at each other, Brand conveyed his distress. It seemed there was nothing they could do to make his daughter warm to them. Even Dave's efforts at friendship had met deaf ears.

Brand stood, yelled his encouragement when Dave's team went on offense. LeeAnn stared, looked at her father as if he'd come from another planet. When Dave threw a short pass that went for the winning touchdown, Dani too came to her feet, shouted with the crowd.

LeeAnn's face contorted, her eyes opened wide. "You're common. Ladies don't yell," she said through clenched teeth.

"Apologize." Brand's terse order carried, its intensity fearsome over the din of the crowd.

"Grandma said." LeeAnn pouted and stamped a dainty foot.

Hands on her shoulders, Brand turned his daughter, forced her to look him in the eye. "I'm your father. I said apologize. Now."

"Sorry." LeeAnn's hateful look made a mockery of the word.

* * * * *

When they got home, Brand followed his daughter into her room. Dani left the door to their suite open, hoped she wouldn't hear LeeAnn howling with pain. She vacillated between wanting to hug the unhappy child and itching to throttle the vicious little brat.

She looked up, saw Brand come in, toe off his shoes and pull his sweater over his head. "If she's smart, she'll watch her tongue a little better now," he said, his expression tight.

"I'm sorry."

"LeeAnn's the one who needs to be sorry. Not that I think she regrets a goddamn thing she did or listened to a word I said."

"You didn't hurt her?" Dani shuddered. Brand was so big, so strong. So gentle. "Of course you didn't."

He rubbed his hand through his hair, mutely shook his head. "No, but I can't say she didn't tempt me to give her a couple of swats on the bottom. Maybe I should have. She needs something to knock some decency into her." He stretched out, stared morosely at the ceiling. "I told you she's a little monster."

Dani couldn't disagree. "Little's the word. Your daughter's only six years old. She's doing what she's been taught."

"She needs to be taught some discipline. I'm through trying to coddle her, cater to her every whim." Brand rolled onto his side, rested his head on Dani's lap. "I won't let LeeAnn insult you," he said, his promise muffled against her jeans-clad belly.

She ran her fingers through his thick light brown hair, massaged his temples. "When LeeAnn says things the way she did tonight, she's just parroting your mother. I try not to pay any attention."

"You're priceless."

She bent, dropped kisses along the furrows in his forehead, on his earlobe and the strong line of his jaw. *I love you.* "So are you," she whispered against his tightly drawn lips.

He traced the curve of her thigh, his touch hard, demanding at first then becoming more sensual. Less angry. When he reached her pussy, he lingered, teasing and taunting her through her jeans until they were damp and she was panting. It felt good, so good she couldn't help but arch her hips, encouraging him to continue.

Rolling, he wrapped his other arm around her then let her go. "At least you don't give me grief when I decide I need to exert a little control. Take off your clothes and bend over the bed so I can fuck your delicious little ass."

"Yes, sir." Trembling at the prospect of having him finally claim her there, she stripped while he released his belt then shucked his jeans and underwear in one impatient motion. Her heart pounded in her chest when she bent over the bed as he'd ordered her to do, but she couldn't deny she was aroused, not with her juices wetting her inner thighs. Not with the scent of sex filling her nostrils. She forgot to breathe for a minute when he walked around the bed and fiddled with the restraints secured to two of the four posts at each corner of the massive bed.

Padded handcuffs clicked first onto one wrist and then the other once she complied, the pressure from the restraints light yet enough for her to know she was well and truly bound. Her nipples tightened as they brushed against the silky Egyptian cotton sheet. "Get up on your knees. I want your ass in the air, waiting for me."

Carefully she brought her legs up on the bed, positioning herself the way she thought he wanted. "Is this all right?"

"It's fine, baby. Just fine. Now, open your mouth for me."

She'd hoped to taste the clean, slightly salty taste of his long, thick cock. Instead she felt the ball gag they sometimes used for sex play filling her mouth, reminding her he'd promised to take her ass this time. The gag's straps caught in her hair, tugged at it as he secured it at her crown. "Mmmm." Being restrained like this excited her…made her eager to serve Brand however, whenever he wanted.

"Like that, don't you?" He moved around the bed once more, and she felt the mattress dip when he settled in behind her. "Easy, now. I'm going to fill your sopping little pussy first." He stroked the insides of her thighs, moving up inch by inch until he spread the bare lips of her sex and spread the moisture there. Her clit swelled and hardened when he pinched it between wet fingers. Slowly he inserted a dildo in her pussy, set it to vibrating and driving her insane.

When he inserted two lubricated fingers into her rear passage, she couldn't help tensing. "Relax. Push out as I push my fingers in. That's right. Oh, yeah, you can take my cock and like it. Easy now."

He pulled out and donned a condom then rubbed his sheathed cock head along her slit. The vibrations increased. She wanted to move, take him in. Belong to him in every possible way. She strained to talk around the gag. "Mmmm."

"I'm going to fuck your pretty ass now. Stay still for me." He grasped her ass cheeks, spreading them apart. His cock head throbbed at her rear entrance. Pushing gently until the sphincter muscle gave way and he was seated inside her. Full. Stretched. Surprisingly aroused. Emotions met, collided, exploded in a burst of colors when he took her fully. "Imagine it's me in your cunt, someone else in your ass…pretend you're sucking a third cock instead of that gag. Would you like that, baby?"

God help her, she would. When he'd told her one night about the ménage he'd enjoyed with Vlad and his wife, she'd been more shocked than aroused. But with it happening to her, with Brand's throbbing cock up her ass and a dildo vibrating in her pussy, Dani had no problem understanding why a woman might want to service two masters. Pressure built in her again as Brand fucked her slow and deep, his fingers moving the dildo and tweaking her clit until she shuddered with another long, hard climax.

"Enough. I want to fuck your pussy now." Withdrawing from her rear, he got rid of the condom and the dildo then took her pussy hard and fast. He grasped her breasts, tugged the distended nipples then soothed them with his fingers. She felt his hot breath on the back of her neck, the bite of his teeth…and his shout of satisfaction as he shot wave after wave of hot semen into her womb. When he knelt and tongued her pussy, she came again.

Once he untied her hands and removed the gag, he kissed her. She loved the taste and smell of him, of her…of the heat and passion they shared. "My God, Dani. Thank you." He buried his face in her hair, let her savor the afterglow. When he rolled to his side, spent, she went with him.

Brand slept, but not for long. A panorama of disturbing dreams disrupted his rest. Concerned, he pulled Dani close, ruffled her sable hair with a gentle hand. He had an overwhelming need to protect her, yet he felt impotent when it was his own flesh and blood lashing out at her with spiteful barbs he knew must cut her to the bone. For the first time he owned up to the blame he deserved because his daughter had become an obnoxious little witch. He should have fought harder, refused to give her up to her grandmothers' tender mercies.

He loved the woman in his arms, had never stopped loving her even when he'd hated her for leaving him. He shut down that thought, dared not risk openly loving her again. But she'd had every reason to make Dave hate him, and she hadn't. She'd even said a few times that she loved him, without him saying the words to her.

He might be her master sexually…but he was afraid she had the power to enslave him. He knew he'd bleed if she ever left. Wouldn't let that happen. Whatever it took, he wouldn't let his mother and daughter turn her love to hate. Losing Dani again would damn near kill him.

Brand closed his eyes. If only he could, he'd keep her like this forever, safe in his arms, away from people determined to drive them apart.

* * * * *

Three days later, Brand came home early, his practice session cut short by a freak late October storm. Freezing rain had made field workouts impossible. Nodding a pleasant greeting to Mrs. Blair, he hurried past LeeAnn's room on his way upstairs. He didn't feel up to dealing with his daughter.

Dani was in their suite, finishing her makeup. Grinning at her reflection in the mirror, he bent down, buried his face in her fragrant, sable curls.

"You're dressed up," he said, wondering where she planned to go in the god-awful weather outside. "That sleet's making it mighty tricky to drive."

"I know. I can't cancel my appointment, though. I'll take a cab."

"I'll drive you." He stripped off his sweats, glanced at the soft, ruby wool shirtwaist dress and high-heeled black suede pumps she wore before taking gray slacks and a navy blazer out of the closet. "We got off practice early because of the damn sleet."

Dani hadn't planned to tell Brand until after the fact that she was visiting a gynecologist. Still, she smiled. When the receptionist had scheduled her appointment, she'd suggested her husband accompany her.

"I'm glad. They really wanted you to come, too, but I told them you'd be working out with the team." As she watched Brand slip a burgundy and navy striped tie under the collar of his snowy white shirt, her heart filled with love. He was magnificent, and he'd chosen her.

Suddenly he stopped in the middle of knotting his tie. "Oh, no."

Dani smiled. "What's wrong?"

"Am I going to be gawked at by a hundred or so ladies at some charity function?"

"No."

"Where are we going, then?"

"To Dr. Farner, Elaine's gynecologist. I have an appointment for a checkup."

"They want me there, too? What's wrong? God, tell me you don't have some awful illness." For a minute he looked as if he might throw up. Then he grinned. "Honey, are you pregnant?"

"I think so. Are you glad?" She held her breath, fearing his reaction.

"I'm delighted." He dropped the blazer he'd been about to put on, grabbed her in an exuberant bear hug. He lowered his head and took her lips in a tender, gentle kiss. As if she were made of spun glass, he helped her into her coat and settled her in his car.

From the mahogany and leather cocoon of the Ferrari's interior, Dani looked at a fairyland of iced evergreens through the gray haze of sleet. Today the world seemed beautiful, despite the autumn storm. She didn't talk, didn't want to break Brand's concentration as he drove on slippery streets. Pulling the soft fur of the mink coat he'd given her against her cold cheeks, she pictured the new baby, vowed she would become the wife and mother Brand apparently believed she could be.

*****

The car stopped. Brand unfolded his long body from the driver's seat. In a few long strides, he reached the passenger door, held it for her. Inside, neither of them had time for reflection. The slim, blonde receptionist hustled them into the doctor's library, so they could fill out reams of forms and wait for the doctor in privacy.

"Here, I'll hang up your coats. You'll be more comfortable in here. If you wait out there, our patients will crawl all over Mr. Carendon for autographs." The woman eyed Brand a bit too hungrily for Dani's liking. And she must have wanted Brand all to herself from the way she was darn near drooling over him. Dani had to get hold of herself, remember when other women ogled her husband, he didn't ogle back. She knew it in her head, so why couldn't she get the fact across to her not-so-confident heart? Why did other women's hungry looks at Brand fuel the insecurity she was trying so hard to overcome?

When the woman left, he whispered in Dani's ear. "Hey, honey. I don't want anyone but you. I don't even know her."

She shrugged. Apparently she hadn't done a very good job hiding the way the receptionist had made her feel. "She'd like to know you, though. Better than she should. You might be safer out in the waiting room with all those pregnant ladies."

"God, no."

"I won't let them at you." She raised her hand, brushed back a windblown strand of blond hair from his forehead. "What kind of questions do you have to answer?"

"Every kind imaginable. How about you?"

"Here's one. 'What methods of birth control have you used?'"

"That's easy. None. Unless you count those condoms I tried, years ago." Brand looked at his questionnaire. "How about this one? 'How frequently do you have intercourse?'"

"Do you really want to answer that one honestly?" Her cheeks turned warm when she thought of the few nights they didn't…and the many fantastic, sleepless evenings they made love again and again.

"How about if I just say at least twice a day, every day, more often on weekends and holidays?"

"Oh, please."

"I'd never thought you believed in 'Once a king, always a king, but once a night's enough', honey." His teasing midnight blue eyes glinted with shards of silver, and his lips lifted in a questioning grin.

"I don't, but you don't need to tell the doctor that. Why don't you just say we do it often enough to get the desired results?"

When the doctor came in a few minutes later, Brand and Dani were still laughing. Looking up and seeing him, Dani tried to affect a certain amount of dignity and decorum.

"Mr. and Mrs. Carendon?"

"Yes. You must be Dr. Farner. You delivered Josh Shearer's twins, didn't you?" Brand asked.

"Yes. I understand Mrs. Shearer referred you to me. Do you have the papers filled out?"

Brand nodded, handed over the forms.

The doctor glanced over the forms, directed them to an examining room. When he finished his examination and confirmed what Dani already knew, he met them in his elegantly furnished office.

"Well?" Brand asked.

Farner looked at a calendar, then at them. She held her breath. "You'll be having your baby around June tenth. I'm sorry for taking up your time with the questionnaires. Most of my practice deals with correcting infertility. Obviously, neither of you has a problem in that regard." He smiled, then gave Dani some instructions for prenatal care.

Brand thumbed through the pages of the booklet the doctor had given them. He paused, stared at a page, then at the doctor. "Are you sure having sex won't hurt Dani or the baby? Some doctors don't allow it."

"I'm positive. You can continue right up until the baby's born. Some positions will be more comfortable for your wife than others as the baby gets bigger, and you might want to keep from letting her bear all your weight, since she's so much smaller than you." Dr. Farner smiled, as if he wondered where Brand might have picked up the archaic notion that caused his question.

"Is there anything we shouldn't do, then?"

"Just be sensible. An expectant mother shouldn't take up contact sports, or any activities where she'd risk serious falls. She should avoid tobacco, alcohol and caffeine, and any medication unless she checks with me first. Otherwise, she can do anything. The important thing is that she be free of emotional stress. You need to shield her from stressful situations, more than from any physical activities."

Chapter Seventeen

Stress. All the way home that word rang in Brand's ears. Stress. A synonym for LeeAnn. For his mother. For the town where he and Dani had grown up.

That night at dinner, he watched the kids, wished he and Dani hadn't decided not to tell them about the baby right away. He wanted to shout out the news, share the joy he felt, knowing he was going to have a chance to do fatherhood right this time, from the start.

Since he'd read her the riot act, LeeAnn had been deadly quiet. The way she stared at him drove him nuts. Dani said she'd been giving her the silent treatment, too.

Dave had taken to staying in his room except for meals. Brand didn't blame him. The atmosphere was tense to say the least.

Only in bed, in the silence of the night, were he and Dani completely happy. They made love and rejoiced at the prospect of their new baby. With luck, the cruise ship would come back on time, and Marilee and Phil would soon take LeeAnn off their hands.

After a particularly trying encounter with his daughter over breakfast, Brand stayed at the clubhouse long after practice was over. He told himself he needed to study the playbook until he almost believed it—even though he'd already committed the entire thing to memory. It was five o'clock, nearly dark outside, when he pulled into the garage at home.

Inside he forced a smile as he shrugged out of his sheepskin-lined parka. He resolved to do something, anything, to break the tension. He closed the door, heard someone sobbing and raced toward the noise. Dani stood in front of the window, her coat half on, half off. She was shaking like a leaf in a storm. Frightened, Brand dropped to his knees, cradled her face in his hands. The fierce wind had chafed her cheeks, tangled her hair. "What's wrong, honey?"

"LeeAnn," she sobbed. "She's gone."

What the fuck? "Where? When? Calm down, baby. We'll find her. She can't have gone far. Take it easy. Please."

"She must have sneaked past Mrs. Blair about four o'clock, maybe a little after. Just before I left to pick Dave up at school, I saw her in her room, sitting by the window and staring out at the snow. Mrs. Blair and Dave are out looking for her. I was out there too, until I had to come back inside to get a warmer jacket."

Brand got up, lifted her damp coat off her shoulders. When she met his gaze, her obvious fear fed his own.

"She's such a little girl, and she doesn't know her way around here. What if she falls into the lake? She'll freeze or drown."

"No, damn it. She won't." He wasn't about to feed Dani's fear even though terror gripped him like a vise. "She's too smart to wander down by the lake. We'll find her." He wished he were certain of that, but Dani was right. It was no time for a child used to warm weather to be traipsing around in six inches of snow. "Did anything happen that made her leave? I mean, did she say anything to you or Mrs. Blair?"

"N-no. Not a word. When Dave and I got back, she was gone. I swear, I didn't do anything to upset LeeAnn."

He knew that. Dani had been nothing but kind to his daughter even when the kid deserved a kick in the pants. "Baby, I know you didn't. Go upstairs and lie down, you look exhausted. LeeAnn will be fine."

"I've got to go back out there. Help find her." She pulled away, started to put on the fleece-lined jacket.

Brand tilted her head back, looked into her eyes. "I'll find her. You're going to rest. You look dead on your feet."

Not waiting for her to protest, he lifted her, carried her upstairs, laid her gently in the center of the bed. He took off her shoes and tossed a blanket over her trembling body.

Furious, he stomped downstairs. He swore he'd ship LeeAnn off to boarding school the minute he found her. The hell with keeping her until Marilee and Phil got back. He'd be doing them all a favor by settling his daughter somewhere where they could curb her rotten spoiled ways.

Quickly, he traded his running shoes for fur-lined boots and bundled up in his heaviest parka. He trotted outside, began looking for his daughter. When he ran into Dave and Mrs. Blair after a few minutes, he sent them inside for a break, told them to call 911 if he wasn't back with LeeAnn in half an hour. No one could survive being out for long in this storm.

As he searched, Brand's anger dissolved, replaced by stark terror. It had stopped snowing, but the cold white stuff swirled all around him. The fragile flakes were no match for a fierce winter wind that caught them up, piled them in drifts as high as a foot or more.

Then he spotted his daughter. She was wearing her hot pink parka, sitting against a tree near the edge of the water. So little, so cold looking, she stared out across the half-frozen lake. Her head drooped against her chest, her shoulders slumped forward from the white-barked ash tree she was leaning against. Brand quelled his urge to call out, order her to come to him. Instead, he went to her, sat down beside her.

"Go away. I hate you. I want to go home." Dried tears streaked LeeAnn's dirt-stained face.

"You're going home, LeeAnn, as soon as Phil and your mother get back from their cruise. Meanwhile, this is your home. Come on, you've worried us all half to death, going off like this." Brand put an arm tentatively around the little girl's shoulders.

LeeAnn jerked away. "I want to go home to Grandma Eleanor an' Grandma Marge. To my friends and my toys and my old school. I hate you, and Mommy, and trashy old Dani, and crippled Cousin Phil. I want my grandmas."

What had those two old women done to his little girl? Brand's fists clenched involuntarily inside his fur-lined gloves, his muscles tensed.

"Baby, hating people hurts the one doing the hating a whole lot more than it hurts the hated ones. It's a lot better to love than to hate. I'm sorry your grandmas never taught you that." Brand tried again to touch LeeAnn. Again, she pulled away.

"You don't love me. You love Dave and Dani. Grandma Eleanor says all you care about is them and your dumb old football games. She said before she sent me to Mommy you'd never come see me anymore, that Dani wouldn't let you come see her either."

If his mother had been there, Brand would have strangled her on the spot. He pulled his hood tighter around his face, hoped to hide the fury he was sure must show in his expression.

"Grandma Eleanor's wrong. You're my little girl, and I do love you. So would Dani and Dave, if you'd give them half a chance. We want you to be happy while you're with us, but you make it awfully hard when you won't even try to be a part of our family."

"You all expect me to do things my grandmas say ladies don't do. Wear boys' clothes, watch boys' games. Things like that."

"Your grandmas are out of line, LeeAnn. Did you know, until I went to college Grandma Eleanor came to every one of my ball games. She yelled when my team did something good, and she wore slacks, too, lots of times. It made her very angry, though, when I decided to play football for a living."

LeeAnn looked up at him, a quizzical expression on her face. "Grandma Eleanor used to watch you play football?"

"Yes. I know it's hard to believe. Come on, sweetheart, let's go home." Brand took her hand again, and this time she didn't pull away. But she made no move to get up off her spot against the tree. "You're going to freeze. Besides, you've scared Dani half to death. Let's go let her know you're all right."

Slowly, stiffly, as though she were pretty much stuck to the tree, she pushed herself up and met his gaze. "Why'd you marry her, Daddy? Why is Mommy marrying Cousin Phil?"

Brand looked down at LeeAnn, lifting her in his arms for the first time since she was a toddler. "Feelings. Special kinds of feelings. The kind of caring that makes two people right together in spite of everything that says they should be apart. Trust me, baby. Your mommy loves Uncle Phil the way I love Dani. And all of us love you."

* * * * *

LeeAnn didn't change overnight, but Brand noticed her opening up more, letting herself enjoy the activities Dani planned to keep her occupied. A week after her foray into the storm, Brand began to relax. Maybe everything would turn out all right after all.

The phone rang. Dave picked it up and handed it over. "It's Uncle Jimmy."

"Thanks." Brand leaned back, put the phone to his ear. "Uncle Jimmy," he said into the receiver then listened to his uncle's news. Laura's husband had finally died. After all the long years in limbo, she was free to marry. They'd have a Valentine's Day wedding then honeymoon on a trip around the world.

Damn. The family firm wasn't likely to run itself for four long months. Brand rubbed his hand across his brow. Maybe Vlad... No, he'd only been working at the firm for a few months. And none of the other associates had been hired to be anything but adjuncts to whatever Carendon was at the helm.

That was going to change. Nepotism had gone on long enough so far as the family business was concerned. But meanwhile Brand had no choice, because he'd gone with the flow, failed to insist the firm would thrive as well or better with someone other than a Carendon in charge. He'd have to go home. Uncle Jimmy had done it for him when his dad had died, given up the trial practice he loved so Brand could follow his own dream. Hell. If anyone deserved to be happy, it was Laura and Uncle Jimmy.

But Dani deserved to be happy, too. He was going to have to take her where she didn't want to go. Ready or not, she'd soon have to face his mother and all her snobbish friends. The people in Carendon who'd called her trash and made her life a living hell. Why now, when she'd come so far toward shedding the insecurities it had taken a lifetime for her to develop, toward believing she was as good as anyone in spite of her lousy family? He'd have given millions if they could have stayed in Milwaukee during the off-season, awaited their baby's birth in peace.

Fuck it. He spent hours trying to come up with a plan so they could do it. But nothing worked. He laid his head in his hands and wished the headache from hell would go away.

* * * * *

"Who was on the phone, Dave?" Dani asked, looking up from the recipe she and LeeAnn were using to make oatmeal cookies.

"Uncle Jimmy. He wanted to talk to Dad." Grinning, Dave filched a finger full of the batter. "I've gotta go work on a book report." That last remark he tossed over his shoulder on the way out of the kitchen.

LeeAnn looked around, followed Dave's lead and stuck her own small finger into the mixing bowl. Dani pretended not to notice her stepdaughter's surreptitious breach of manners as she shuffled through boxes in the pantry for raisins to add to the dough. There! She brought it out and measured out a cupful. "Here, LeeAnn. Would you like to stir these into the batter?"

"Yes, ma'am." When the little girl smiled, she looked like Brand. Since he'd had a long talk with her after she tried to run away last week, she'd been behaving for the most part, although she had the occasional lapse.

"Then let's get these into the oven. It's almost time for you to go to bed."

* * * * *

Brand helped eat nearly all the cookies before they settled down for the night. Though he'd been jovial to everyone, he'd seemed preoccupied, almost like he'd been the first few weeks after LeeAnn arrived.

"What's the matter?" Dani asked once they'd undressed and gone to bed.

Brand hesitated. Every day she seemed more self-assured. Still, he hated to tell her until he had to. He wasn't at all sure she was ready to face the not-so-friendly faces in their hometown. He'd wait to tell her, at least for a little while. He couldn't stand the thought of making her unhappy. "Nothing's wrong. I was just thinking about Uncle Jimmy and Laura. Her husband finally died. He called to tell me and said they'd be getting married on Valentine's Day."

"You'll fly to Atlanta for the wedding, won't you?"

"Yeah." Afraid she'd read more in his expression, he buried his face against the fragrant, satin warmth of her shoulder. "I'm glad I found you, honey." He stroked her back, lost himself in the silky feel of her skin against his calloused palms.

"I'm glad, too. I love you." She moved as close to him as she could get and pressed her tiny body against him. The faint scent of apple blossoms filled his nostrils, and her small sigh when he nudged her legs apart let him know she wanted him, too. When she cupped his face in her hands and dragged him to her for a kiss, he took over.

Gently, for he'd never been as conscious of how small and fragile she was until now, when he knew she was pregnant, he rolled her over onto her back, came over her. He nudged her legs apart, settling himself between them. "I want inside you, baby."

"Oh, yesss." He loved her eagerness, the way she welcomed him into her body…and her heart.

He braced himself on his elbows and slid into the moist haven of her pussy, bending his head to nip at her lush lips. "You feel so fucking good. Put your arms around me and let me love you."

Her pussy contracted around him, milked him. Vanilla sex had never been so good. His balls tightened, and his cock swelled more inside her hot, wet sheath. He felt her hands on his shoulders, grasping, digging in, listened to her breathing grow ragged. When he looked down at her, he saw love in her eyes, passion in the slackness of her mouth, the sheen of sweat on her brow. "Come for me, honey. Now."

She whimpered, bucked her hips, took him deeper, changing the angle of penetration just enough to bring her clit in contact with his pelvis. Then she shuddered, her climax starting in the wild pulsation of her pussy around his cock, spreading through her like wildfire. "Yeah. Like this. Oh God, I'm coming, too."

He closed his eyes, let instinct take over. Came in short, steaming bursts that left him drained. So drained it was all he could do to roll off her, drag her into the protective arc of his body. Murmur words of love and sex as he gently caressed her swollen breasts.

As they lay there, Brand thought again of Uncle Jimmy and his urgent request. He wished they could stay like this forever, Dani in his arms, the center of his world. But he couldn't. He had no choice but to assume his family obligations. Still, the idea of hurting Dani was more than he could bear.

Chapter Eighteen

Time passed quickly. Dani was almost sorry when Marilee and Phil arrived to take LeeAnn home. The little girl had done a turnaround in attitude, become her daddy's biggest fan. As they drove to the airport, Dani looked at Brand, smiled. His daughter's enthusiastic recounting of how he'd led the Marlins in the game that clinched the division championship had to have him bursting with pride.

"And the Marlins are gonna go to the Super Bowl. Daddy says it's gonna be in Houston. I wanna go."

Phil ruffled LeeAnn's hair. "If your daddy can get us tickets, we'll take you to the game," he told her.

Brand grinned. "No problem. Just keep your fingers crossed we make it through the playoffs." He pulled the Mercedes up to the curb at the airport terminal, put it in park and got out to help a skycap get the luggage and Phil's wheelchair out of the trunk. Then he opened the back door, held out his arms to his daughter. "Come here, baby, give your daddy a hug."

Although she'd never have believed it possible a few weeks back, Dani knew now she was going to miss LeeAnn. The little girl seemed happier, surer of her position in all their lives, and that change of attitude made her much more pleasant to be around. She was still a handful, though. Dani grinned at Marilee when her daughter balked about getting out of the car.

Brand teased LeeAnn until she got out, lifted her high in the air then held her for a hug and kiss. "See you soon," he said as he set her on Phil's lap. Then he turned to Dani, clasped her hand. They watched LeeAnn, her mother and her new stepfather until they disappeared from sight.

* * * * *

Brand sprawled across the bed, tried to relax. The sound of water beckoned him to the bathroom, but he wouldn't join Dani in her shower tonight.

He'd delayed telling her as long as he could, and there would be no talking if he stripped off his sweats, stepped under the warm, pulsing stream of water and let nature take its course.

Staying out of the shower gave him no guarantees. He was already half hard, just thinking about her dripping wet, luscious body and how she always responded to him. He rolled off the bed, padded barefoot on the plush carpet to her walk-in closet. There it was, a white terry robe that would cover her from head to foot. Without letting himself look inside, he looped it over a towel rack just inside the bathroom door.

"Put this on before you come out," he told her. Then he lay back on the recliner and waited. He looked up when she appeared a few minutes later looking puzzled, swathed in the shapeless garment he'd picked out for her.

He waited until she sat down then took a deep breath. "Honey, we have to go home for the off-season," he said, trying to sound casual.

Dani's eyes widened. She clutched her belly protectively. "Oh, no! You promised. You said we could stay here until I felt ready to go back home. I don't know—"

Brand sensed her distress, wished he could tell her he was joking. "We have to go. For Uncle Jimmy. He wants to take Laura on a long trip after their wedding." Brand brushed an errant strand of hair back from her brow.

"What does that have to do with you?" Her voice quivered. "You told me—you promised me—we wouldn't go back there until I wanted to go. I don't want to go."

Brand rubbed the back of his hand across his brow, met his wife's tortured gaze. "There never has been a time when there wasn't a member of one of the founders' families in charge of the firm, honey. Uncle Jimmy and I are the last ones. If I don't go home and work, he won't take the time off."

"I'll stay here with Dave, then. Brand, I can't go home, not yet."

Twelve years ago, Brand had seen people hurt Dani. He'd thought when he married her the first time that they'd accept her as his wife. They hadn't. They'd followed his mother's lead, made it crystal clear that to them Dani was as much trash as her mother, would always be trash no matter who she married or what she might accomplish. He had no doubt a lot of the people still felt the same. He'd rather stay away, never go home again if doing so would cause Dani pain.

But she'd come so far, conquered most of the insecurities she'd formed, growing up the way she had. He'd watched her with LeeAnn, Marilee and Phil, noticed how comfortable she seemed to be. He'd practically convinced himself that now, carrying his baby, Dani was ready to follow him anywhere, defy anyone who'd try to interfere with their happiness.

"You and Dave belong with me, Dani, wherever I have to go. I couldn't stand us being apart. I hate this as much as you do, but I can't turn my back on Uncle Jimmy, not after all he gave up for me." His words were sharper than he'd intended. Dani looked as if he'd slapped her.

"If I decide to go with you, when will we have to leave here?" The tentative smile on her lips didn't make up for the stricken look in brown eyes liquid with tears.

"After the playoffs and Super Bowl."

"What about Dave's schooling? He's worked so hard to catch up with the rest of his class at Eastover."

"He can transfer to Trinity Prep in Atlanta. Their curriculum's similar. I can drop him off every day on my way to work."

"That was why you picked Eastover?"

"I'm sorry, baby. How in hell could I have known this would be the year Laura would finally be free to marry Uncle Jimmy? Damn it, her husband lay in a coma in that nursing home for nearly twenty years. No, I did not choose Eastover for Dave so he'd be ready for my old prep school. We went over all the reasons for his being there when he first started." Brand raked his fingers across his brow, stared at Dani.

Knowing only one way to still her fears, he gathered her in his arms, carried her forcefully to their bed. Once there, he bent to kiss away her tears. When he felt her grasp his shoulders he set her gently on the bed, unfastened her shapeless robe.

He stripped off his sweats, smiled when she looked at him, settled her gaze on his rock-hard cock.

"It'll be all right, honey," he promised, stretching out beside her and meeting her heated gaze. "No one will dare mess with my wife. No one but me, that is." Turning on his side, he pulled her to him. "I'm going to keep you so hot and wet you won't care where we are, as long as we're together. And if I have to tie you up to keep you with me, I will."

He felt better when he saw a smile cross her lips. "Maybe I should fight you, then. You haven't been playing our bedroom games lately."

Grabbing both her hands, he held them above her head. "And you've missed them, haven't you? Just wait until our baby's born, and we'll resume the games. Maybe invent some new ones." He took her lips, tongue-fucked her hard and fast, until they both were panting and ready. "Ride me, now," he ordered, lifting her over him and settling her onto his cock.

She looked so fucking gorgeous, with her breasts starting to swell, her belly with just a little paunch. He stroked her silky skin from throat to hip, stopping to caress her breasts and pinch the rosy nipples. Then he found her clit and played with it while she rocked on him. Together. That's where they belonged. Never again would he let her get away.

Impatient and afraid he'd tire her, he rolled them over, increased the pace. Soon he felt her spasming around him, heard her whimper with pleasure. And he came in her, his climax more an act of male possession than one of animal lust.

* * * * *

Early the next morning, Brand slept while Dani lay next to him and stared miserably at softly lit shadows moving amidst the icy trees outside their window. In silent desperation, she held his hand.

She loved Brand more than she loved her own life. He protected her, made her feel cared for, almost loved. He gave Dave the father's love he'd missed for so long. No way could she stay here, sulk alone while Brand did what he had to do. She just wished they had to go anywhere but Carendon.

Dave. Would the people who knew her sordid beginnings punish him for being her son as well as Brand's? Dani couldn't stand that.

She pictured Eleanor, rejecting Brand's son because she was his mother. That might not happen. The woman could just as easily accept Dave and do her evil worst to turn him against his mother. Maybe Brand as well.

Would Brand still want her after all was said and done, or would his mother and her friends persuade him his feelings for her weren't real?

Dani had only questions. She needed answers. She got up, cooked, and served Brand his breakfast. He smiled, complimented her for the muffins she'd made. Acted as if everything were perfectly normal. As far as he was concerned, she guessed everything *was* normal. After all, it wasn't he who'd become the butt of cruel jokes and snide remarks.

"What about Dave? How will your mother and her friends treat him?" It was hard to keep her voice steady, but she managed. She poured more coffee into Brand's mug, staying behind him to avoid his gaze.

Brand sighed, set a half-eaten muffin back on his plate. "Dani, we've been over this before. I've pushed my mother. She's pushed back. We're both adults now. This will work out. You don't really think she'd set out to destroy her own grandson, do you?"

"Yes, I think she might. She warped your daughter's mind then tossed her away like last year's dress when it suited her purposes. And she hates me. She could easily take out that hatred on Dave."

Brand shook his head. "That won't happen. I won't let her hurt Dave. Or you." He paused, met and held her gaze. "I know I said that before, and it turned out that I lied, but I'm no longer a seventeen-year-old boy who believed she and Dad would support me in what I wanted to do. I know what Mother's capable of now. I can handle her."

"But—"

"Don't worry about trying to placate my mother. Don't worry about stupid things other people may say or believe. Believe this. The only people you need to please are yourself and me. And you please me, honey, God knows how much you please me." His tone was frankly sensual, his look heated. Then his expression turned serious.

"Dave will get along fine at Trinity. With the folks in Carendon, too." He stood, shrugged into his parka. "Look, I know the idea of going back home scares you, but trust me. It will all work out. We'll be there just a little over four months. Then we'll come back here before I start next year's preseason training." He looked at the clock, frowned. "I've got to go, honey, or I'll be late for practice."

"You'll be home early?" Dani stood on tiptoe to give him a farewell kiss.

"About four, unless Coach has us stay longer. If he does, I'll let you know." He wrapped his arms around her, hugged her as though he'd never let her go.

* * * * *

Day followed day, punctuated by Christmas decorating and shopping trips. Dani shoved her fears about going home again into the deepest corner of her mind. The holidays, she vowed, would be the best ever, the first for her and Brand and Dave as a real family. She loved that they'd be celebrating it in a winter wonderland...that this would be the first white Christmas she or Dave had ever seen.

"Do you have anything else for LeeAnn?" Dani finished arranging gaily wrapped packages in a big box, found a bit of room left over. "I want to get this shipped tomorrow so it will get to Houston in time for Christmas."

Brand looked up from the chess game he was losing to his son. "Not me. You wrapped up the pendant I got her, didn't you?"

"Let me get those computer discs I promised to copy for her," Dave said, sliding his chair back and hurrying off to his room.

"The pendant's here, along with some other things I bought for us to give her." Dani glanced at the tiny box that held the pendant, thought it symbolized a new beginning, a bright future for the relationship between Brand and his daughter. "I got Marilee and Phil a pretty brass planter from all of us. Is that all right? I thought it would seem funny to send things to LeeAnn but not to them."

"That's fine." Brand studied the pieces on the marble chessboard. "Hey, honey, what do you want for Christmas?"

"Maternity clothes. I really can't think of anything else I need."

Brand chuckled. "I think I'll let you pick those out yourself. Christmas is for giving people what they want, not what they need."

Dani smiled. After nearly five months of marriage, she still couldn't get used to Brand's expansive, expensive lifestyle. He'd already given her jewelry, a fur coat, a Mercedes. Not to mention the thousands of dollars she'd spent to replace her bedraggled wardrobe with nice clothes.

She couldn't imagine what more he could find to give her on Christmas morning, unless it would be an announcement they wouldn't be going back to Carendon after all. And she didn't really want that, wouldn't love him as much if he blew off his obligation to Uncle Jimmy.

"I can't think of a thing you haven't already given me," she said softly. "Or Dave, either, for that matter."

"I got Dave a Rolex sports watch, from both of us. With the games and sports equipment Santa is bringing, that should be enough. Dave pointed the watch out to me one day when I took him shopping."

"Brand, he's not even twelve years old," Dani said, aghast. "What if he breaks it or loses it? A Rolex is too expensive for a kid. They cost several hundred dollars, don't they?"

"Make that several thousand. But Dave will take care of it. If he loses it, we can get him another one. I doubt if he'll be able to break it. The sports model is almost indestructible." He glanced down at his wrist. "I've had this one for years, and it's good as new."

Dani shrugged helplessly. Her reluctance to spend money, she knew, stemmed from her lifetime of poverty and deprivation. For that reason, she'd defer to Brand in this. He knew what he could afford and what was appropriate to give children in the world they lived in.

Dave bounded into the great room, carrying two small square boxes of computer disks. "Here, Mom. I copied all of

LeeAnn's favorite games. The discs are labeled and ready to go. Is there room in the box?"

"I think so." Dani rearranged the packages and added the disks. "Hey, will one of you come here and hold the box together while I put tape on it?" She looked over the bright, plentiful boxes under their towering Christmas tree. Just this morning she'd arranged the most recent packages that had come via UPS. Marilee and Phil had sent a big box of glittering packages for Dave, Brand and herself.

The huge pile of gifts awed Dani. They'd been arriving nearly every day for the last week, from Brand's fellow players, the Marlins' front office, even from fans who'd sent Brand presents at the clubhouse. Laura and Uncle Jimmy's box had come yesterday. Dani looked at the little square package they'd sent for her, wondered what it contained.

Her gaze wandered from the tree to the expanse of windows behind it. The scene outside took her breath away. Trees, naked of their leaves, held powdery snow in the crooks of their branches, while the massive spruces boasted caps of white. The ground sparkled, and the sun reflected brilliant gold off a blanket of pure white atop the frozen lake.

Dani loved it. The snow, the presents. The magic of a Christmas season like she'd never experienced before. She grinned, pictured a sassy snowman standing guard outside over the sparkling Christmas tree.

* * * * *

That afternoon, Brand and Dave helped Dani build Frosty. She couldn't imagine anything making her happier than seeing that lopsided snowman list drunkenly between the two men she loved. Determined to record memories of joy she feared were too good to last, she used up two discs for the vidcam before they went inside.

"Hands off until Christmas morning." Brand stretched out on the sofa, tired after their romp in the snow.

"Aw, Dad," Dave groused. "I'm too old for Santa Claus, anyhow." He sneaked a greedy look at the pile of presents under the tree. "Why can't we open them tonight?"

Brand grinned down at his son, recalled having asked the same question when he was Dave's age. "Because. Just because. That's what my dad always told me when I asked him. Did you and your mom used to do your gifts the night before Christmas?"

"No. I mean, no sir. Santa always brought whatever I was going to get, and it was sitting under the tree when I woke up on Christmas morning. I just thought, with all these presents, we'll miss out on our turkey dinner if we have to open 'em all up tomorrow morning."

Brand tried to picture the meager Christmases Dave and Dani had shared for so many years. He'd thought often, while he shopped for their gifts, that they'd done without so many things he would gladly have given them. Instead of resenting the years they'd lost, he focused on how happy it made him that they'd found each other, that they were together at last.

Chapter Nineteen

"Next year there'll be four of us." Brand rested his head on Dani's lap. "Maybe more." He'd been teasing Dani lately about her rapidly expanding waistline, telling her he'd heard twins had popped up occasionally on his family tree. He liked watching her get flustered at the possibility of her family growing faster than she anticipated.

Noticing Dave had fallen asleep on the other end of the leather pit group, he slid a hand under Dani's cashmere sweater and slipped a finger inside her bra to rub her nipple. "You think Dave would be insulted if I carried him to bed?"

"Maybe, but why not do it anyway?" Dani ran her fingers idly through Brand's hair. "Why not just carry me upstairs and let Dave sleep down here beside the Christmas tree?" She let out a tiny moan of pleasure when he cupped her breast, plucked at the taut nipple with his fingers.

"Your wish is my command." He stood, scooped her up. Her hands went immediately around his neck, and she tangled her fingers in his hair. His pulse quickened. When he bent and teased at her lower lip with gentle nips, she begged him to hurry. He did, straight upstairs.

A fire crackled in the fireplace, casting its gold-and-orange glow through the room. Snow fell outside, visible in its pristine beauty through windows that kept out the cold. "Merry Christmas, baby."

When she smiled up at him he felt ten feet tall. "Merry Christmas to you, too."

He felt an urgent tightening inside his jeans. Still, he told himself he'd go slowly, love her thoroughly, tenderly on their first Christmas Eve together. No BDSM play, not now when she was carrying his child. He set her onto her feet beside their bed, breathed in her apple blossom fragrance made musky with the scent of desire. As though she were a precious package addressed to him alone, he unwrapped her, leaving her clothes in a heap at her feet. He'd never felt so possessive—so protective as he did now, when she stood naked before him in the firelight, her body just now beginning to show signs that their baby was growing inside.

He bathed her slender neck with tiny, open-mouthed kisses. At the same time he traced the perfect curve of her back, stopping when he reached her rounded ass cheeks. He pulled her against him. "Feel what you do to me." His cock throbbed against her belly as he found her lips, plunged his tongue deep inside when she opened to him.

Her breathing shallow and rapid, she returned his kiss, tangling their tongues in a sensual dance. When he pulled away to steady his own racing pulse, she stroked his chest, teasing his nipples through his shirt and sweater. Apparently frustrated by the barriers, she jerked the shirt loose from his jeans. She slid her small hands up the skin she'd bared, circling his navel before moving up, stroking his flesh, tangling her fingers in his chest hair. Knowing she wanted him got him hotter, harder. His heart beat faster and his pulse raced.

He groaned. Got rid of the offending garments. Tossing them onto the floor on top of hers, he gave himself up to her loving hands. Her eager touch, the way she frankly admired every inch of his body, made it damn hard to go slow. Particularly when she slipped her hand inside his waistband and circled the tip of his cock with a searching finger.

"Let me get these pants off." He reached for his belt and loosened it then freed the button and zipper of his jeans.

Dani's breathing turned ragged when he stood before her, naked and completely still but for his throbbing cock. God but he was perfection, except for the colorful collection of bruises and lacerations that seemed to come with his job. With gentle fingers and searching lips, she explored every corded muscle, each inch of the silky, taut skin above his waist, soothing the small hurts when she came to them. She ran a finger around his navel first then bent and tongued it while she cupped his hot, hard sex in her hands.

Her mouth watered when she noticed the slick bead of lubrication at the tip of his cock. "May I?" she asked, accustomed to having him tell her what he wanted.

"Oh, yeah. Feel free." He looked down at her, heat in his eyes as she knelt and took his cock in her mouth. He tasted good, so good, she couldn't help licking him as she cupped his balls in both hands. If only he loved her…if only he'd say the words she'd sensed in his touch but never heard. Wanting to consume him, she took him deeper, swallowed.

"Stop that. If you don't, I'm going to come. And as good as your mouth feels on me, I want more from you tonight than a blowjob." His voice was ragged as he stroked her throat, tickled her earlobes. "I'm going to touch and taste every inch of your beautiful body. I'm not going to stop until you scream with pleasure." He set her on the bed and knelt, using his fingers to massage her toes, her instep. His hot breath tickled, made her want to beg him to stop…no, never stop. She wanted him to sink his teeth into her flesh, make her take every bit of pleasure he had to offer.

When he moved up her calves, she discovered there was a spot behind each knee that set her nerves on fire, made her want to scream for him, to ease the tension, to sink his big, beautiful cock in her throbbing pussy. But he kept on with his leisurely exploration, using his fingers to tease his way up her outer thighs.

He had to ease the fire he was building inside her. Soon. She looked down at him, on his knees before her, lighter strands of his hair catching the firelight as he bent his head, slid her legs apart and took her swollen clit between his teeth, his expression intent when he glanced up and met her gaze.

As though he knew she needed more, he found her with seeking fingers, slid them along her wet, hot slit. When he exhaled, even that slight motion of moving air against her sensitized flesh set her nerves on end. She wanted him to take her, force her body over the precarious edge where it teetered yet didn't plunge overboard. But he seemed in no big hurry, flicking her clit with his tongue then worrying it between his teeth while he finger-fucked her. "Please fuck me now," she whimpered when the pressure became too much to bear.

He stood and pulled her to her feet, dragging her hard against him. His heart pounded against her ear when she laid her head against his chest. His breath came in ragged gusts, and his rock-hard cock throbbed against her belly. When he let her go, she lay down, spread her legs. Her pussy clenched with anticipation as she watched him follow her down, cover her body with his own and kneel in the spot she'd made for him between her thighs.

"You want this, honey?" he asked, rubbing his cock slowly, tantalizingly just outside her hot, aching sheath. "Do you want me inside you as bad as I want to be there?"

"Oh, yes." She wriggled beneath him, trying to capture him.

He obliged her, capturing her wrists and holding them above her head with one big hand while he nudged her legs farther apart and positioned himself between her wet, throbbing pussy lips. With one quick, hard thrust he filled her to the hilt. He fucked her slowly, with smooth, deliberate flexing of his powerful hips. The pressure built inside her, threatened to overflow. She whimpered, moaned. "Please, Master."

"Please what?"

"Please...I need to come." Babbling now, out of control as sensations bombarded her, she begged him to take her hard and fast, push her over the edge into sexual oblivion.

"Soon, baby. Soon." He shifted onto his haunches, careful now as he'd been ever since learning she was pregnant to avoid having her take the bulk of his weight. Grasping her hips, he held her for the hard, fast thrusts she needed, controlling the depth of his penetration when she'd have killed to take all of him. She strained to take him deeper, clamped her inner muscles around him every time he pulled back.

"Take it easy. Squeeze me. Yeah, I know you want it all, but you're not getting it. Not as long as there's a chance I could hurt you or that little guy who's growing inside you."

She had to keep him in her, loving her. Powerful waves caught her, carried her to a world full of brilliant color, incredible sensation. She panted. Dug her fingers into his shoulders. Clamped her legs around his waist. Had to hold him there, take him with her.

He sank deep inside her, the first bursts of his hot semen triggering another climax. "That's right, baby, come some more." His muscles tensed as he held himself above her, sparing her his weight until finally he rolled over and collapsed at her side, spent. "I love you."

Still quivering in the aftermath she clung to him, his words echoing in her head. He couldn't have given her a better Christmas present if he'd tried.

* * * * *

Brand woke first, untangled himself from Dani and the twisted bed linens. He opened the nightstand drawer, found a brightly wrapped, tiny box that he set gently down beside her outstretched palm. "Merry Christmas," he whispered before he got up.

He hoped she'd sleep a while longer. She needed more rest now that she was pregnant, and God knew she'd gotten little enough of that last night. He smiled, remembering they'd awakened twice in the night to make love. He couldn't think of a Christmas present he'd have liked any better.

Looking in the mirror while he shaved, he glimpsed her standing behind him, still half asleep. She was naked, he noted with rising interest, except for the ruby and diamond pendant he'd left beside her moments earlier. Except for the small bulge of their child in her belly and her swollen, blue-veined breasts, she was as tiny as ever. More desirable than ever before.

You're an insatiable bastard. You had her three times last night, and you want her again now, first thing on Christmas morning.

Christmas morning. This was their first Christmas as a family. He fought off his attack of lust and tried to concentrate on scraping the stubble off his face while Dani looked on with loving amusement.

"Merry Christmas to you, too," she said, her eyes sparkling with happiness. "Close your eyes."

"I'll cut myself." Brand laid his razor down, let his eyelids droop.

Standing on tiptoe, she threaded a heavy chain around his neck and fastened the clasp. "Now open your eyes."

He looked down and saw a perfectly detailed, gold marlin suspended from a heavy rope chain. She must have searched all over to find it. "Thanks, honey." He turned around, held his arms out, closed them around her when she stepped into them.

"Do you like this?" he asked, nudging the pendant he gave her away from a luscious breast with his lips.

"Uh-huh. Do you like the little marlin?"

"Uh-huh. You'd better go get dressed. We can't be spending Christmas morning in bed while Dave waits downstairs to open his presents." Hating to let her go when what he wanted was to take her back to bed, he released her and patted her rounded backside.

It felt right, celebrating Christmas with Dani and Dave, anticipating the new member of the family who'd be with them this time next year.

* * * * *

Bountiful. Happy. Warm, in an icy wonderland. That was how Dani saw Christmas. The best Christmas she'd ever had.

She'd watched the two people she loved playing with Dave's new games, shared the traditional Christmas dinner Mrs. Blair had prepared. They'd wished Brand's Uncle Jimmy a happy holiday, talked on the phone with LeeAnn. She hadn't let fear or sadness intrude. There hadn't been room, not with all the happy, loving feelings in her heart.

The next day, after Brand left to work out with his team before the first playoff game on Sunday, Dani left the fantasy world, returned to reality. Alone, for Dave had joined a couple of school friends so they could compare loot, her thoughts took her back to Carendon. She was determined to handle the problems when they arose, no matter how hard it might be.

You're not a skinny kid with thrift store clothes. And you're certainly not a carbon copy of the woman who gave you life but not much else.

No. She was a woman people respected, not only because she was Brand's wife but because she was a successful homemaker, a good mother. A good person. She had as much right to hold her head high as anybody in the narrow-minded little town that bore Brand's name.

Why was it, no matter how many times she told herself she had no reason to be afraid of going home, doubts cropped up in her mind, undermined her confidence?

By the time several weeks later when she and Dave got on the plane to fly to Houston for the Super Bowl, Dani was a bundle of raw nerves.

Chapter Twenty

Still pumped up over the Marlins' win and his selection as Super Bowl MVP, Brand left the locker room and went to celebrate with Dani. Tonight, she'd be beside him when the league presented him with his spoils—the coveted ring, the MVP car, and of course the fat check that he and all the members of the team would get for being the best in the league.

Then they'd go home. He'd hang up his pads for five months and do his time satisfying the clients at Carendon, Brandon and Smith in Atlanta. Always honest with himself, he knew those clients could do better with a lawyer who devoted all his time to his practice. They chose him to represent them for one of two reasons. Some chose his family's venerable firm because of its name, him instead of one of the full-time associates because he was a Carendon. Others, probably more now since he'd won new accolades on the field this year, wanted the Marlins' star quarterback to handle their legal problems.

When Brand saw Dani and Dave elbowing their way through the crowd, he forgot everything in his haste to get to them. He elbowed his way through, oblivious to reporters shouting questions at him as he passed by.

"You were great, Dad." Dave rushed ahead of his mother, hugged Brand. "You got MVP and everything!"

"Hey, son, you're supposed to be watching out for your mom." Brand pushed through the crush of press people, caught Dani in his embrace. "Did you enjoy the game?" he asked her after lifting her high in the air, bringing her face level with his for an exuberant kiss.

Dani nodded, held onto his neck as he kept moving through the sea of bodies. "Marilee said to tell you they were going straight home as soon as they could make their way out of the stadium. She asked if you'd call LeeAnn later."

"I will. Were they okay?" Brand had tried but failed to find seats in one of the sky boxes, which would have been a lot more comfortable for Phil than the fifty-yard-line open air seats he'd managed to reserve for them.

"They're fine. LeeAnn sat with Dave and me for most of the game."

Brand was glad. He spied the row of black limousines that would take the team and their family members back to the hotel where they were all staying.

Tonight, they'd party until dawn. Tomorrow they'd return to Milwaukee. Next week they'd go back to Carendon, but he wouldn't worry about that now.

* * * * *

Until last summer, Dani had never been on an airplane. In the past month, she'd flown thousands of miles. Brand had insisted she and Dave come to all the playoff games, so she'd flown to Denver, Los Angeles and finally to Houston for the Super Bowl. Now they were airborne again, heading for Atlanta. There, they'd pick up a rental car and drive the thirty-some-odd miles to Carendon.

As the hours ticked away, Brand sensed her escalating discomfort. She put on a brave face, but he saw through it. When the pilot announced their imminent arrival in Atlanta, he held her hand, felt her tremble. "It won't be so bad, honey," he said, hoping he was telling the truth.

Dani loved him for trying to calm her fears, but she couldn't help worrying. She knew Brand, the football player. She remembered the teenage boy she'd fallen for so long ago. But she didn't know Brand, the socialite attorney. Didn't have a notion how he'd react if she made some social snafu. She didn't want him to suffer because he'd married her, hated the idea of messing up his image in staid, conservative Carendon, Georgia. She wouldn't fit in there, no matter what he said. "When do you have to go to work?"

"Monday. Uncle Jimmy wants to go over some cases I'll be handling for him. He and Laura are getting married in two weeks, and if I'm not going to make a fool of myself, I need all the help he can give me."

"All right." She pasted on a smile for Brand's benefit, felt a lurch as the big plane hit the runway and began taxiing toward the terminal. She tried to squelch a sense of foreboding. She'd come home, something she'd sworn she'd never do.

* * * * *

While Brand skillfully maneuvered the rented SUV around hills and curves on the narrow highway, Dave chattered nonstop. Not having seen where both his parents had grown up, he seemed enthralled with the redness of the Georgia clay, the bleak look of winter-naked gum trees with their pale bark. "Dad, are all the rivers reddish brown like this one?" he asked when they clattered over an old, metal grate bridge.

"It's not the river that's red, Dave. It just looks that way because of the clay riverbed. This is the Big Cat River. Our house is on the Little Cat. There's good fishing there, if you're interested."

Dave's face lit up. "Yeah. Roger's dad took us fishing in Tampa once, out on the bay. All we caught was catfish. Speed told us they weren't fit for humans to eat, so Roger fed 'em to his cat."

Brand explained the difference between saltwater and channel catfish. The talk of fish distracted Dani, made her forget to worry about where they were going until they'd almost reached the little town of Carendon. Then it hit her. The winding road, the school bus stops. Familiar redbrick houses set back from the highway, half hidden by towering trees even now when their branches were bare. Tumbledown sharecropper shacks perched closer to the road. Skeletons of cars and tractors mired in mud, worn garments hanging to dry on sagging clotheslines. Her throat tightened, and she twisted the leather handle of her red Coach handbag, an involuntary protest at the reminders of her past. Though she tried to hold it back, an anguished gasp escaped her lips.

"Don't do this to yourself, honey. You'll love the house, I promise." Brand reached across the seat, held her hand.

"Aren't we staying in the lodge? I mean, when we come here for visits from Atlanta?" Dani had assumed they'd spend most of their time in Georgia at Brand's condo in the city. "Surely we aren't going to stay with your mother."

For years, that cold, antebellum mansion had figured strongly in her nightmares. She'd been there only once, the day Eleanor had made it clear that Danny Sue Murdock would never belong in her hallowed world.

She couldn't breathe. Her heart constricted in her chest. A chill ran down her spine. Brand was taking her home, really home. Eleanor would tear them apart again. Trying to hold back tears, she stared out at the road, the same road she'd last seen from the smeared windows of a Greyhound bus that night she'd fled Carendon and all it stood for.

"No, baby, we're not going to my mother's." Abruptly, he turned off the highway onto a brick, single lane road whose gate stood open.

Where was he taking them? Dani searched for familiar landmarks, saw the old hunting lodge, the spot where she and Brand had spent their few, happy days of marriage so many years before. "I thought you said we weren't staying here."

"We're not. There's not enough room for all of us in that one-room antique. Look up ahead." Brand slowed the car, gave Dani her first look at a house built of native cedar and fieldstone, all graceful lines and angles that merged into a prepossessing whole.

"Our house. The one we talked about." Dani shed tears that she couldn't hold back. "When did you build it?"

"I arranged to have it built last summer. Before I found you and Dave. But since I'd told you we didn't have to come back here, I didn't say anything. I even had the contractors stop doing finish work on the interior. But when I knew we'd be staying here this spring, I had the place furnished as a surprise."

"It's beautiful." As soon as he stopped the car, Dani opened the door and got out, impatient to see if this part of their childish dreams really had come true. When Brand opened the front door and let them in, she could barely believe her eyes.

He'd remembered. There was the cozy fireplace, complete with a fan-shaped fire screen she'd wished for long ago. A big oak china cabinet full of the blue willow-patterned dishes she'd told him how much she liked. Brand hadn't neglected anything. Dani felt foolish for having so many reservations about coming home. She stepped into the kitchen and looked out the windows that faced the Little Cat River.

"You said you wanted to enjoy that view when you cooked," he said when he came up behind her, laced his fingers together over her expanding tummy.

"Where's Dave?"

"I sent him to wash up."

Dani opened the refrigerator, found it already stocked with food, noticed someone had set three places at the round oak table in front of a glass wall.

"I want you to be happy, honey." When he squeezed her, she felt a tiny bump against her ribs. "Our baby?" he asked, his tone reverent.

She nodded, smiled. "This is the first time I've felt him move."

"I'm glad he let me feel him, too. What's in there?"

"Food. Lots of it. Some looks as though it's ready to heat and eat."

Brand hugged her. "I asked Bessie to come out this morning, bring the food. She said she'd fix us some supper, leave it so we could heat it up. What do you think?"

"That I love you. I love this house, too." She turned, buried her tear-streaked face against Brand's broad chest. "You and Dave must be starving." They'd hardly eaten a bite of the food they'd been served on the plane.

"A little. Let's see what Bessie made." He took the containers as she handed them to him, lifted the lids one by one. "Looks good! Ham and red beans, it looks like, and rice. A fruit salad of some kind, and a bowl of greens. Cornbread. If I'm not mistaken, there will be a coconut cake under that dome on the table. Bessie must be trying to make points with Dave before she even meets him."

"Who's Bessie?" Dani imagined it more likely that the woman wanted to make points with Brand.

"Mother's cook. The best cook in the whole damn world."

"Your mother had her do all this?" Dani couldn't help hoping that Eleanor had decided to welcome them. All of them. But she wasn't ready to take that leap of faith. either.

"Not exactly. I called Bessie last week, asked her to buy some food and bring it out here. She volunteered to cook us a meal. Today's her day off at Mother's."

Dani hid her disappointment, busied herself in the kitchen, heating the food and setting the salad on the table. She was relieved when Dave came in, demanding his father's attention for a guided tour.

Later, as they ate, she listened to Dave's excited monologue about the fishing he hoped to do with Brand in the Little Cat River. If she'd believed in herself, believed in Brand, her husband and son wouldn't have lost twelve years they could never reclaim. Because of her own foolish fears, she'd cheated both of them.

Brand focused his attention on his son, talked with him as if he considered the boy his equal. She'd thought Brand would spoil Dave. Instead, his love and attention had changed Dave for the better, brought him out from the shy, quiet shell he'd lived in before he knew his dad.

For the sake of them all, she'd make herself fit in. She'd face everyone, even Eleanor, prove she deserved her place in her husband's privileged, charmed life. In Carendon, in Milwaukee. Anywhere life might take them.

* * * * *

It was with almost grim determination that Dani set off the following morning for Carendon's quaint old shopping district around the courthouse square. Brand had taken Dave with him, and was to drop him off at Trinity Prep on his way to work.

She'd been alone in their beautiful new home when the car dealership had delivered a second leased Mercedes and handed her the keys. Denied the excuse of having no transportation, she'd gone upstairs.

Determined to bolster her courage, she dressed carefully. The soft rose wool dress she chose flowed from a simple yoke, skimmed her expanding breasts and belly, fell in loose pleats to a crisp hem just below her knees. She put on her ruby earrings and the pendant Brand had given her. After discarding several gold bracelets, she decided to leave her wrists and fingers unadorned except for the tailored cuffs of her dress and her wedding band.

She took her mink coat off its hanger, gave it a fond look. No, it wouldn't do, not in Carendon, where the gentry had always seemed to disdain ostentatious displays of wealth. She put the fur back, chose a plain black coat and draped a silk scarf in tones of rose and gray around her neck inside the coat's shawl collar.

With hands gloved in soft gray leather, she clutched the steering wheel. Her nerves stood on end as she approached the ramshackle frame house where she was born. She stopped, put the car in park, stared out at the dismal scene she'd sworn she'd never face again. The old shack still looked the same, even after ten years of sitting vacant. Paint had long since flaked away, leaving raw wood grayed by years' exposure to the elements. One wall listed at a precarious angle, perhaps now a little more pronounced than she remembered.

Why on earth hadn't whoever owned it torn it down, wiped out the blight folks had always said it put on the town?

She opened the car door, started to get out. No, she wouldn't go any closer. Slamming the door shut, she laid her head against the leather seat. Inhaled the new-car smell as she stared at the place she'd never wanted to see again.

The porch still sagged. The rusted-out pickup truck she'd used as a playhouse when she'd been LeeAnn's age still rested on its side next to the house. Its carcass, bare when she'd left, was nearly hidden now by a tangle of kudzu vines that looked as if their next target might be the shack itself.

Except for the pervasive vines, nothing had changed. But Mama was long gone, Grandpa dead and buried. Maybe, after all this time, people would have forgotten them. Forgotten her.

Dani laughed, the sound bitter to her own ears. What on earth had she been thinking of, coming back here? If she couldn't forget, how could she imagine anyone else would have put the past to rest? No matter how hard she tried, she couldn't help thinking about the years when she'd shared this rotting shack with her mother and grandpa, sometimes with whatever man her mother had taken up with for more than a night's supply of alcohol.

She tore her gaze away, told herself this wasn't real. That it hadn't been her life since she'd walked away nearly thirteen years ago. She wasn't the skinny little girl who'd slaved away at the Dairy King and worn castoffs from the Salvation Army store. She'd made something of herself.

She'd done it. Not Brand. She'd been on her own, holding her head high and proud a long time before he'd burst back into her life. This shack wasn't home, wasn't where she belonged. It hadn't been for a long, long time.

Her confidence restored, she pulled back onto the highway, crossed the bumpy railroad tracks. Soon she reached the square, parked in one of the slanted, narrow spaces in front of the old courthouse. As she was locking the car, she noted the curious looks the foreign sedan received from passersby. Steeling herself against the stares that felt like needles prodding at her skin, she walked into a small, old-fashioned grocery store she remembered from her childhood.

With unhurried efficiency, she selected items from the list she'd made. Since Bessie had stocked the kitchen with all the real essentials, the list was short. Soon, she stood at the old-fashioned checkout counter, surprised to see that the clerk was one of her old classmates from Carendon High School.

"'Mornin', ma'am," the woman said, her manner servile. "Will this be all for you today?"

"Yes, I think so. Aren't you Dorcas Sutter?"

"Yes, ma'am. Do I know you?" Her shoulders slumped, Dorcas searched Dani's features, seemed unable to recognize her.

"We went to high school together. I'm Dani Carendon." Even now, Dani couldn't make herself volunteer her maiden name here, where it had once evoked certain contempt.

Dorcas' manner became even more obsequious. "I don't remember no Carendons goin' to school with me. Only one I knowed of was the boy, the one that run off to play football somewhere when he coulda had everything anybody could want right here in his old hometown. He didn't go to high school here, though. He went to some fancy school in Atlanta."

"Trinity. Our son's going to school there now. Brand's my husband." Dani smiled. Dorcas had come from a poor family, too, but her folks had been hardworking, honest sharecroppers. Still were, Dani guessed, taking in the woman's clean but worn white sweater, the faded cotton dress beneath it. She decided to take a chance. "I was Dani Murdock when we were in school."

Dorcas' pale, thin lips tightened, and her respectful manner evaporated into thin air. "Wasn't necessary to admit that, I knowed you was Danny Sue Murdock th' minute you said you was married to *him*. Everybody in town knows you snagged him, even if it were years after you used your mama's wiles to trick him into knocking you up. It almost broke old Mrs. Carendon's heart. You may priss around in your pretty clothes, brag about your new husband's name, but you'll always be trash to the decent folks around here."

She paused, glanced at the cash register. "That'll be forty-six dollars and twenty cents."

Her hands trembling, Dani extracted three twenty-dollar bills from her gray leather purse. When Dorcas handed her the change, she blindly stuffed it back in the purse, gathered the grocery bags in her arms. It was all she could do to hold back tears when she murmured the obligatory, "Thank you."

"By the by, you might want to do your shopping at the new mall about five miles the other side of your big, fancy house. That's where the folks that live in the new subdivisions go. Folks won't be knowing you there."

When she got back to the car, Dani let herself go. Tears ran down her cheeks as she mulled over the woman's parting suggestion. Though cutting, her words were almost kind, as though her old schoolmate woman wanted to save her the humiliation of showing her face where people would undoubtedly remember.

For a long time she sat, staring out at the cracked concrete statue of some Confederate officer that sat in the middle of the town square. Try as she might, she couldn't figure how to prove to the townspeople she wasn't the living reincarnation of her mother. Then it came to her. She didn't need to win Dorcas over.

She belonged with Brand now, in the circle of people he knew. Not with people like Dorcas, even though she might have hoped for friendship with the woman when they were kids if decent folks hadn't warned their kids to stay away from the town whore's daughter.

Dani was pretty sure Marilee liked her though she could just as easily have hated her because Brand treated her with consideration he'd admitted he never showed toward his former wife. It stood to reason other women who'd grown up with Marilee and Brand might like her too. How could she meet them?

Eleanor. No way. Dani shuddered at the thought. If she dared approach Brand's mother, the woman would eat her alive. But maybe...

The more she thought about approaching her mother-in-law, the more she felt that might be the only way. A voice in her head kept saying no, that she could do as Dorcas suggested and avoid Carendon like the plague, shop at the new mall instead. She could live without other women's friendship, concentrate on pleasing Brand and Dave.

But Brand needed a wife, not an ostrich. And Dave needed a mother who'd go to school functions, do things with him away from home, not just one who would provide him with chocolate chip cookies and brownies for his lunch box. As much as she might want to do it, there was no way Dani could write off this town or its people.

What was the proper thing to do? According to the etiquette guru who ran the website she'd studied so carefully, she should reach out to older relatives, make the first move toward establishing a relationship. Okay. She'd do it. Brand's mother couldn't do any more than toss her out on her backside. Could she? Dani started the engine, her decision made. She'd go see Eleanor Carendon, invite her out to the house to see Brand and meet Dave.

Chapter Twenty-One

Dani pulled away from the town square, her hands shaking against the leather-covered steering wheel. She tried hard to steady them as she drove down tree-lined streets, past stately homes that somehow seemed less intimidating now than when she was a kid. She pulled into the circular drive in front of the Carendon house, shut off the car and walked to the door. *Don't shake, Dani. Don't let her know you're scared stiff at the thought of seeing her.*

The melodic chime when she pressed the doorbell brought back memories of the only other time she'd been here, but she held her head high while waiting for someone to answer the door. Once inside, her coat and purse whisked away by a uniformed maid, she sat in the parlor, in the couch the maid had indicated.

Determined not to show fear, Dani held her hands in her lap. Looking around, she realized this was the same room where they'd talked—rather where Eleanor had talked and she'd listened—nearly thirteen years earlier. On the same exquisitely upholstered, hideously uncomfortable antique sofa where she'd perched back then, terrified dirt from her jeans would rub off on the cream brocade.

Apparently Eleanor didn't care a lot for change. Dani recalled the lace doily on the end table, the cut crystal ashtray she doubted if anyone would dare actually use for the purpose it had been designed. A familiar looking vase, filled with hothouse roses now, had held a mixed summer bouquet back then. She unclasped her hands, saw she'd dug her nails into the flesh so hard they'd almost drawn blood.

Before she saw Eleanor, she felt her presence and looked toward the foyer. Like the objects in her living room, the woman hadn't changed much. She was still tall and slender, her posture ramrod straight, short silvery hair impeccably styled. Her navy dress with its pristine white collar smacked of timeless good taste. The only sign of aging Dani saw was a papery fragility of the skin around Eleanor's eyes, mouth, and chin that hadn't been there thirteen years ago.

"You really didn't need to call," Eleanor said without preamble when she came into the room. "In a town this size, I'd have known you were here, even if my son hadn't phoned to tell me." She sat on the love seat across from Dani—the same spot where she'd sat years ago.

Dani doubted Eleanor's choice of seats was coincidence, but she forced herself to meet her steely gaze and smile politely. "Since I had to come into town for groceries, I thought I'd stop by, invite you to come see our new home and meet Dave."

"Did Brandon send you on this errand?"

Brand wouldn't have done anything so cruel. His mother had to know that. "No. He didn't. I thought you might want to see him, meet your grandson."

Eleanor smiled, a gesture that didn't make it to her cold, gray eyes. "I would like to see my son. I'd like to meet my grandson, in spite of the fact he's your child, too. You may tell Brandon he may bring David to the club next Saturday morning."

"You're welcome to come to the house before the weekend. I mean, it would be a more private place for you to meet Dave." Dani tried to sound confident, but she was afraid her mother-in-law had seen right through her.

"Perhaps we should talk, Dani." Eleanor spoke softly, but her voice had an edge of ironclad determination. "Would you care for tea?"

"That would be nice." Dani wondered if she'd be struck dead for lying.

Getting up, her back rigid, Eleanor crossed the room, tugged none too gently on a needlepoint bell pull. When the maid appeared, she ordered tea. Then she sat down again, this time closer to Dani on the other end of the tapestry covered sofa. Dani practically squirmed under the woman's close visual scrutiny.

"You're expecting another child." Eleanor looked a little green, as if she might have to excuse herself.

That gave Dani perverse pleasure. She smiled, touched her hand to her tummy. "In June. Brand didn't tell you?"

"He neglected to mention it. Was this child conceived before or after your most recent wedding?"

"After." The woman's rude question surprised Dani so much that she didn't think to reply it was none of her business.

Eleanor said no more until the maid had rolled in a silver tea cart and disappeared. Reluctantly, as if she thought her daughter-in-law might break the fine Limoges china plate and cup, she poured tea and set two small cakes on the plate beside it.

"You may add sugar, milk or lemon if you like," she said finally, taking her own cup and balancing it expertly on its saucer. "You'll enjoy Bessie's tea cakes, I'm sure."

"Thank you, Mrs. Carendon." Dani nibbled daintily at one of the cakes before assuring Eleanor they were indeed delicious.

"I am an honest woman, Dani. I didn't want my son to be married to you when you were children. I didn't want him to marry you last summer. Nevertheless, Brandon chose to make you his wife, not once but twice. Despite the embarrassment he has put me through, I love my son. Since his father was killed before he finished college, Brandon is all I have left."

"Both of us want you to know Dave and our new baby, when he's born." Dani set her plate back on the tea cart, wondered what Eleanor was going to propose.

Eleanor stood, motioned regally for Dani to follow. Above her rosewood writing desk, she pointed out, was the history of Brand's family. While Dani tried to follow the fine lines back to thicker branches, and finally to the trunk itself, Eleanor spoke reverently about a lineage somebody in her family had traced back to Norman England and beyond.

"As you can see, Brandon's father and I were distant cousins. Not close enough to remark on, of course. When we married, we brought together not only the two most important families in our fathers' law firm, but also the most prestigious branches of this family tree.

"I had hoped for many children to strengthen our line. But that was not to be. Brandon was the only one, born at a time when I had despaired of having even one son to carry on the Carendon name. The Brandon name died out with my father."

Eleanor returned, stiff-backed, to her spot on the sofa. Dani stared at the framed, yellowed family tree for a moment longer then turned back to her mother-in-law. She couldn't understand the woman's obsession with family trees and bloodlines. But then, considering the ancestors she'd known, Dani thought it logical that she had no burning desire to learn about the ones who'd lived and died before her time.

She paused, tried to think of something appropriate to say. "Did you want Brand to marry one of his cousins, the way you did?"

"No. There were none of suitable age for him. I wanted him to marry someone like Marilee, whose lineage was complementary to his own. A lady who could stand proudly beside him, give him fine sons."

"Brand has a fine son, Mrs. Carendon." Dani clenched a fist until she felt her nails dig into her palms again. She reminded herself she'd come here on a mission, and that mission wasn't to alienate Brand's mother any further than she had managed to do by her presence in Brand's life.

"That's what Brandon says, what the headmaster at Trinity tells me, too. I intend to see David takes his rightful place in society here. With my help, people will forgive him his maternal background, accept him as his father's son." Eleanor sat back, as if relaxing after a long vigil.

Dani held her tongue, seethed silently as she waited for the older woman's next pronouncement.

"Perhaps you're right," Eleanor said after a moment. "I shall accept your invitation for dinner tomorrow. I agree, I should meet my grandson before our outing Saturday at the club."

Eleanor rose, effectively dismissing Dani. She followed her mother-in-law into the entryway and retrieved her coat and handbag from the ever-present maid.

When she got back in her car, she guessed she'd escaped relatively unscathed.

* * * * *

At home, Dani changed into baggy sweats and put her groceries away. Her visit had gone less well than she'd hoped, better than she'd expected. She'd accomplished one thing, at least—getting Brand's mother to come here so Dave could meet the woman for the first time in the security of his own home.

Eleanor hadn't warmed to her, but Dani hadn't expected her to. She had been disdainful but coldly polite for the most part. Much like she'd acted the other time they'd met.

The old Dani had cringed and knuckled under, tossed away everything she'd wanted because she'd believed Eleanor's lies and half-truths. The woman Dani had become had stood up for herself, at least as much as she could and still achieve her goal.

She smiled, leaned back in a kitchen chair. Oh, no. She'd actually invited Brand's mother for dinner, and she hadn't a clue what to serve. For hours she planned and discarded menus. Once she'd settled on the food, she spent the rest of the afternoon cooking. Before Brand and Dave got home, she'd baked two cakes from scratch, made a fancy molded salad, and glazed a ham Bessie had left in the refrigerator.

Humming with pleasure at working in the kitchen of her dreams, Dani looked up from the spaghetti sauce she was stirring for tonight's dinner when Brand and Dave came in through the garage door. "Welcome home."

"Been busy, honey?" Brand took in the delicious aromas that wafted through the house. He kissed Dani then lifted the lid off the pot she'd been stirring, sampled the rich, red sauce. "I thought I smelled ham."

"You do. It's for tomorrow night. We're having spaghetti tonight." She wrapped her arms around his waist, tilted her head back. "Your mother is coming tomorrow for dinner, to meet Dave."

When Brand had called Eleanor last night, she hadn't indicated she would be visiting anytime soon. As a matter of fact, she'd given him the distinct impression she'd never set foot in the house he shared with his wife and son. "Tomorrow?"

"When I went to town for groceries, I stopped by and invited her. It wasn't wrong for me to ask her here, was it? I mean, I thought I should go, try to make peace with her."

Brand ran his hands over Dani's shoulders, felt the tension there. He'd never have asked her to face down his formidable mother alone, but he was damn proud of her for doing it. He rubbed her cheek, cupped her chin in his hand. "I'm glad you made the effort to go see her. I'm just surprised she took you up on your invitation. Can I help you get anything ready?"

"You might try to get home early tomorrow so you and Dave can visit with your mother while I get dinner ready," she said, her expression serious.

"How about if I ask Uncle Jimmy to bring Laura and come, too? That way, you won't have to knock yourself out twice, fixing fancy meals for family."

When Dani nodded, her lips curving into a smile, Brand silently congratulated himself for thinking of a way to diffuse a potentially explosive situation. "I'll call Uncle Jimmy now."

* * * * *

On the surface, the dinner party went well. Brand, however, wasn't so sure it had been a success, although Dani had acted the gracious hostess to his mother's queen of the manor. While he showered off sweat after his workout, he thought about the family gathering that had ended two hours earlier.

To be sure, his mother had charmed Dave. While she hadn't been overtly rude to Dani, he'd felt an eerie underlying coldness pervading the warmth of his home and family. He shrugged. Maybe, he thought, he was reading his mother wrong. He hoped so.

"Everything was perfect, honey," he told Dani a few minutes later when he stretched out in bed beside her. "God, I'm beat."

"Was your workout that hard?" She rolled onto her side and faced him.

"Not hard, just a pain to do at eleven at night. I like to hit the weights in the morning."

"Why don't you, then?"

"No time."

"Are you that busy at the office?"

"Uncle Jimmy has a heavy caseload. He expects me to take over a lot of it while he and Laura gallivant around the world."

"Certainly someone else can do some of the work."

"He's assigned as many cases as he can to other lawyers at the firm. I have to take my share, and I have to bone up enough so I don't come across sounding like the dumb jock I am." His gaze locked with hers. "I'm a hell of a lot better quarterback than I am a lawyer. And I don't like not being the best at anything I do."

"You will be. Your uncle wouldn't leave you with his cases if he didn't know you could handle them."

She had more confidence in him than he had in his own ability to jump in on the complicated cases Uncle Jimmy had dumped in his lap. Brand gathered her in his arms. Slowly, his tension drained. Their baby moved around, poked at him. Content, he splayed his hand across Dani's swollen belly, kept it there until they fell asleep.

* * * * *

The following Saturday, Brand needed to go to work, but he wasn't about to let Dani brave his mother and her friends alone, and he knew she'd promised to take Dave to the country club for lunch. He pushed the troublesome case he needed to prepare to the back of his mind, concentrated on finishing his workout.

At noon, he handed over his car to a grizzled black attendant and escorted his wife and son into the dining room of a small, exclusive club some of his long-dead ancestors had founded years before he was born.

Dave gawked at a huge pair of deer antlers on a wall above a large round mirror. "Awesome."

"Be quiet, Dave," Dani whispered.

She sounded stressed, and that bothered Brand a lot more than his son's childish comment. The opulently furnished clubhouse, with its huge fireplace and gleaming dark wood-paneled walls, might have been transplanted from some English castle. It actually did look pretty awesome.

He squeezed her arm, smiled down at her. "Dave's okay, honey."

They followed a stoop-shouldered waiter toward a table by the fireplace where his mother waited with Marge Sheridan and several others of her friends. Brand thought about retreat but reminded himself he was a grown man, not a kid Dave's age. His hand at the small of Dani's back, he stopped when they reached the table.

"Mother," he murmured as he held Dani's chair, motioned for Dave to sit between her and Eleanor. When he sat at Dani's other side, he introduced her and Dave to the other women.

She had to be at least as uncomfortable as Brand was. After less than fifteen minutes, he felt as though his mother and her cronies had skewered him on a pin, stuck him under a microscope, and zeroed in for a cell-by-cell examination.

"What?"

"Brandon, your mind is somewhere far away," his mother said.

Not far enough. Brand shot an apologetic look at Dani before turning to meet his mother's gaze. "I'm sorry, Mother."

"I asked when your new baby is due," Marge Sheffield said. Brand noticed, not for the first time, how his former mother-in-law's eyes got brighter when she thought she was making points at someone else's expense.

"June. We'll have been married ten months by then." Brand didn't bother to conceal his disgust at the accusation presented under the guise of polite conversation. He felt bad when he noticed Dani's gaze settle on the glazed carrots on her plate, saw her cheeks turn pink. Until he could engineer their escape, he'd try harder to be civil. Embarrassing his wife was the last thing he wanted to do.

Would Dave never finish the triple-chocolate mousse he'd ordered for dessert? Brand made a mental note to suggest to his son that he might skip dessert the next time he went out to eat with his grandmother and her friends. He'd taken all he could of the company, felt the same undercurrents he'd thought he felt when Eleanor had come for dinner—undercurrents that tugged less subtly today when she had her cronies in tow.

"Mother, I'd like to speak to you in private," he said as they got ready to leave.

Eleanor gave him a questioning look, but she followed him to a deserted alcove in the clubhouse foyer. "Couldn't this have waited? It's rude to exclude others in one's party from conversation."

Brand struggled to hold onto his temper. "It was rude for you and your friends to make my wife uncomfortable too, but that didn't stop you. I intend to."

"I don't know what you're talking about, Brandon."

"Yes, you do. Mother, I realize I've made you unhappy about many of the choices I've made. It's possible I've intentionally exaggerated those choices, done some things because they make you angry. But you've made me unhappy too, by refusing to accept the way I want to live my life, the woman I've chosen to share it. I'm willing to bury the hatchet, respect your feelings, let you enjoy Dave, LeeAnn, and the other grandchildren Dani and I may give you."

Eleanor looked him in the eye. "I sense conditions I'm certain I won't like."

Determined to get his point across, Brand sat down, drew his mother beside him on the padded window seat. "One condition, Mother. Accept Dani as my wife. Make certain your catty friends know you accept her. Stop the sniping, stop dredging up her past. It's my past, too. A past I'm not proud of, one that contains twelve lost years I'll always hold you responsible for."

"And if I don't accept your terms?" Defiance flashed in Eleanor's cold gray eyes.

"I'll write you off. You won't see me or my children. I won't have a mother. And you won't have a son. Think about it." Brand got up, strode across the room where Dani and Dave were waiting.

* * * * *

Days merged into weeks, weeks into months. Brand looked up from the papers on his desk. He raised his hand, stroked his brow. It was a beautiful day, and he longed to be back home, enjoying this first day of May with Dani.

She'd been wonderful, never complaining about the long hours he had to spend here at the office. Many a night he'd gone home too late for dinner, stripped, thrown on sweats, hit the Nautilus equipment in his home gym then staggered into bed, too tired to do more than give her a quick kiss before he fell asleep.

Other nights, he'd stayed in town and fit in his workout at the health club there. A lot of those nights, Dani drove in to meet him for one of many business-social functions he couldn't avoid. She'd played chauffeur to Dave too, determined her son wouldn't miss out on the juvenile social life that abounded at Trinity Prep and the Carendon Country Club.

Although she never complained, Brand sensed she still felt isolated, outside the mainstream of the lifestyle he'd known all his life. She'd withdrawn into a quiet, polite surface of herself at the banquets and charity balls they'd attended. Dave had even commented, asking him why his mom dropped him off at social functions but didn't stay and socialize with the other boys' mothers.

Briefly, Brand wondered if his mother had ignored his ultimatum, if she'd failed to set her stamp of approval on Dani. Because she hadn't mentioned having had any unpleasant encounters at the club or in town, he told himself his worries on that score were probably unfounded.

Frowning at the work that still kept him prisoner, he tossed his pen down on the legal pad where he'd been scribbling notes, tried to formulate a logical argument in favor of his client's position. For all he'd managed to get done today, he might as well have stayed home. Thank God Uncle Jimmy would be back in another two weeks.

Chapter Twenty-Two

Two more weeks.

On the wooden deck outside the master suite, Dani stared out at the rolling Little Cat River. With spring's bright new growth, the place looked much as it had when Brand had brought her here thirteen years ago. Smiling, she savored bittersweet memories, memories of two happy teenagers learning the mysteries of their eager bodies on the grassy riverbank.

She looked down at the bulging mound that was their child. She missed Brand. It had been days since he'd held her. Weeks since he'd reached for her at night, wanting her. His law practice kept him so occupied he could barely find time to keep his magnificent body honed for the coming football season, let alone find time for her.

When she took a look at herself in the mirror, though, she couldn't blame him. She felt fat, ungainly, much too ugly to compete with the elegantly slender socialites who stared her down at the parties they had to attend. She sensed they thought she was beneath them, read scorn in their spiteful glances. A tear made its way down her cheek.

She didn't have time for this self-pity party. Determined to think positive, she got up and went inside. Glancing at the calendar she'd had to start using to keep up with her obligations, she realized she'd have to hurry, pick Dave up from a birthday party he'd been invited to by the Granger boy whose parents lived next door to Eleanor. After struggling to get the seat belt fastened over her belly, Dani drove out onto the highway toward Carendon. She let out a sigh of relief when Dave came outside at the first sound of her horn.

"Hi, Mom. I thought Dad was going to come get me," Dave said as he climbed in and fastened his seat belt.

"Your dad's still at work. He had his secretary call and ask me to pick you up. How was the party?" Dani noticed Dave seemed unusually preoccupied.

"Fine. Uh, Mom. Can I ask you something?" He twisted his hands together as he wriggled on the seat.

Dani smiled as she turned the car back onto the highway toward home. Then she noticed her son's agitated state. "Sure. What's wrong?"

"Is it…well, is it unusual to have a baby when you're as old as you are?" Dave asked, his voice unsteady.

"Not really." Dani's hackles rose. What had someone said to Dave? "Why?"

"Well, Mrs. Granger said something that made me wonder," Dave said, his manner evasive.

"What did she say, Dave?"

"Uh, well…well, she said no lady with a twelve-year-old kid would go and have another one on purpose, or somethin' like that." Dave hung his head. "Why'd she say that?"

Dani could imagine what else Susan Granger might have said, things Dave wouldn't repeat for fear of hurting her. "I don't know. I can't explain how other people feel. I did plan to have this baby, though. Your dad and I both want it."

"Then you didn't get the baby so Dad would marry us again?"

Her heart constricted at the anguish she heard in her son's voice. So that was what Mrs. Granger had intimated. That she'd deliberately gotten pregnant to trap Brand into marriage. She tried to hold onto her temper as she stopped the car, got out and followed Dave into the kitchen.

"Sit down, Dave." Dani didn't know what, or how much to tell him. "Do you know how babies are made?" she asked, her voice almost a whisper.

"Like puppies and kittens, I guess. Except it takes longer." Dave's face turned red, he stared at the floor.

"It takes nine months, give or take, and it takes a month or so for a man and woman to be certain there's a baby on the way. How long was it between the time you found your dad and the time he and I got married?"

"Less than a week. I'm sorry, Mom. You didn't know I was coming when you and Dad got married the first time either, did you?" Dave sounded so hopeful she almost cried.

"Yes, we did." There was no point in lying. Not when so many people in Carendon knew the only reason Brand had eloped with her thirteen years ago was because she'd been pregnant. "Dave, I know that's not something to be proud of, but it isn't all that awful, either. Lots of couples, particularly ones as young as your dad and I were then, find themselves getting married after they learn a baby's on the way."

"Then you are poor white trash, just like everybody here says." Dave spat out the hurtful words as tears welled up in his eyes. "You really did use me to trap Dad. I hate you."

She sat, stunned, as her son shoved his chair away from the table. Her mind whirling, she tried to figure out where this had come from. Susan Granger? Probably, but Dani doubted she was the only one to have made snide comments. She recalled how Dave had been acting a little withdrawn lately, how she and Brand had attributed the new attitude toward his being a pre-teen, not the little boy he'd been just a short time ago. Susan might have said something that triggered the outburst, but it had been coming. She should have realized it.

First things first. She had a feeling her son was going to do something foolish, and she had to stop him. "Listen to me, Dave. No matter what, your dad and I both wanted you. We were awfully young, and we may not have been married, but we were in love."

"You're nothing but trash, and I'm sorry I'm your kid." He slammed the kitchen door on his way outside.

Numb, she watched Dave take off down the path toward the dock. She'd lost her son. No, the Susan Grangers, the Eleanor Carendons, even Dorcas Sutter and people like her, had stolen Dave, seduced him away to a world where she couldn't go.

They'd used the dirtiest of dirty tricks, the one weapon she couldn't defend against. The weakness of a couple of lonely kids who'd fallen in love, let their hearts and bodies take them where it hadn't been wise to go. She started to cry but fought back the tears. No. She wouldn't sit back any longer, take whatever Eleanor Carendon and her mean-spirited cronies decided to dish out.

She was strong. She'd survived hardships those women never dreamed of, rough times that would have broken most of them. She'd come out on top, had her son and kept him. Against the odds, she'd gotten an education, found a decent job. At the same time, she'd raised Dave alone for eleven years, until Brand came back on the scene. She'd taken damn good care of him, too. Dave had no reason to hate her.

Dani straightened her shoulders, held her head high. She'd done nothing to be ashamed of, nothing at all. She'd set Dave straight, show every small-minded witch from Dorcas Sutter to Susan Granger, even Brand's own self-important mother. She was no doormat for them to stomp into the ground. Upstairs, in the bedroom she shared with Brand, she looked out the window toward the dock that jutted out over the Little Cat. There was Dave, staring down at the water. He'd be all right.

But the walls were closing in on her. The house Brand had built, the one they'd dreamed of together years ago, suddenly seemed small. The fresh spring air hung around her, as though waiting for a breeze to come along and ruffle the still curtains at the windows. She took a deep breath of that pine-scented air, looked down at the setting she'd always associate with her and Brand and those few hopeful, happy days they'd had so long ago.

"I've got to get away." Her words echoed off the walls, reverberated in her head. Yes. She had to take a few days for herself, get out of this town for a short respite. Breathing room. That's what she needed. A getaway. Not forever. Not for long. Just for a week. Even a day would work. She had to figure out whether she could carve a niche for herself in this place that so often seemed to hold nothing for her but pain, the residue of unhappy memories. She had to decide whether she wanted to try.

Determined to escape, she packed one small bag. Milwaukee, that's where she'd go. She'd give herself the chance to think things out away from Brand. Dave, too, even though it would nearly kill her to leave him. She'd get away from the people she loved as well as the townspeople who couldn't see her except in the context of her contemptible relatives and childish mistakes she'd made. She'd stay just a few days, fly back before the weekend. Hopefully by that time Dave would realize she was okay. That one foolish mistake hadn't turned her into an evil person.

Picking up the phone, she watched her son through the window while she called for an airline reservation then tried to reach Brand. Disappointed when his secretary told her he'd gone to see a client, she tried his cell phone but got no answer.

Downstairs, she found a pen and paper, sat at the kitchen table. She wrote a note, scrunched the paper in her hand, started to write again. No. She'd left a note for Brand thirteen years ago. She wouldn't do that to him again. She'd tell Dave where she was going, and call Brand again as soon as she got to Milwaukee. Now, she'd stop by his mother's house, ask her to come here, check on Dave. While she was there, she'd tell Eleanor where she was going, when she'd be back. And she'd tell the woman a few things she should have said long ago instead of trying to keep the peace.

"Dave!" she called out as she walked to her car.

"Yeah?"

She should have scolded him for his rudeness, but she didn't have the heart. "I'm going to Milwaukee for a few days."

"So?"

"So you're my son. I love you very much. That never stops. I'm going to take a few days because I need them. Because..." She wouldn't burden him by telling him how much he'd hurt her. "You talk with your father about this and see what he has to say. Then we'll talk some more when I get back. Your grandmother will be here in a little while. Stay in sight of the house and be good for her."

Dave dug the toe of one sneaker into the gravel on the drive, his expression still angry but also, Dani thought, a little sheepish. "Okay," he said as if he didn't care, and when she tried to give him a kiss and hug, he stiffened perceptibly.

* * * * *

Her heart ached. She loved Brand so much, she couldn't bear to make him suffer. Would he understand she needed space, time, or would he think she'd deserted him again? She'd try to make him understand, let him know she still loved him, that she'd be back as soon as she made sense of her battered emotions.

On the way to Eleanor's, Dani pondered decisions she'd have to make. Hard decisions, considering she loved Brand with all her heart, loved Dave and wanted the best for him, loved the unborn baby who deserved both his parents. She'd need to decide, too, if she was willing to stay here and face down people who couldn't or wouldn't see her for what she'd made of herself, not what her mother had been.

She stopped in front of her mother-in-law's house, got out of the car, squared her shoulders. She marched to the door. This time she didn't ask to see Eleanor. She told the maid to take her to her mother-in-law and followed while the woman did her bidding.

"Eleanor." Somehow the sunroom seemed friendlier than the stiff parlor where she'd talked with the woman before.

Brand's mother looked up from the embroidery on her lap, stared at Dani as though she'd suddenly grown two heads. "I beg your pardon…"

"I'm certain you do. Dave's at home alone. He's understandably upset, considering Susan Granger told him today I used this baby as well as him to trap his father. She passed along her opinion that I'm nothing but trash, along with other hurtful information, most of which wasn't true."

"What?"

"You heard me. It was Susan Granger who said the hurtful words, but we both know you're the one who's kept the gossip going, made certain no one in this town ever forgets the story of how you got Brand off the sinful hook set by the kid who belonged to the town drunk. You've let those same people know how you hated it when we got back together, too." Dani kept her voice low, but she was certain from the pallor that crossed Eleanor's face that her message came through loud and clear.

The older woman got up, looked across her yard toward the estate where the Grangers lived. "I haven't spoken with Susan Granger in months," she said.

"You haven't had to. You've made your feelings clear at the country club, the grocery store, God only knows where else. I'm sick of it, and Brand's had it with your petty nonsense."

Eleanor whirled around, met Dani's gaze. "You can't talk to me like this. And you can't speak for my son."

"No, but he can speak well enough for himself. I know he's told you he expects you not only to treat me and Dave with respect, but to make sure everyone else does."

"I can't control what others think or do." Eleanor's mouth had a stubborn set to it, and her eyes burned through Dani as if she weren't there.

Somehow the woman's haughty expression made Dani angrier than her words. "You don't give yourself anywhere near enough credit," she said, her tone deliberately sarcastic. Then she sobered. "This has gone entirely too far. It's touched my son. Hurt him. If it doesn't stop, it's going to touch this baby who's not even born."

"Surely you don't think I would intentionally hurt David, or an unborn baby whose only sin is that he will be—"

"My child as well as Brand's?" It was all she could do to keep her tone halfway civil. "That's no sin, just like it wasn't my sin for me to have been born to my mother. I couldn't help it, any more than this baby will be able to help having me for his mother."

"The sins of the father—"

"Please. I know all about having to live with the results of my mother's sins." Dani wasn't about to let Eleanor take the upper hand, not this time. "Still, those sins didn't become mine—and my sins won't become my children's, either."

"You're the one who became pregnant at sixteen. Surely that wouldn't have happened if you'd had decent parents—a good home."

"Really? Your son had as much to do with me getting pregnant as I did. I'm sure you'd say *he* had a good home. Caring parents. All the advantages I didn't have."

Eleanor looked as though she might explode. Dani checked her watch, decided she'd pushed enough. She had a plane to catch. She moved toward the door, turned, met her mother-in-law's gaze. "I'm flying to Milwaukee for a few days. Can I count on you to go check on Dave? I couldn't reach Brand before I left."

The older woman nodded, followed her to the door. When she looked back at the house from the street, Eleanor was still standing in the doorway, watching. Then Dani headed for the airport, doing her best not to think about her mother-in-law or what she might say to Brand and Dave.

* * * * *

When Brand got home, he didn't see Dani's car. He stuck his head inside and called out. Silence. A chill ran up his spine in spite of the warm breeze. What the fuck was wrong? The baby? He checked his cell phone. He'd missed her call, but she hadn't left a message. Maybe she left a note inside.

He went inside and set his briefcase down, looked everywhere he could think of that she might have left him a message. Nothing. Where the hell was she? From his bedroom balcony, he spotted Dave. He'd thought the boy would have gone with Dani. Since he hadn't, he damn well should have been studying for final exams instead of sitting on the dock and staring at the Little Cat. Since he wasn't with her, though, maybe Dave knew where Dani went.

"Fuck." He shed his suit, put on shorts and an old football jersey and hurried outside. "Where's your mom?" he asked when he sat on the bench beside his son.

"She said she was going to Milwaukee. I don't care. Do you?"

Brand could see Dave had been crying. Still, the boy's disrespectful reply infuriated him. "Damned right I care. If you said or did something to upset your mother, you're going to regret it. Come on. I want to know exactly what's going on."

"She took off about an hour ago." Dave looked his father in the eye, his expression belligerent. "I don't care. You shouldn't care either. She's nothing but trash. She used me to get you to marry her. Everybody says so. She admitted it."

Chapter Twenty-Three

~

"What the hell are you talking about?" Brand felt like grabbing his son, shaking him until his teeth rattled.

"She admitted you both knew she was going to have me before you all got married the first time. Mrs. Granger said so, but I didn't believe it 'til Mom told me it was true. Dave sounded so self-righteous, Brand wanted to shake him.

"So you're mad because we weren't nice, because we let ourselves get you on the way before we stood up in front of a preacher?" Brand's fingers itched to strangle Susan Granger. Maybe he would.

Dave fixed his gaze on the toes of his Nikes, fidgeted as though ants had crawled up his ass. "I'm not mad at you. Boys take what they can get. Nice girls don't let them. Trashy girls do. Mrs. Granger said."

"Susan Granger's full of—" Brand caught himself before saying what he meant. "She's nuts. I never went around, taking what I could get from every girl willing to dish it out. And your mom didn't sleep with me intending to get pregnant, either. We were young and impatient, damn it. We made love, and you just plain happened. I'd have wanted to marry her even if you hadn't been on the way."

He paused, gentled his tone. "Your mom grew up poor, but she was never trash. I guess her mom and grandpa fit most people's definition of poor white trash, but your mom never wanted to live the way they did. She worked hard from the time she wasn't much older than you. Then we met, and we fell in love."

A sharp, sudden pain hit Brand in the gut. He and Dani had been incongruous soul mates, both lonely and a little isolated from the other kids in Carendon. He'd been the only child of rich older parents who rarely spoke to each other, she the unwanted daughter of a woman whose main interest in life apparently had been in getting her next drink. Their home lives had been dissimilar but equally dysfunctional.

Together, they'd fought loneliness, and in the process they'd fallen in love. Dani had made him feel complete, the way no one else ever had. She still did. He looked at their son, fought the tightness in his throat. "Your grandmother—my mother—chased your mom away. She sent her out in the world alone with no money and not much of an education. But Dani made it.

"She had you, kept you, loved you. It had to have been damned hard for her to finish school and take care of you at the same time, but she did it. Did a good job, too. She took good care of you until you found me. The way I see it, you should be damn proud of your mom. And damn ashamed of yourself."

"But Ms. Granger said Mom trapped you into marrying her twice. Once because I was going to be born, the second time because she wouldn't let you have me unless you took her, too." Dave's shoulders drooped. Brand didn't know whether to reassure his son or throttle him. The second option held more appeal. He needed to strike out, hurt someone for hurting the woman he loved.

He loved Dani, and he had no intention of losing her again. "Come inside. I have to find your mom." He resisted the impulse that made him want to jerk Dave roughly to his feet. Instead, he stood and waited for his son to precede him up the pathway to the house. A house that seemed deadly empty when Dani wasn't there.

In the kitchen, Brand ordered Dave to sit. He picked up the phone. The second call he made to airline reservation agents paid off.

"She's already on a plane to Milwaukee. I'm going to grab the first flight I can get, go to her. I hope to hell I can talk her into giving us another chance." Furious, he got up, headed upstairs. Turned, saw Dave still sitting at the kitchen table. "Get a move on. Grab your toothbrush and some clean clothes. *You* are going to stay with your grandmother."

As he tossed some jeans and shirts into a duffel bag, Brand punched out his mother's phone number. When no one answered, he let out a string of curses.

A few minutes later, Dave cowered against the passenger door of Brand's car, as if he thought Brand might hit him at any minute. His fear wasn't far off the mark. Brand's temper flared, his control wavered. "Your mother loves you, although after you talked to her the way you did, God knows why. What were you thinking? That Mike Granger's idiot mother is some kind of oracle, that whatever bullshit she spits out is fact? I can't believe you're so gullible."

He shut up, pulled into the drive at his mother's house, turned off the ignition. "Get out," he snapped. "And get inside." In four long strides, he reached the door and punched the bell. No one answered. What the fuck was going on? He rang again then glanced at Dave. From his expression, Brand figured he was terrified. He deserved to be afraid, as afraid as Brand was.

He pushed the doorbell again but didn't let it go until he heard the screech of tires. His mother's Cadillac, fishtailed to a stop behind his car, practically ran it down. "Brandon, thank God you're both here," she gasped, practically running to get to them. "You look awful. Tell me what's going on."

"We'll talk, Mother. Count on it." Brand turned to Dave. "You, get upstairs. Find my old bedroom, go in there and don't even think about leaving until your grandmother says you can." His son's dark eyes glittered, as if tears were going to flow at any minute.

"Dani's gone to Milwaukee," Eleanor said when Brand turned back to her. "I was on the way to your place when I saw you coming this way. Brandon, you drive much too fast."

He planned to drive even faster when he took off for the Atlanta airport. "Dani called you?"

"She came here. Threatened me. Made all sorts of ridiculous accusations." Eleanor moved into the living room, sat down.

"Good for her. I thought I made it clear what you had to do if you wanted any kind of relationship with us." He paced around the elegant room, feeling like a caged lion. "You have until I bring Dani home to set Susan Granger and all your other friends straight. And to persuade my son how much you care for and respect his mother."

Eleanor sniffed. "I have never said anything in David's presence that would make him think I dislike Dani."

Taking the only halfway comfortable chair in the showcase room, Brand explained what Dave had told him about his confrontation with Dani. "I'm going after her. I pray I can persuade her to come back, but I wouldn't blame her if she refused to set foot in this damn town for the rest of her life."

"If she won't…"

Brand loved Dani. He'd loved her since they were kids. Unconditionally. She loved him that way, too. He had to go to her, let her know what he hadn't said in words, reveal emotions he'd buried under layers of resentment and distrust. He hoped to hell he hadn't waited too late to come to his senses.

His emotions raw, Brand met his mother's gaze. "If she won't come back here, I'll take her wherever she wants to go. Dani's my life. Nothing else matters except her and our children. I'm going to give her our son back, minus the crazy ideas folks have put in his head about his mom. You're going to help me do that, if you want to be part of our lives."

Brand held his mother's gaze, refused to look away when she leveled a blank stare at him. Then she nodded and her expression softened visibly. "What do you want me to do?"

When he looked into her eyes, Brand thought he saw love. Could his mother care, beneath the meanness and snobbery she'd nurtured so long? Had he opened her heart when he'd told her Dani was his life, made her care in a peripheral sort of way for the woman he loved?

He spoke, conscious of the tightness in his throat. "I want you to give my son some insight into family loyalty. And if I can get Dani to come back, I want you to get to know her, learn to love her."

When he got up to leave, Eleanor followed. For the first time in longer than Brand could remember, she reached up, drew his face down, brushed a self-conscious kiss along his jaw. "I'll set your son straight. Go bring Dani home. You may not believe it, but I do love you, Brandon."

If he hadn't seen the glistening hint of moisture in his mother's eyes, he'd have had a lot of trouble believing her parting words.

* * * * *

Fish jumped in the crystal clear water of Lake Marion, stirred the water by the dock. Irises of a dozen or more colors had sprung to life beneath trees sporting pale, new leaves. Most people, Dani imagined, would be rejoicing at nature's rebirth after a long, icy winter.

But she missed the red-gold hues of autumn, the stark ice and snow that had followed—vivid reminders of those first days she'd spent here with Brand and Dave. The joys they'd shared, learning to be a family.

With difficulty she knelt, felt the early morning dew against her bare knees. She sniffed a golden iris, the loveliest of the flowers under a towering maple tree. Nothing. It had no fragrance. Even the Christmasy smell of the blue spruce trees seemed faint, muted. Suddenly tired, she heaved her heavily pregnant body up, went inside and climbed the stairs to the master suite.

She'd never felt so alone. Not since the lonely months before Dave's birth had she been without another soul to cherish, to nurture. Somehow, the baby growing below her heart seemed unreal, the remnant of a fantasy she'd nurtured in vain. A dream that Brand would come to love her again, as much as he had when they were kids.

Maybe, like people said, she *had* trapped Brand with sex. She turned, looked at the big bed where they'd shared so many sensual pleasures. Where he'd taught her about the ecstasy that lay in her submission…his mastery. She'd never felt so secure, so confident in herself, as when she'd lain in the warmth of his embrace. She'd been certain Brand had felt it too, that mystical bond that formed between them every time they touched, even if he seldom put his emotions into words.

But all the magic in the world beneath the sheets couldn't compensate Dani for the pain she'd felt that awful moment yesterday afternoon when she realized she'd lost her son's love.

* * * * *

Exhausted physically as well as emotionally, Brand got off the flight he'd had to wait six hours to connect with in Chicago, strode through the Milwaukee airport. Eight in the morning. Dani had been gone thirteen hours. Thirteen hours, plenty of time for her to decide he wasn't worth the heartache she'd suffered because of him, his mother — fuck it, he might as well claim blame for the whole damn town.

At one of the kiosks, he grabbed a coffee, swore when it scorched his throat. After he rented a car, he tried to relax, slow down, but he made the trip home from the airport in forty minutes. Another rental car sat at an angle in the driveway of the condo, confirmed this was where Dani had come.

Quietly, he turned his key in the lock, let himself in. She'd be upstairs in their bedroom. He didn't know how he knew, only that he did. He slipped off his shoes, went silently up the stairs. *Please God, don't let me be too late to let her know she's my whole damn world.*

There she was, staring out the window. He came behind her, whispered her name.

Her breath caught, the sound a muted echo of the way she always sighed in the afterglow of their lovemaking. He reached out, sifted his fingers through her windblown sable hair, stroked along the curve of her neck, down her arm. Laced her fingers with his and brought them to his lips.

She sighed again, this time louder, moved toward the window as if she were in a dream world. "Baby, why'd you go?" He spoke softly, intent on coaxing her back from a place she must have found somewhere deep in herself, a place where she'd feel no pain. He dropped soft kisses in her hair, along the sensitive nape of her neck, laid his hands over where their unborn child rested, oblivious to his parents' pain.

"Brand." His name on her lips was a silken plea, for what he didn't know, was afraid to guess. Part entreaty, part rebuke? Need? She tugged his hands up, pressed them against her swollen breasts. She still wore his ring, as he wore hers. Two hands, fingers entwined, bound by circles of gold and precious stones.

He held back the desire that rose when he tasted her satin skin, smelled the mixture of apple blossoms and musk that was uniquely Dani. At her touch, he trembled, answered her mute plea, fondled her full breasts that soon would nourish the child they'd made.

As if she were in a trance, she turned, buried her face against his pounding heart.

"Dani. God, Dani, I love you. Don't ever leave me again." The words came out ragged, torn straight from his heart.

She looped her arms around his neck, tilted her head back, met his gaze with eyes that brimmed with tears. "I love you, too. So much. Please don't ever let me go."

The fear that had his chest tight lifted, left him lightheaded with relief. "I won't," he promised, tightening his hold on her, providing the physical closeness he sensed she needed. Hell, he needed it, too. Needed to bury himself inside her, remind her in the most elemental way that they were one. Inseparable no matter what obstacles stood in their way. "You're not going anywhere, ever again, unless we go together."

Words weren't enough. Brand knew it. She needed — they needed — an affirmation of that elemental attraction that had brought them together years ago, drawn them back to each other more even than the son they both loved. She craved to feel the desire he'd suppressed too long, not as much out of concern for her pregnancy or because of demands made on him at work as to put some distance between them. To deny the depth of his emotional dependence on the tiny angel who'd captured his heart. Who'd become as necessary to his life as the air he breathed.

He wouldn't deny it anymore. Ever. Gently he skimmed his hands over her ripe breasts, her rounded belly, stopping to feel the thump of his baby's strong, insistent movement against his palms. He moved lower, lifting the silky fabric of her only garment and claiming the warm flesh of her inner thighs, the dampness of her swollen pussy as he brought the nightie up and off.

She craved more than the love he'd never again let her doubt. More than the gentle vanilla sex they'd shared because he'd given in to what he'd told himself was fear for her safety and that of their unborn child. God help him, he wouldn't deny her again. "Lie down on our bed. First I'm going to spank you for giving me the scare of my life. Then, baby, I'm going to love away the hurt. I'm going to show you so much pleasure you'll never dare think of leaving me again."

Dragging his keys from his pocket, he opened the toy closet, chose a flogger with braided silk strands that would sting but never mar his darling's lush ass cheeks. And restraints he looped around the bedposts in case she needed to feel as well as sense she was under his control.

As he undressed he watched her watch him, felt her admiring gaze when he shucked his jeans and briefs. Her hands went over her head, and she slid her legs apart. Yeah. His loving sub was begging to be controlled, and it got him incredibly hot to bind her willing body to the bed for their mutual pleasure.

Once she was confined, he knelt at her side and deliberately let the strands of the flogger slide along her silky skin, over her full breasts, her growing belly, the smooth, pale mound she still kept waxed at his command. He moved the handle in a slow arc, watching her expression turn rapt as the knotted ends bounced off her clit and swollen pussy lips. "I think you like this too much."

When she whimpered and spread her legs farther apart he stopped, lifted the flogger and laid several stinging blows to the insides of her thighs. At the first sign of redness, he stopped, tossed the flogger away and brought his lips down to soothe the little hurts away. More than ever before, he wanted never to hurt her, only to bring her to the heights of sexual pleasure.

Mindful of her pregnancy, he loosened her bonds and positioned her on her side, knees raised, pillows positioned to support her belly and legs. Lying on his side behind her, holding her steady, he sank his aching cock into her sweet pussy and fucked her gently. When she'd have had him fuck her harder, deeper, he resisted, stimulating her instead with hot words of love and sex...and a gentle finger in her ass, moving in tandem with the slow motion of his hips, fucking her gently. With love.

When she moaned with satisfaction he gave her the knuckle of a finger on his free hand, absorbed the mild discomfort from her bite along with her pleasure.

God but he'd been a fool and almost lost her. Never again, he swore as he gathered Dani in his arms and held her.

* * * * *

When Dani woke up, it was dark. She'd had a dream. A wonderful dream.

Determined not to wallow in self-pity, she tried to get up, but she couldn't. Something warm and heavy bound her to the bed. She ran her hand over a muscular, softly furred arm. A big hand with long, calloused fingers, splayed across her swollen belly. She shifted. So did the hand, and the hard, male body she was using as a backrest.

She must still have been sleeping, dreaming. But she was real. Brand seemed real, as well, so very real. If she turned, looked at him, would he disappear?

She looked down, straining her eyes to see in the dim pre-dawn haze. His hand was real enough. Lifting it, she inched away, turned her head. This was no fantasy, no figment of her imagination. He'd come for her.

She couldn't resist peeling back the covers, admiring every inch of his hard, well-honed body as he slept beside her. When the cool air prickled the skin on her arms, she wrapped up in the top sheet and pulled a blanket up to Brand's muscular neck.

The baby protested the way she'd stretched, gave a vigorous kick. For the first time in weeks, she didn't feel like a clumsy cow. Brand hadn't acted turned off by her body. As a matter of fact, he'd sworn he liked her swollen belly, and he'd rested his head on their unborn child. He'd made her laugh when he chided the baby good-naturedly for pounding on his cheek.

Before that he'd bound her to the bed, swearing he'd never let her go, and they'd made love with an intensity like never before. Her skin still tingled from where he'd used the flogger then rubbed his beard-roughened cheeks over it. He'd brought her close to climax over and over with his mouth and hands, refusing to let her come until she'd begged him to give her his long, thick cock, to fuck her until she couldn't tell where she ended and he began.

She smiled down at him, recalled how carefully he'd untied her hands, helped her turn onto her side. Her skin still tingled where he'd cradled her belly in his hands while entering her ever-so gently from behind. When she'd finally come, she'd seen shooting stars in her head. But he hadn't finished yet. He'd brought her up again, stroking her wet, swollen clit while fucking her pussy with tender care, until she trembled and exploded again as his triumphant yell heralded his own explosive orgasm.

And he'd told her over and over that he loved her, held her as if he'd never let her go. The words she'd needed him to say. The protection of his strong arms.

"We can't have a marriage based on sex." The words just popped out, filling the silence of dawn. Hearing them made her jump as if they'd come from a stranger's mouth. She nearly died of embarrassment when Brand rolled onto his back and shot her a questioning grin.

"Why not?" he asked, his sleepy voice sexy enough to make her tingle. "I kind of like it myself."

"Oh, you! That's not what I mean. I meant I can't keep my hands off you. You don't seem to be able to keep yours off me, either, but that's not a good enough reason for us to be together." She loved the lazy grin he aimed her way.

"It's not?"

"No. Last night you said you loved me, but I guess what you mean is that you love to have sex with me."

"And don't you love to have sex with me, too? Don't you enjoy the games we play?"

"Of course." Her cheeks grew warm at the insinuating tone of his voice. "But we can't spend our whole lives in bed. Dave hates me now because everyone's told him I deliberately got pregnant to trap you—twice."

"Come off it. You and I both know that's not so. What other people think doesn't matter." He reached out, brushed an errant lock of hair off her cheek. "I set Dave straight before I left. And he doesn't hate you. He's just a kid. A kid who didn't know better than to listen to vicious gossip."

"Where is he?" What had Brand done with their son?

"With Mother. Getting a lesson in family loyalty, among other things." He wrapped a long arm around her shoulder, pulled her close and cradled her against his broad, softly furred chest.

"You'd both be better off without me. All of you," she amended, her heart breaking as she clutched her hands over the little life now kicking her in the belly.

"Baby, you can't mean that." His arms tightened around her as if he feared she would disappear. "You and Dave and this little one have made my life complete. I love you all the time, and I won't allow you ever to doubt it."

She turned, met his solemn gaze. All at once, a weight lifted from her heart. She felt alive again, younger than she'd been at sixteen, almost like a newborn with no past and only a shining future. "You really do love me, don't you?"

"More than life. I know I haven't said it enough, but I do." He sounded so sincere she couldn't help believing him. She brushed a tear from her cheek, met his gaze. He caught her hand, brought it to his lips.

"I'm sorry, baby. Sorry I put you through all the pain of going home. God, I didn't know they'd be so cruel as to use our son that way. I can't believe that after thirteen years... Why, Dani? You never did anything to hurt any of them, then or now."

She laid her palm against his beard-shadowed cheek. "They weren't looking at me. They were seeing the ragged little girl whose mother would sleep with anybody for a drink, the sixteen year old who trapped their golden boy by getting pregnant. The woman they thought used her son to get to his dad, her body to hook him.

"I was okay with it when they accepted Dave as if he was yours alone, as if I hadn't had any part in creating him. As long as I had both of you, it didn't matter what they thought of me." She paused then continued. "I tried so hard not to embarrass you."

"Embarrass me? You've never made me anything but proud. And happy. It's as if I was only existing before you came back into my life, marking time and playing the roles people threw at me. If you want, I'll wind up things at the office and we'll come back here as soon as Uncle Jimmy and Laura come home."

Smiling, Dani thought of the home Brand had built for them on the banks of the Little Cat. A home that poignantly mingled their past with the present. And their future. That future wouldn't be perfect, but they'd fill it with the kind of love that could weather storms, last forever and longer. "Let's go home. To stay. Let's go back there when football seasons are over, and when you retire, put down roots for Dave and our other children."

"You're sure?" For all that he loved Carendon and the rolling, red clay hills where he'd grown up, Brand loved Dani more. "Is this what you want or what you think will make me happy?"

"Both. Take me home, love."

Epilogue
Two months later

At the altar of a church that had survived Sherman's fiery march to the sea, Brand stood solemnly at Dani's side, listening as the snowy-haired pastor who'd baptized him admonished them to bring their child up with love and devotion.

A glow of red and gold reflected on Dani's face from a stained glass window. The air-conditioning system hummed audibly now that the organist had paused.

His gaze shifted to the wriggling baby cradled in his godmother Elaine's arms, and his heart filled with pride. His infant son, born of his love for the strong, beautiful woman at his side. He'd been with Dani, scared to death but determined to witness the miracle they'd created together, when Brent had made his appearance two weeks earlier.

They had everything that was important. Their family. Dave, and now Brent. Even LeeAnn, who sat on the front row with Phil and Marilee, being good during the christening because Brand had promised her she could hold her baby brother afterward. It would be good practice for his little girl, learning to take care of a newborn. Phil had caught him alone yesterday and told him Marilee was pregnant, that they'd have their baby around Christmas.

His mother, her silver hair coiffed to perfection, sat in the Brandon pew one of her ancestors had first claimed before the Civil War. She was still stiff-necked and frequently a pain in the neck, but she'd moved firmly to their side. Since he'd brought Dani back, Eleanor had been working as hard to make people around here accept her as she'd once tried to drive her off. When he'd laid Brent in her arms at the hospital, Eleanor had shed tears of joy.

They were home. Wherever they were. Here where their love had begun, as well as the home they'd found with the Marlins back in Milwaukee.

Friends. True friends like Elaine and Josh, who had flown here to be Brent's godparents. Marilee and Phil, who had brought his daughter here to share their joy. Vlad Ivanov, who'd be taking over management of the firm now that he and Darlene had settled in and decided Atlanta was where they wanted to live and raise their family.

As the pastor baptized Brent, Brand counted his blessings. He curved his fingers around Dani's hand. Tilting her head, she met his gaze. And smiled up at him.

He needed no words. Neither did she. They had a forever kind of love, and a marriage no one ever again would declare out of bounds.

The End

Also by Ann Jacobs

༄

A Gift of Gold
A Mutual Favor
Another Love
Awakenings
Black Gold: Dallas Heat
Black Gold: Firestorm
Black Gold: Forever Enslaved
Black Gold: Love Slave
Captured (*anthology*)
Colors of Love
Colors of Magic
D'Argent Honor 1: Vampire Justice
D'Argent Honor 2: Eternally His
D'Argent Honor 3: Eternal Surrender
D'Argent Honor 4: Eternal Victory
Dark Side of the Moon
Enchained (*anthology*)
Forbidden Fantasies (*anthology*)
Gates of Hell
Gold, Frankincense & Myrrh (*anthology*)
Haunted
He Calls Her Jasmine
Heart of the West 1: Roped
Heart of the West 2: Hitched

Heart of the West 3: Lassoed
Lawyers in Love: Bittersweet Homecoming
Lawyers in Love: Gettin' It On
Lawyers in Love: In His Own Defense
Love Magic
Loving Control
Mystic Visions (*anthology*)
Storm Warnings (*anthology*)
Switching Control
Tip of the Iceberg
Topaz Dream
Unexpected Control
Wrong Place, Wrong Time?

About the Author

Ann Jacobs is a sucker for lusty Alpha heroes and happy endings, which makes Ellora's Cave an ideal publisher for her work. Romantica®, to her, is the perfect combination of sex, sensuality, deep emotional involvement and lifelong commitment—the elusive fantasy women often dream about but seldom achieve.

First published in 1996, Jacobs has sold over forty books and novellas, some of which have earned awards including the Passionate Plume (best novella, 2006), the Desert Rose (best hot and spicy romance, 2004) and More Than Magic (best erotic romance, 2004). She has been a double finalist in separate categories of the EPPIES and From the Heart RWA Chapter's contest. Three of her books have been translated and sold in several European countries.

A CPA and former hospital financial manager, Jacobs now writes full-time, with the help of Mr. Blue, the family cat who sometimes likes to perch on the back of her desk chair and lend his sage advice. He sometimes even contributes a few random letters when he decides he wants to try out the keyboard. She loves to hear from readers, and to put faces with names at signings and conventions.

Ann Jacobs welcomes comments from readers. You can find her website and email address on her author bio page at www.ellorascave.com.

Tell Us What You Think

We appreciate hearing reader opinions about our books. You can email us at Comments@EllorasCave.com.

Why an electronic book?

We live in the Information Age—an exciting time in the history of human civilization, in which technology rules supreme and continues to progress in leaps and bounds every minute of every day. For a multitude of reasons, more and more avid literary fans are opting to purchase e-books instead of paper books. The question from those not yet initiated into the world of electronic reading is simply: *Why?*

1. ***Price.*** An electronic title at Ellora's Cave Publishing and Cerridwen Press runs anywhere from 40% to 75% less than the cover price of the exact same title in paperback format. Why? Basic mathematics and cost. It is less expensive to publish an e-book (no paper and printing, no warehousing and shipping) than it is to publish a paperback, so the savings are passed along to the consumer.
2. ***Space.*** Running out of room in your house for your books? That is one worry you will never have with electronic books. For a low one-time cost, you can purchase a handheld device specifically designed for e-reading. Many e-readers have large, convenient screens for viewing. Better yet, hundreds of titles can be stored within your new library—on a single microchip. There are a variety of e-readers from different manufacturers. You can also read e-books on your PC or laptop computer. (Please note that Ellora's Cave does not endorse any specific brands.

You can check our websites at www.ellorascave.com or www.cerridwenpress.com for information we make available to new consumers.)

3. ***Mobility.*** Because your new e-library consists of only a microchip within a small, easily transportable e-reader, your entire cache of books can be taken with you wherever you go.

4. ***Personal Viewing Preferences.*** Are the words you are currently reading too small? Too large? Too… ANNOYING? Paperback books cannot be modified according to personal preferences, but e-books can.

5. ***Instant Gratification.*** Is it the middle of the night and all the bookstores near you are closed? Are you tired of waiting days, sometimes weeks, for bookstores to ship the novels you bought? Ellora's Cave Publishing sells instantaneous downloads twenty-four hours a day, seven days a week, every day of the year. Our webstore is never closed. Our e-book delivery system is 100% automated, meaning your order is filled as soon as you pay for it.

Those are a few of the top reasons why electronic books are replacing paperbacks for many avid readers.

As always, Ellora's Cave and Cerridwen Press welcome your questions and comments. We invite you to email us at Comments@ellorascave.com or write to us directly at Ellora's Cave Publishing Inc., 1056 Home Avenue, Akron, OH 44310-3502.

COMING TO A BOOKSTORE NEAR YOU!

ELLORA'S CAVE

Bestselling Authors Tour

UPDATES AVAILABLE AT
WWW.ELLORASCAVE.COM

MAKE EACH DAY MORE *EXCITING* WITH OUR

Ellora's Cavemen Calendar

♄ WWW.ELLORASCAVE.COM ♄

Cerridwen, the Celtic Goddess of wisdom, was the muse who brought inspiration to storytellers and those in the creative arts. Cerridwen Press encompasses the best and most innovative stories in all genres of today's fiction. Visit our site and discover the newest titles by talented authors who still get inspired - much like the ancient storytellers did, once upon a time.

Cerridwen Press
www.cerridwenpress.com

Discover for yourself why readers can't get enough of the multiple award-winning publisher
Ellora's Cave.
Whether you prefer e-books or paperbacks,
be sure to visit EC on the web at
www.ellorascave.com
for an erotic reading experience that will leave you breathless.